THE NARCISSIST

Anne Wedgwood

The Book Guild Ltd

First published in Great Britain in 2023 by
The Book Guild Ltd
Unit E2 Airfield Business Park,
Harrison Road, Market Harborough,
Leicestershire. LE16 7UL
Tel: 0116 2792299
www.bookguild.co.uk
Email: info@bookguild.co.uk
Twitter: @bookguild

This work is entirely fictitious and bears no resemblance to any persons living or dead.

Cover art based on an original design by Hannah Williams.

Typeset in 11pt Adobe Garamond Pro

Printed on FSC accredited paper
Printed and bound in Great Britain by 4edge Limited

ISBN 978 1915853 479

British Library Cataloguing in Publication Data.
A catalogue record for this book is available from the British Library.

For all who have acted and worked at East Riding Theatre

ONE

She's dead. There's none of the rubbish you see in films about thinking she might be asleep. People don't take afternoon naps slumped all over their dressing-room chairs with huge bullet holes in their heads. I sniff the air, thinking there'll be a smell of gunpowder – or cordite, that's what makes the smell, isn't it? It should smell like Bonfire Night, right? But it doesn't. I'm hit by the stench of eggs, with something else underneath – a flowery trace of perfume which seems familiar. I can't think about it now, my brain's frozen. I always wondered what it would be like to find a dead body and now I know. My heart's dropped into my stomach, I'm shivering while I feel the dampness of sweat creeping into the thin fabric of my dress, and I think I'm going to fall down so I look for something to grab. Not the chair – it's full of dead body. It's a tiny room, with just a clothes rack and a dressing table, so I have to slide down the door and crouch on the floor. I don't feel faint exactly, but I put my head between my knees anyway. Just for a minute. I'm not supposed to be here, and I have to get out. Just as soon as I can stand.

I need to get some air into my lungs. There's a posh fan whirring quietly in the corner, but it's fresh air I need. It's hard to take deep breaths when you're crouched over and your head's upside down, so

I make myself straighten up, holding on to the doorknob in case my legs give way again. Looking at her doesn't help, so I shut my eyes, count to twenty and take the breaths first. Okay, that's a bit better. Now what? I have to tell someone. Alert the authorities – isn't that what they say? I turn round, my hand on the doorknob, ready to rush out into the corridor, to find someone to tell, and never mind that I wasn't supposed to be there. No, Billie, wait, you can't. You know what happens to people who report crimes – they become suspects. And from what I've seen on the telly, it's all too easy for suspects to get searched. I can't risk that happening, not with those pills lurking in the bottom of my bag. Why on earth did I let Vanessa persuade me to sell them to her? It felt cool at the time, hanging out with a famous actress, sharing my 'stash' with her, but they were never even my pills to sell, and now look where it's got me. I've been a total idiot, but it's too late now. I'll just have to leave the way I came. Without anyone knowing.

I can't risk the corridor. It might have been all right with Vanessa around to explain what I was doing here. Getting into trouble for visiting her here, dodging her security detail, is one thing, but finding her dead body's another. I make myself look around the room in case there's something I'll need to know later on, but I've never been here before so I don't know what I should be looking for. It's just a dressing room. Clothes on a rail, a muddle of makeup on the counter, light bulbs around the mirror, half-blinding me with their glare, and the inevitable bottle of water. Nothing out of the ordinary. Except for the obvious. And then I see the gun. It's on the floor beside the chair. I know that gun. It's Vanessa's. She's shot herself. I have no idea why I didn't see it before.

The brain freeze is back. It's no good, I've got to get out. I can't think straight or make sensible decisions in this state. A fluttering net curtain catches the corner of my eye, and I look more closely at the window. It's an old sash one from when the building was a church. It's raised just a little, and I'm surprised it's not been pulled up all the way on a roasting day like this. Perhaps too much breeze would have spoilt Vanessa's hair, although I guess she won't have to worry about that now. I tiptoe round the chair, not wanting to touch the body, pull back the net curtain and see the car park. It's not perfect, but it has to be less risky than walking out through the theatre. The window's stiff and I can't stop my fingers trembling as I try to push it upwards. I may look small but I've got strong arms, and panic gives me added strength. It suddenly shifts, giving me plenty of space to climb out, pulling my bag behind me. Instinct tells me it's best to leave it as it was, so I take a minute to pull it nearly shut again. The car park's shimmering in the heat, busy with people going to and from their cars with their Saturday shopping, and even though my legs are screaming at me to get out as quickly as possible, I leave slowly, pulling out my phone from my bag and pretending to check it as I walk out and past the entrance to the theatre. I want to call Jay, but I can't. I can't talk about it where people might hear. My mind won't take in what's on the screen, it's too full of what I've just seen, and I put the phone away as soon as I'm away from the building, mind racing, feet walking blindly, just following the pavement away from the theatre and the horrors inside.

I should tell the police. I will tell the police. But only after getting rid of the pills. The image of the body, the gun, the blood, fills my mind; my head starts to spin, and I know I'm either going to faint or be sick. I can't go back to the theatre, but the library's almost next door, that'll have to do. I only need to hold on for a few minutes before I'm in the building and rushing into the toilets, which are handily placed on the ground floor. There's someone in the first cubicle – someone who's not too well from the sound of things – and I don't want to be next to them, so I go to the far end, locking the door with shaking fingers.

Deep breaths, Billie, deep breaths. And water. My mouth is parched, and I take big gulps from the bottle in my bag, perching on the closed seat, still shivering, still sweating, with my bag on my lap. I rummage around for the pills, flush them down the toilet and sit down again, draining my water bottle and waiting for the cistern to fill. I lift the seat again – the pills are gone. I heave a sigh of relief and take more deep breaths. My body starts to feel more like itself and I tell myself it's time to get a grip. I can't stay in here all afternoon, and now I'm feeling better and my bag's free of illegal substances, I need to get going. It's all very well not wanting to get into trouble, but the responsible thing to do is to let someone at the theatre know about the dead actress in their dressing room, if only to spare some other poor person the shock of finding her.

The person in the first cubicle flushes and unlocks the door. I can hear them washing their hands. I can't manage polite conversation right now, so I wait for the sound of the hand dryer and the swing door flapping behind them before coming out. I wash my hands over and over, I don't know why, but it helps me feel calmer. I look at my face in the mirror. I can't believe how normal it looks after what it's just seen. My mind flicks back to Vanessa, in the chair with the bullet hole and the gun and… why did she shoot herself, anyway? She didn't have anything to worry about; she had a perfect life. She was always going on about how lucky she was and what a great career she'd had; she'd be the last person to kill herself. My head feels as if it's going to burst. No. I can't go back to the theatre – if I report it now they'll want to know why I was there in the first place, how I got in, why I didn't tell them or call 999 straight away. I'll be there – or, even worse, in a police station – for hours, there'll be questions about Vanessa and who knows what else. And all the time, I'll be having to work out what I can and can't say, even if it was suicide.

The thought brings me up short as I dry my hands. Surely it doesn't matter much anyway, if Vanessa killed herself? It would be different if it were a murder – it would be a crime scene then, but it won't be, will it? Telling myself it's fine, I've been fussing over nothing, it's nothing to do with me, and I shouldn't have got rid of the pills after all, I walk down the library steps, trying to remember what I'd planned to do after seeing Vanessa. My mind's a blank. I can't think of anything other than what I've seen. Some kind of primal instinct is telling me to go home and hide, so I turn back towards the centre of town. The shortest route is past the theatre, but I can't make myself go that way.

The town's heaving but the back roads are always quieter, even on a Saturday afternoon, and ours is deserted. I can't wait to get into the house, but my footsteps drag as I approach it in anticipation of having to talk to people. I stop at the corner and roll a smoke with shaking fingers. It's a mess, but I get there in the end, and it's worth it – I don't want to go into the garden and risk someone being out there. I'm ready with a story of a headache, which even Alex can't spend too long questioning, but I really don't want to see anyone. There's no open fire door here to sneak in through, but at least I've remembered my key, and with a bit of luck I'll be able to avoid too much family contact for a few hours. I close the door as quietly as I can behind me and take off my shoes. I thought I'd calmed down, but my fingers are shaking as I untie the laces. I can't stand the heat any longer, and rip off my socks, thinking that perhaps I should have ditched the habit of a lifetime today and worn something lighter than Doc Martens. The tiles are smooth and cool beneath my bare feet, and I stand for a minute in the shaded hall. Silence. I don't wonder where everyone is, just thank my stars they're not here, and nip into the kitchen to refill my water bottle from the fridge before retreating to the study. Blinds drawn, fan on, I stretch out on the sofa and close my eyes.

TWO

'Billieeeee, it's readeeeee.' Alex's voice and a hammering at the door wake me from a dozy dream about getting lost in a forest. It's the one in the play, I've forgotten my lines, and I can't find my way out until I remember them. It's a relief to be woken, even if abruptly. And then it isn't. I remember Vanessa, and a stream of questions rushes through my brain. Someone must have found her by now, so what's happening? Does Dean know? Is it on the news yet? What do I say when I 'find out'?

Alex isn't known for his patience, and respect for privacy isn't in his repertoire either, so it's no surprise when he flings open the door and marches straight in, looking at me with disgust and amazement.

'Why are you asleep? It's nowhere near bedtime.'

'I wasn't asleep, I was just resting. I got hot and tired walking back from town and needed a lie-down.'

'Liar, I've been calling you for ages. Never mind, you've got to come now, it's ready. It'll burn soon if you don't hurry up.' I remember the barbecue we're having this evening. Early evening, because of Alex. Is it six o'clock already?

'And we can't have that, can we?' I swing my legs off the sofa and wait a moment for the blood to leave my head, thinking it's sleep

I need, not food, but it's not worth the hassle of explaining that to Alex. My phone's on the table. I need to phone Jay, check my social media feeds and post a photo or two. I can't risk losing followers now, especially with a new tour coming up. Everyone says having loads of followers helps you get work, and it's the only free marketing I'm likely to get for myself.

'Alex, I just need a moment, okay? Can you give me a couple of minutes to check my phone? I'm expecting a message.'

'All right. Two minutes.' He pulls a stopwatch out of his pocket and fiddles with the controls.

'I need the two minutes alone, Alex.'

'Aaaall right.' He goes out, still fiddling. My little half-brother's obsessive about time, and I know that two minutes is exactly what I've got. I pick up my phone and press my thumb to the screen. A little row of squares pops up to tell me I've got some Instagram likes. The symbols always give me a buzz but it's the number beside them I'm interested in. Forty-two – the answer to the question of the universe, as Dad would say. There's nothing on my news app about Vanessa, but there's a text from Jay asking how my meeting went. Conscious of the seconds ticking away, I call Jay and open Instagram at the same time. I'd better post quickly or someone's bound to ask what's up. I've got a photo ready to upload from some I prepared yesterday. I'll have a good excuse to make myself absent in a few hours' time, but it might look odd if I stop now. I almost laugh at myself for being so calculating. Why am I behaving as if I'm a murder suspect? Vanessa killed herself – there won't be any suspects. Perhaps it's because I thought it was a murder at first. Before I saw the gun. On the other hand, it's better to be safe than sorry, as Nora likes to say. I add the picture to my feed while Jay's phone is ringing and click a few likes for good measure. He doesn't answer. I need to talk to him so badly it hurts, and it would have given me an excuse to stall Alex, but there's nothing I can do.

'Time's up!' Alex barges back in, waving his stopwatch triumphantly.

'I'm coming, I'm coming.' I push my feet into a pair of sliders and grab my phone.

'No phones, Billie, remember? Not at mealtimes.' It's a new rule and it's a pain. All because Ellie won't let Alex have a phone. It's supposed to 'demystify' the idea for him, but I'm really not sure it's working.

'Okay, okay, look – I'm putting it down.' I'll have to sneak back in later to call Jay. It'll be easy enough to pretend I'm going to the loo in an hour or so.

'Come *on*,' says Alex, pulling me up with both hands. 'We've got sausages and burgers and corn on the cob, and we've done you some fish kebabs, specially. It's really cool.'

'I thought barbecues were supposed to be hot,' I say, as we make our way into the kitchen.

'It is hot, I just meant… oh, you're joking, aren't you?' Alex and humour don't mix very well, but he's learning.

'Yes, well spotted.' I glance at the clock on the kitchen wall. Two hours since I came home and the house has returned from a silent place of refuge to its normal state of a not-so-big house crammed with too many people. Dad's outside, piling food from the barbecue onto serving plates, and Sandy's in the kitchen, putting the final touches to one of her famous salads. Ellie's at the sink, her back to me, bashing an ice tray in what seems to be a futile effort to release the cubes into a metal bowl.

'Why do Americans need ice with absolutely everything?' she says to no one in particular. 'It would be easier to go next door and get some out of his fancy fridge…'

'Let me help,' I say, making her jump as I come up behind her.

'Oh! There you are! You gave me a fright.' Ellie hands me one of the plastic trays. 'Where have you been? We thought you were out but then Alex spotted your boots in the hall and worked out you must be in after all.'

'I was in my… the study.' It still rankles. Why did Nora have to come and live with us? She's got plenty of money to buy her own house and I'm sure she'd be able to look after herself perfectly well if Ellie and Sandy stopped fussing around her. 'I was having a little doze. What did you mean about Americans?' Now that the clatter of ice cubes has stopped, I can hear voices drifting in from the garden. Dad and Alex, of course, and another voice, one with an American accent. It's Dean – how can he be here? What's going on? How can he be in our garden swigging beer when his wife's lying dead with a bullet hole in her head?

'Oh, your father bumped into Dean on his way back from his bike ride. He's on his own tonight, with Vanessa working late at the theatre and the children away for the weekend with their grandparents. Mike asked him to join us for the barbecue.' She doesn't sound too pleased about it, although whether it's Dad or Dean she's annoyed with, I'm not sure.

'Did he?' It doesn't sound likely to me – he might have been living next door for the last six months, but Dad and Dean aren't what you'd call the best of friends.

'I expect Dean invited himself. You know what he's like, he can't stand being alone. Anyway, he's here now. He's been "helping" set up the barbecue and drinking beer for an hour already. I'm surprised you didn't hear them come in.' She scoops a few stray cubes into the bowl and turns towards me at last. 'Are you all right?' she asks. 'You're looking tired.' Far from being a wicked stepmother, Ellie always knows when something's wrong, even when I try my best to hide it.

'I'm fine, I had a bit too much sun this afternoon, that's all. I'll be better once I've had something to eat.' I pick up the ice cubes and grab a wine glass. My stomach's not sure about the idea of food but I'm going to need a drink to get me through this evening.

'Hey, Billie,' says Dean. 'How're you doing?' He's leaning back in his chair as if he owns the place, a beer in one hand and a cigar in the other. He's nearly old enough to be Ellie's father, but it doesn't stop him wanting to look 'cool', as his oh-so-youthful golf gear demonstrates.

'Good. You?'

'Great, Billie, great. I've been playing golf all day, and now here I am with you fine people, relaxing like I haven't done in a long, long time. I've even had my phone turned to silent – it's not "good form" to leave it on while you're on the course, you know.' He looks round the table as if waiting for a round of applause, although it's not clear whether it's for the momentous decision to ignore his phone or his attempt at a posh English accent. He doesn't get one – no one in this family is much impressed by ageing Hollywood producers anymore. Dean's quick to 'read the room', as he'd say, and barely misses a beat before ploughing straight on. 'And then I bumped into Mike outside the house and he invited me over, and I know the rules here – no phones at the table, right?' He winks at Alex, who nods approvingly.

I'm not in a state to cope with sitting next to him. Never mind he's a self-important creep – I'm sure Vanessa only married him for the sake of her career – how can I make polite conversation knowing it's only a matter of hours, maybe minutes, before someone tells him his wife is dead? I pick a chair as far away from him as I can manage and try a bit of seafood kebab, watched anxiously by Alex, who's refusing to touch his burger until he knows I like it.

'It's great, Alex,' I reassure him. 'What's in it?'

'Ummm… seafood,' he says, busying himself with ketchup and bread roll.

'You mean Sandy made it.'

'Well…'

'Sandy made it and you cooked it, and it's cooked to perfection. Well done, Alex, nice one.' His face lights up and Sandy gives him a nudge.

'New king of the barbecue,' she tells him. 'You'll be doing your father out of a job. I'll just pop inside and check on Mother. The heat's tired her out today, but she needs to eat.'

'I'll go.' Ellie's half out of her chair but without any great sense of purpose.

'Don't worry, it'll only take a moment. Save me a sausage – I won't be long.' Sandy's already halfway across the garden, looking competent, and I feel a twinge of guilt for not asking where Nora is. Not a big twinge, though. If she hadn't come to live here I'd still have a room of my own to come back to instead of having to camp out in the study. The lack of space is driving me mad, not to mention the noise from the stairs and the rooms above. Ellie's sitting with Dad and Dean at the other end of the table, and she's joined in the turning-off-your-phone conversation.

'I totally agree that it's good to switch your phone off, Dean. Too many people are glued to their screens all day. I turn mine off completely when I'm working – I can't think creatively if I know there's even a chance of an interruption.'

'Sure thing.' Dean helps himself to salad. 'But what if there was an emergency? How would Mike or anyone else get in touch with you?'

'It's not that hard! We all managed without them for years, you know that. And anyway, there's always someone around in this house to answer the landline and come and find me.'

'That's all very well for you, but we're not all lucky enough to work from home,' says Dad. 'And you wouldn't want me to fall off my bike and not be able to call for help, would you?'

'I daresay you'd manage.' Ellie avoids his eye as she helps herself to salad. 'But seriously, Dean, if you've had it off all afternoon, shouldn't you check it? How do you know the children haven't been trying to call you?'

'They haven't got phones, Ellie – George only turned nine this month.'

'I know that, but what if their grandparents were trying to get hold of you? What do you think, Billie? You're the phone expert here. Should Dean carry on in blissful ignorance of who's been messaging him all afternoon or should he check?' She turns to Dean in a playful aside. 'We'll give you special dispensation, Dean, just for two minutes – Alex can time you.'

'I…' Ellie has no idea what she's asking me. As soon as Dean looks at his phone he'll see a hundred messages and missed calls and his nightmare will begin. I don't want to be the one who tells him to – I can't do that to him. 'Leave it, Dean. I know you think I'm one of those "glued" people, Ellie, but it's only for promotional purposes. Look…' I hold both hands in the air. 'No phone!' They all laugh, and Dean's hand, which has been straying towards his pocket, comes up to clap Ellie on the back.

'Sorry, Ellie, you lose. I'll check it soon but not before I've had one of those excellent fish kebabs.' He winks at Alex, who beams with pride. Everyone laughs and Dad goes to get Dean his kebab. I'm starting to wonder how long I can go on making polite conversation when Alex jumps up, nearly knocking the table over.

'Alex! What on earth are you doing?' Ellie grabs his plate, which is teetering on the edge of the table, as he dashes inside.

'Doorbell!' he shouts over his shoulder. Alex likes to think that being ten makes him grown up, but he hasn't grown out of his obsession with answering the door, which is strange when you consider how much he dislikes talking to strangers. Maybe it's a protective thing, like you get with dogs.

'Who's that?' Dad asks. He always does that, as if one of us might have X-ray vision or super-sensory awareness. We've not got one of those fancy doors with a video camera, so it really is a very silly question.

'I can't see from here,' says Ellie. She always says that, too. It drives me nuts sometimes, the way they always say the same things, but it feels strangely comforting today. My heart's racing, knowing it must be the police, come to tell Dean Vanessa's dead. I can't let Alex deal with them on his own, and I want to get it over with, so I follow him in before anyone else has a chance to.

'I'll go – it's probably a delivery van getting lost. We don't want to leave them at the mercy of Alex's directions, do we?' They let me go, Dad looking for marshmallows to cook on the embers, and Ellie reaching for the wine bottle to top up her glass.

I'm only a few seconds behind Alex but the door's already open, revealing two people on the step. There's a woman with blonde hair tied back in a messy bun and a tall guy who looks more like a sportswear model than a policeman. They're not in uniform, and this only emphasises the difference between the two of them – her in a linen shirt and trousers, and him in a preppy open-necked shirt. She flashes a card at me and peers over my left shoulder as if looking for a grown-up to talk to.

'DI Ronnie Twist, Humberside Police. I'm sorry to disturb you, is this Mr and Mrs Preston's house?' I knew it'd be the police, but it's still a shock. My mouth goes dry and my mind's a blank, but fortunately Alex isn't fazed at all by the presence of two detectives on our doorstep. As far as he's concerned, a question's a question and needs an answer, and he's always keen to provide those.

'Yes, it is. What do you want? And who's he?' He clearly thinks her rude not to have introduced her companion, and after the initial shock of being spoken to by such a small person has worn off, I can see the twitch of a smile cross the detective's face before she bends down a little to address Alex directly.

'This is my sergeant, Luke Carter. We're looking for someone called Dean Westerby. A neighbour told us that she saw him coming into your house a little while ago, so we've come to see if he's here.'

'Have you come to arrest him?'

'No, we just need to talk to him.' She straightens up, looking beyond me again towards the back of the house, no doubt hoping a competent person will emerge if she waits long enough.

'He's here,' I say. 'We're in the garden. You'd better come through.' I open the door a bit wider to let them in and lead the way through the kitchen and outside, leaving Alex to lock the front door again in the precise manner in which he thinks it should be done. Sandy comes out of Nora's room with a half-empty plate and almost bumps into us. There's no time to explain properly, but I manage to nod furiously in the direction of first Alex and then the living room. She's quick to take the hint and heads swiftly towards the front door, still clutching the remains of her mother's meal as I take the people who have come to shatter Dean's life into pieces into the garden.

THREE

It takes a moment for them to register that I'm not alone. The three of them – Ellie, Dad, Dean – are clustered around the barbecue, laughing about something, and it's only Dad who turns round when I clear my throat, thinking I have to get their attention somehow.

'So was it a delivery? Has Alex wangled us a free pizza?' He's got a smile on his face, and it soon drops, but in puzzlement rather than dismay. 'Oh. Hello.' He doesn't echo Alex's 'who's this?' but it's there, hidden in his tone. Dean and Ellie turn round quickly, and straighten up with the air of naughty schoolchildren, although I can't think what they've got to feel guilty about. It's not against the law to have a barbecue in your own back garden, is it?

'Um, this is DI…' Her name's gone right out of my head and I feel like a complete idiot. Here they were, thinking I'm a child, and now I'm behaving like one.

'DI Ronnie Twist,' she says, holding out her hand towards Dad. 'And DS Luke Carter.' He gives a little nod but stays a step behind her. 'I'm sorry to disturb your evening. We're looking for Mr Dean Westerby. We've been trying to contact him throughout the afternoon. A neighbour said she'd seen him coming in here a couple of hours ago.'

'I'm Dean Westerby.' Dean steps forward but doesn't offer his hand. 'I'm sorry you've been put to all this trouble. I've had my phone switched to silent. We were just joking about it… I'm sorry if it's caused a problem. What's up? Nothing's happened to my kids, has it? Please don't tell me it's that?' He's suddenly gone pale, and he takes a step towards a chair, putting out his hand to steady himself.

'No, it's not about your children. Would you like to sit down, Mr Westerby?'

'Come on, Dean, sit down.' Ellie's at his side in no time and she pours him a glass of water. She looks up at the detective. 'Do you need us to leave? Is a private matter? We can go inside if you want.'

'That's up to Mr Westerby,' she says, looking at him. 'You may find it helpful to have a friend with you, sir. I'm afraid it's not good news.'

Dean looks around and nods. 'Stay,' he says. 'Please.' Everyone takes a seat, Ellie and Dad on either side of Dean as if to protect him, and me next to Ellie. DI Twist moves a chair round so that she can sit in front of Dean rather than look at him across a table full of food, and DS Carter stands close behind her.

'I'm sorry to have to tell you that your wife received a gunshot injury this afternoon.'

'A gunshot? How? They weren't using guns on set, were they?' It's an understandable assumption, especially in Dean's world of action movies.

'It didn't occur on set, Mr Westerby. It happened in your wife's dressing room.'

'Her dressing room? How could she be shot there? They have security, bag checks, how could anyone get a gun in there?'

'It would seem that someone – possibly your wife – managed to do so, Mr Westerby.'

'Vanessa? Vanessa smuggled a gun into the theatre? Why would she do that?'

'I'm afraid I can't answer that question, Mr Westerby.' She pauses, her gaze sweeping across the rest of us and perhaps thinking that this is an inappropriate setting for such a gruesome conversation. 'Mr Westerby, it really would be best if we could continue this conversation at the station. Would you mind coming there now? You'd be welcome to bring someone with you.'

'What? You're not arresting me, are you?'

'No, of course not. But you might prefer to continue what is going to be a difficult conversation in a more private location.' She looks over at the garden fence as if wondering if eavesdropping neighbours might be lurking behind them, and I suppose she's got a point.

'No. Say what you've got to say here. Say it now.' Dean's face is tight with strain, and I suppose he thinks hearing the news straight away will somehow make it less awful.

'Very well.' DI Twist looks directly at Dean, her expression deliberately blank. 'The initial assessment at the scene was that your wife appeared to have taken her own life. We're—'

Dean cuts across the inspector while she's still speaking. I guess he's used to behaving like that in his production meetings. 'Vanessa? Vanessa… what did you say? Took her own life? Are you saying she shot herself?'

'A gun was found by her side, indicating that the wound to her head was self-inflicted.' It's official police speak, I know, but it sounds so cold and unfriendly. At the same time, a wave of relief washes through me. It's not at all hard to look shocked when I hear the scene lodged in my mind described like this, and I can stop trying to behave normally at last. The inspector opens her mouth to continue, but Dean interrupts her again before she has a chance to speak.

'Self-inflicted? Vanessa? Why would she do that? Did you find a note? Anything to say why she did it?' He's shaking his head in bemusement and disbelief.

'I don't believe it,' Ellie says, looking at Dad. A look passes between them that isn't shock – it's something more like a smile, but that can't be it. My brain's in no state to work out what unspoken signals might mean right now.

'Neither do I,' says Dean, straightening his back. 'Vanessa wouldn't kill herself in a million years. Your guys must have missed something. How many gunshot deaths do you deal with around here anyway? Are you even qualified to handle something like this?' He's out of his chair, looming over DI Twist, but she's quick to get up too, and she stands her ground in front of him.

'Please stay calm, Mr Westerby. I appreciate how difficult this is, but I must ask you to let me finish.' Dad puts a gentle hand on Dean's arm, and he subsides resentfully into his chair. DI Twist does likewise, and I notice that the sergeant has quietly taken a seat himself and is making unobtrusive notes on a small tablet. She continues speaking calmly, ignoring Dean's interruption.

'What I was going to say is that although the scene suggests suicide, it is by no means certain. Initial observations have led us to keep an open mind.' What does she mean, an open mind? I saw her. I saw the gun. It was obviously suicide. My thoughts are so clear in my head that I can't believe I've not said them aloud, but she's carrying on, her blue eyes wandering around the garden as if looking for answers in the shrubbery. It's weird, but maybe it's designed to put people off their guard.

'The post-mortem will tell us more, and the theatre has been cleared and sealed off until the cause of death is confirmed. In the meantime, we need to ask you to formally identify your wife. And it would be very helpful if you could help us with the weapon.'

'The weapon?' All the bluster has leaked out of Dean. He's looking as pale as is possible for a man with a California tan, and his eyes have filmed over with tears as the reality of the situation sinks in. Whatever their problems, it must be a huge shock, and I guess he must have loved her once.

'Did your wife own a gun, Mr Westerby? It's important, as I'm sure you can appreciate, to establish this as early as possible and, if so, to find out if the weapon found in her dressing room belonged to her. Our next steps depend on this, and we need your help.'

'Um, yes.' Dean's in shock, I can tell. Both he and I know that

Vanessa had a gun, but it wasn't strictly legal. Is he going to deny it?

'Yes, she had a gun, or yes, you'll come to identify the body?' She's looking at Dean now, and there's a hint of compassion in her eyes. Perhaps it's to encourage him to trust her, and if so, it seems to work. Dean heaves a sigh.

'Yes, of course I'll come to see Vanessa.' He pauses, as if weighing up his next answer. 'And yes. She did have a gun.' The detectives exchange glances, but Dean's too distracted to notice.

'Thank you for your honesty, Mr Westerby,' says the inspector. 'We appreciate how difficult it must be for you discuss such matters. Before we go to see your wife's body, I must ask you more about this so that we can proceed as quickly as possible with our investigation. I'd like to show you a photograph of the weapon found with your wife this afternoon. We need to establish as quickly as possible if it belonged to her.'

'Sure. Show me the picture. It won't be hers. Vanessa would never do such a thing, so let's clear that up now and you can start looking for whoever murdered her.' Dean's regained his composure now, but he's in for a shock if he thinks it's not Vanessa's gun. Sergeant Carter produces an envelope from a folder I hadn't noticed him carrying before and hands it to his boss. She places it on the table in front of Dean, who is perhaps wishing he'd gone to the station after all.

'Please take your time, Mr Westerby. It can be hard to focus clearly when you're under stress. We're happy to wait for an accurate response.'

Dean reaches for the photograph as if it's burning and pulls it towards him by its corner. I can't see it from where I'm sitting but he doesn't waste any time.

'It's hers. That's Vanessa's gun.' He pushes it back, but he can't tear his eyes away from it. 'I don't understand. I just don't understand…' He turns to Dad and then Ellie in turn. 'Can you? Can you understand? When did Vanessa ever look unhappy? Tell me! Did she ever look anything other than full of life to you?' They shake their heads, apparently lost for words. Dean turns back to the detective.

'She didn't kill herself,' he says fiercely. 'I know she didn't. She wouldn't do it to me and she wouldn't do it to her kids. Someone else shot her. I know it. You've got to believe me.'

'As I said, Mr Westerby, we are keeping an open mind. Your views will be taken into account, I can assure you, and we're grateful for your help in looking at the photograph. Can you come with us now? To see… your wife?' She's speaking kindly now. It can't be easy dealing with situations like this, and I find myself taking mental notes in case I get to play a detective one day. Dean seems to have run out of steam, and he stands up slowly, refusing Dad's offer to go with him, but saying yes, he'll be in touch. Dad gets up to see them out. Ellie and I look at each other, and then wordlessly follow in his wake, Ellie to sort out Alex and tell Sandy what's happened, and me to the study to call Jay.

* * *

Jay's tiny face is on my screen – he's left a message asking why I've not called, and telling me I'd better do it soon while he's in a café with Wi-Fi. I try to imagine a parallel universe in which the only exciting thing to have happened to me today is a friendly chat with a famous film star, in which she's promised to get me a part in her next movie. Not that I ever expected that to happen, but a word in the right direction – specifically towards her agent – would have been nice. Part of my brain – the wishful part – had hoped she might wangle me a walk-on in *Bess of the Blitz*. The more realistic part had hoped for a photo of the two of us – not some desperate fan selfie, a proper friends-together picture – that I could tag her in. I bet Jay a tenner I'd get one, and he'll be wanting to know who's won. I press his face and lie with my eyes shut while I wait for him to pick up so I can pretend I'm on a French beach rather than a poky office with my clothes in a suitcase. It rings for what seems like ages.

'Bills?' He's out of breath.

'Who else? What took you so long?'

'I was in the bog.'

'Of course you were. Great timing, Jay.'

'It was your timing, not mine!' I can hear the smile in his voice, and I hold the phone a bit tighter. If he's not in the hotel, the signal won't be good enough for a video call, and I wish I could see him properly.

'Tell me what you're looking at.'

'The sea. The beach. A nice cold beer. French girls in their bikinis.'

'I'm sure they're all very ugly.'

'Of course they are. Everyone's ugly compared to you, you know that.' I can hear him taking a sip of his beer. Why did I spend all my money on clothes and clubbing? I could be there now if I wasn't so stupid. Maybe next year…

'Yeah, yeah, sure they are.'

'Bills? Are you all right?' The banter's nice, talking to Jay like this makes me feel like I've been wrapped in a hug, but it's no good, I can't keep it going for long. Jay has the best ear in the business – he can do any accent you like and he can always tell if something's wrong, just from my voice.

'No. I'm…' I can't put it into words. There's too much to say and I don't know where to start. I've got this far on adrenalin, and now that I'm on my own with Jay's voice in my ear, it's hitting me properly. Vanessa's dead. She's dead. She shot herself. I don't care what Dean thinks – he didn't see her. It's the only explanation. And I found her. It's way too late to tell the police what I saw, but now the news is out, I can't resist the overwhelming urgent to tell someone, and the obvious person is Jay.

'Has something happened?'

'Yes. I… I don't know…' I can't help it: the tears have started, my nose is running, I've not got a tissue, and this suddenly becomes the most important problem in my life. I sit up, blinking in the gloom. 'Wait a minute, Jay.' I put the phone down and grab the box of tissues from the desk. One's not going to be enough. I sort out my nose, but the tears won't stop. It must be some sort of delayed shock.

I drink some water, keep wiping my eyes – I must look awful, it's just as well it's not a video call after all – and arrange cushions to lean on so I don't choke on my runny nose by lying down flat.

'Billie? Are you there?' It's all taken a while and the phone's been squawking, but I can't talk yet. I lean back and take a deep breath.

'I'm here.'

'What the hell's going on? Is it Vanessa? Has she upset you?'

'No. Yes. She…' All I can see is Vanessa. In the chair. With the gun. And the blood. I want to throw up, but I can't hang up on Jay. It's not fair on him. I stop and reach for my water bottle. Why didn't I think to bring something stronger in here? I need something for the shock – brandy, isn't that what they say? Or whisky – or anything really.

'What? You're not making sense, Bills. Take a deep breath and start again.'

'Okay. Sorry.' I blow my nose again and sit up straight. It feels better somehow. 'I went to see Vanessa. Like I told you I was going to.' My voice is wobbling but I've completed a sentence. That's a start.

'Yes. Good. Take a breath, Bills, take it slowly. In your own time.' He's using his calm voice. It usually irritates me, but it's helping for once.

'Yes. In my own time. I went to the theatre; the fire escape was open, like she said. I found her dressing room. And… and…'

'Come on, Billie, you can do it.' He's sounding serious now; he must have guessed something really bad has happened, even though he won't have a clue what it is.

'She… she…' Deep breath, spit it out, better out than in. 'She was dead.' There. Done. Now it's Jay's turn to be incoherent.

'Dead? What do you mean, dead? Are you sure? I mean, she hadn't just had a heart attack or a stroke or something? Are you sure?'

'She had a bullet in her brain, Jay, so yes, I'm sure.' He didn't mean to make me cross, but he has, and for some strange reason it's making me feel better.

'Billie!' He's shocked now, although whether it's by the description or my bluntness I'm not sure. There's a silence while he takes it in. I can hear a seagull in the background and people talking, laughing, although I can't tell if it's in French or English. It's surreal, thinking of him in such a different place without a care in the world. I suppose it's the same for him, trying to imagine me and what's happening here.

'Oh, f—ck, Billie, that's unreal.' He doesn't know what to say. He's even forgotten not to swear. He's usually good about it, doesn't tease me, knows it's important, but I suppose it's understandable.

'Yeah. Only it isn't. It isn't unreal. It happened.'

'Yeah.' There's a pause. More seagulls. I take some deep breaths, lie down again, wait for him to talk.

'So, I guess you didn't call because you've been with the police, right? Did you have to give a statement or something?'

'Um, no. I didn't.'

'Didn't give a statement? Why not? Don't they do that anymore?'

'I haven't been with the police. Well, I have. They came to the house. Dean was here and they came looking for him. So everyone knows.'

'But didn't you report it? Why not? Isn't it against the law not to report something like that?'

'I don't know, Jay. It probably is. But I didn't, because I had those pills you gave me in my bag, and they're definitely illegal. I told you I didn't want them and now look where it's got me.'

'Why were they in your bag? Why didn't you stash them somewhere safe?' He's angry, I can tell, thinking he could have been pulled into trouble if I'd been caught with the pills and had to say where I got them.

'Because I'm living in a tiny room with no storage in a house with five other people! And you can hardly talk – if you hadn't had them on you at the airport I'd never have had them in the first place.' That shuts him up. I won't tell him that Vanessa was going to buy them off me, things are bad enough already.

'Okay, I'm sorry, all right? Look, Billie, you can't just leave it. You have to tell someone, I'm sure you do. You've not still got the pills, have you?'

'Of course not. I went to the library and flushed them down the toilet. But what would be the point? It wouldn't help anyone.'

'No. All right. Sorry. It's just a shock, right?'

'Tell me about it.' We're both thinking. There's more chatter at his end, the chink of glasses. I can almost hear the sound of the waves crashing on the shore, but it's just wishful thinking. 'Look, Jay, you can't tell anyone about this. Not yet anyway, and definitely not about me being there. It'll be online soon enough, but please – please don't say anything until it is.'

'Of course I won't.' His voice has softened again. 'Look, Billie, I've got to go. Get some rest, eh? It's horrible, I get that, but you'll feel better soon, I promise. And I'll be back in three weeks. It'll all feel a million miles away by then.'

'Yeah. I know. It's just… three weeks feels a long time right now… Call me soon. Please?'

'Sure. Take care, Bills.'

'You too.' The phone chirrups his goodbye and I wonder how long it will be before he says he loves me. And why he had to go. And who else was there.

* * *

There are more likes popping up on my phone but I'm not posting again. I open all my accounts in turn, say I'll be taking a break from social media for a while for family reasons, and mute all notifications. It seems a shame not to carry on just as I was getting some good responses, but it might look insensitive to keep posting right now. I'll start again in a few days, with something about Vanessa's tragic death and how much I'll miss her. By the time I've finished it's starting to get dark, and I hear the front door opening and Dad and Dean's voices in the hallway. He must have called or texted ahead to avoid

Alex doing his doorman act. I can't help it – I've got to know what's been happening, so I pull my dress straight and follow them into the kitchen. It's a warm night, and Ellie and Sandy are outside, sipping wine with a candle on the table in front of them. Dad grabs a couple of beers and we join them to listen to Dean.

We go through the shocked and horrified stage while Dean sips his beer nervously and tells us about the morgue and the gun in more detail than we might have wanted. There's a pause while Ellie and Sandy see to Alex and Nora, neither of whom cope well with variations in their bedtime routines. Dad and I bring out the barbecue leftovers, since no one managed to eat much before the police arrived, and our tummies are starting to rumble, and Dean checks his phone to make sure the children are okay. Ellie comes out with a bottle of brandy, saying it will help with the shock. They must have some sort of sisterly routine for this, because Sandy comes out two minutes later with another bottle for the same reason, giving us a brief and guilty opportunity to laugh. We move on to the incredulous stage, wondering why Vanessa would do such a thing. Despite his denials earlier, Dean's accepting the police's original assessment, and his identification of Vanessa's gun doesn't suggest they're likely to change their minds. Then it's time for coffee and a practical discussion of what will happen next and how Dean's going to tell the children. The brandy's going to my head, and it starts to feel like a carefully planned social event with a drinks list to match.

Eventually there's nothing left to say – at least nothing that anyone wants to say. We sit awkwardly in the gloom, no one feeling able to break the silence. The midnight chimes of the minster float across the air as if giving us permission to leave, and Dean stands – a little uncertainly – and says thank you, he doesn't know what he'd have done without us, and he should let us get to bed. We try not to follow suit with too much alacrity, and Ellie walks him to the front door, telling him that we'll do anything to help, and the children are welcome to come over any time. The rest of us clear up in silence, and with three of us it doesn't take long to stack the dishwasher, put the leftovers in the fridge and wipe the surfaces. We hear the front door shut quietly but Ellie doesn't come back, and I'm sure I'm not the only one feeling relieved that we're not going to have to make polite conversation before the morning. We say our good nights and go our separate ways – Sandy to her room, Dad to join Ellie in their bedroom and me to put up my sofa bed and scrub my teeth in the downstairs loo.

I don't sleep. My brain seems to have taken a series of photos of Vanessa: from behind, slumped in her chair, her head, her hand drooping towards the gun, and – most vivid of all – the horrible hole in her head. As soon as I close my eyes, they flicker in front of me on a continuous loop, and I can't get rid of the smell of eggs in my nose. It's no good. Trying to sleep won't work. I'll have to do the best I can to rest, and hope to make it up tomorrow. I rummage in my bedside drawer for a spray that Sandy gave me ages ago when I was stressed about auditions. It's lavender and it's supposed to help you relax. I squirt it on my pillow and find a playlist of what Dad would call smooth sounds on my phone. I do a search for images of Vanessa and find a picture of when she was younger, telling my eyes to take a photo of that. It is – was – one of her favourites, and she had it framed in the snug. It's from one of her first films, and she's looking very young and happy and pretty.

I lie back again and tell my body to relax, one muscle at a time, starting with my toes. It works pretty well but my brain won't follow suit. I conjure up the latest image of Vanessa, and tell myself to think about her life, not her death. But this isn't much better. It's not as if I liked her; in fact, hardly anyone liked her very much as far as I could tell. She was self-obsessed, arrogant and manipulative, and I have to admit it – I'm not sorry she's gone. It's a relief to know she won't be living next door anymore. Does that make me a bad person? And if it does, what about the rest of them? Sitting round drinking brandy and saying how sorry they were? Only they didn't say they were sorry, did they? It was all about why did she kill herself and what about the children. Not one of them said they were sorry she'd gone.

25

FOUR

'Who's taking me to the minster today?' Alex doesn't understand the need to turn the volume down on Sunday mornings. The concept of a lie-in hasn't registered yet, and I doubt it ever will.

'No one,' comes the muffled reply, followed by the sound of Ellie and Dad's bedroom door opening and Ellie going into the upstairs bathroom. 'Give me two minutes, Alex, okay?' There's a pause, followed by the sound of the toilet flushing and the tap running, and I can imagine Alex sitting on the landing, tapping his toes in frustration.

'So how will I get there? It's too far to walk.' It's not much more than half a mile, but Ellie's not ready to let Alex loose on his own yet, so she's let him carry on thinking it's miles away.

'Ssh, Alex, you'll wake everyone up.' Ellie's herding him downstairs, and I listen to the mumble of their voices as they go into the kitchen, wondering what excuse she'll come up with. She won't want to be anywhere there's a risk of people gossiping about Vanessa until she's had a chance to explain what's happened to Alex and answer his inevitably insensitive questions. I must have slept in the end but it doesn't feel like it. My eyes are gritty, my head's thumping and my mouth's dry from the brandy. I got out of the habit of late mornings a long time ago, thanks to the combination of Alex and drama school, and I know I won't go back to sleep. I'm desperate for a cup of tea, even if it does mean talking to Alex, so I make my way into the kitchen, wondering if Ellie's told him everything yet.

'But you said she was ill last night, not dead.' Alex's spoon is sitting in his cereal bowl, abandoned in favour of his need for clarity.

'I know. I didn't want to upset you by telling you she was dead. I thought it might stop you sleeping.' Ellie is sitting opposite my half-brother, knowing he'll need her full attention for this conversation.

'Why would it stop me sleeping?'

'When people get a shock – like hearing someone's died unexpectedly – it can make it hard to get to sleep at night.'

'Did that happen to you when Grandpa died?'

'Yes, it did.'

'Oh. Okay.' Alex eats a few mouthfuls of Weetabix and Ellie gives me a nod as I mime a letter T at her. She waits patiently for the next question, knowing it's only a matter of time.

'Where is she now?'

'I'm not sure. I think she'll be at the hospital. That's where they take people when they've died.'

'Why? They can't make her better if she's dead, can they?'

'No, but that's what they do.'

Alex considers this and returns to his breakfast, thinking hard. When his bowl is empty he drinks his juice and sits back in his chair. 'I have two questions to ask.'

'Go ahead, you can ask them,' Ellie says. I can't believe she's so calm. I'd be terrified of what Alex's crazy questions might be. I put her tea in front of her and stay where I am by the kettle, hoping to stay out of the discussion.

'My first question is: how did Vanessa die? It can't have been a bomb because we'd have heard it. And she wasn't ill. So was there a fire at the theatre? Or was she in a car accident?' Trust Alex to think of every possibility other than what actually happened.

'It was none of those,' says Ellie. 'It was a gun. She was shot. In the head.' It sounds brutal put that way, but Alex would only ask for the details anyway. Alex is a big fan of detail.

'Who shot her?' I'm sure that wasn't question number two, but it won't help to point it out.

'The police think she shot herself.'

'Why would she do that?'

'I really don't know, Alex. That's something they're trying to work out. As soon as they tell us, I'll let you know. What was the second question?' Ellie's voice is beginning to sound strained, and I'm not surprised.

'My second question is: who will look after Heidi and George? They won't have a mum now, will they?' The disconnect between the content of his words and the almost scientific manner of their delivery brings tears to my eyes. Alex can't moderate what he says in the interests of the feelings of others – it's not his fault, and I love him to bits – but he understands what the most important things are in life, and I feel terrible. I've been stressing about what to do, what to say, how awful it was to find Vanessa's body, but that's nothing compared to how her children will feel, something I should know better than anyone.

'Dean will look after them,' says Ellie, blinking back her own tears. 'And Tess, of course. And I'm sure they have aunts and uncles and grandparents just like you do. And maybe we can help them too. By having them over and being kind to them.'

Alex is nodding thoughtfully. 'I'll let them on the Xbox before I have a go.'

'That would be kind.' Ellie takes a sip of tea. It looks like the inquisition might be over now, but Alex isn't finished.

'Maybe Dean will get married again and have another child, like you and Dad did. And then George and Heidi will have a new mum.' He turns to look at me. 'That's what happened to you, isn't it?'

'Yes, Alex, it is.' I hadn't anticipated the conversation taking this turn, but I suppose I should have. I sit next to Ellie and give her hand a squeeze. 'I was very lucky to get a new mum when Dad met Ellie, and you for a brother. But that was a long time after my mum died, and I don't think it's something you should mention to George and Heidi just yet.'

'That's all right, I won't.' His questions might go on for ever, but at least Alex is easily satisfied with the answers, and he thankfully reverts to more practical matters.

'Is that why we're not going to the minster today? Because Vanessa's died?'

'Yes. We need to stay here in case Dean needs any help.'

'Okay. What will I do instead?' Alex lives by his routines. Everything's written down on a chart in his bedroom, and there'll be a space in his mind now where 'minster choir' usually is.

'One hour of piano, one hour of Xbox and one hour of reading. How does that sound?'

'In that order?'

'Reading first. Not everyone wants to be woken up by Bach first thing in the morning.'

'All right.' Reassured by having a plan, Alex clears his dishes and trots off to brush his teeth. Ellie heaves a sigh, leans back and closes her eyes.

'Well done.' I sit down in Alex's recently vacated chair. 'That can't have been easy.'

'No, but it's done. He won't ask much more now.'

'Not now you've answered his two questions.' I smile. 'You got off lightly there, I thought.'

'I know.' Ellie gets up and heads for the toaster. She sounds unexpectedly upbeat. She seems to have moved past the shocked stage with remarkable speed. Maybe having to deal with Alex has helped her to feel more normal. And she looks different somehow. Less wrinkled round the eyes and something else I can't put my finger on. Maybe she finally got around to using face cream – I've been telling her long enough, and so did Vanessa. Or maybe that's what's helping – no more Vanessa.

* * *

With Alex fully occupied, the rest of us can get going at a civilised pace. I take my tea and toast into the study and check my phone to see how far the news has travelled. There's nothing on my news app, but a search produces a reference to Vanessa's 'sudden death' on the local news page. It will only be a matter of time before my friends make the connection, and I'm glad I turned my social media off last night. The thought of having to see their comments and the inevitable online storm that's bound to follow is all too much.

I need to make myself do something normal, if only to take my mind off Vanessa. I'd set aside today for learning lines. I've got a month before rehearsals begin, but I want to be word-perfect when we start, and it's a big part. Sundays in our house aren't the old-fashioned conventional sort. Alex has to eat the minute he gets back from singing, so it's easier to have sandwiches than a roast. Afternoons were always family time in the past, but since coming home I've found the routine's changed. Dad's joined a new cycling group and he's out all day on his bike, and Ellie spends the afternoon in her studio while Alex is practising or on his computer games. Sandy often takes Nora out on Sundays and she asked if I'd like to join them. I suppose it was kindly meant, but she just doesn't get that even though Nora may be a lovely old lady, I don't want to spend my afternoon looking round some boring stately home with the woman who stole my room. My clothes are still in my suitcase, and I've refused to hang them in Sandy's room on principle. The thought of having to iron something yet again to make it look half decent irritates me even more than usual. I won't be able to learn lines like this so I pull on running shorts instead of a dress. Exercise will do me more good than moping, and it should clear the last of my hangover. It was too hot to run yesterday, and I know I'll feel better if I can go out while it's still cool.

Running's not as much fun as bouldering, but it's free, and I have to keep fit somehow. Five miles round the town and over the

30

Westwood does me good, but I get a shock when I come back. There's a crowd – not a big one, but definitely a crowd – of people outside Dean's house. It's obvious from the cameras and microphones that they're reporters. They weren't there when I left – the news must only have just broken – and I wonder how Dean's doing. Maybe he'll go away for a while to avoid them – I know that's what I'd do in his position. They're facing away from our house and I manage to let myself in without attracting any unwanted attention whilst noting that some of the other neighbours have been more than ready to provide information for the press. Although what Millie Cooper thinks she can tell them about Vanessa when she never goes anywhere other than the shops is a mystery to me.

The run's done me good, and the worst of the wrinkles come out of my dress after hanging it in the bathroom while I shower. It's one of my favourites, a floaty floral print, perfect for a hot day, and just putting it on improves my mood. Maybe I will manage to learn some lines, but I might be better off doing it in the garden rather than cooped up in here. I need coffee first, and head for the kitchen. Once the kettle's on I wander down the garden path to the studio, and Ellie waves at me and nods to say she'll join me. The doorbell rings as I'm pouring the water into the pot. Alex will have his headphones on by now, so it's up to me to answer. It's Dean. Wearing an un-ironed shirt, a baseball cap and dark rings under his eyes.

'Billie. Hi. Um… is your dad in?' He looks over his shoulder in what I can only think is a shifty manner, and I realise he must have come round the back of his house and detoured along the other side of the road to avoid the reporters. I take a step backwards and we stand awkwardly in the porch, out of sight of the crowd opposite.

'He's out on his bike. Ellie's here, though. Can we help?'

'Well… maybe. That is…' I don't know how to help him get whatever it is he wants to say out of his mouth, but Ellie's come up behind me and she's better at this sort of stuff than me.

'Dean. Come in – how are you doing?'

'Ellie, I need some help. I was hoping Mike…'

'He's out cycling.'

'Yes, Billie said.' Dean pauses. He seems to be making up his mind about something. 'Look, Ellie, can I come in? The police have been over asking questions and I feel like I need some advice. I can't talk to Vanessa's parents, they're upset enough as it is and they're busy with the kids, anyway. And it's the middle of the night back home.'

'Of course, come in.' Ellie hustles him in, shooting me a look that says 'please don't leave me alone with him', and we all troop into the kitchen.

* * *

Dean sinks into the first chair he finds, and as soon as he sits down a rush of grief and something else – is it fear? – sweeps across his face and he puts his face in his hands. It's a gesture I'd have expected from Vanessa rather than Dean, but I suppose he's picked up some actorly traits over the years. There's an awkward silence while Ellie and I look at each other, not sure whether to say something or not. We busy ourselves with getting out the nice mugs, pouring the coffee and finding some biscuits. Despite Ellie's signal for support, I'm not sure I want to be part of this conversation, but she's placed my mug very firmly on the table and I don't have a good excuse to leave. Dean's finally lifted his head and is staring into the middle distance, thinking about goodness knows what.

'So, Dean,' says Ellie. 'How can we help?' Her unexpectedly direct approach seems to shock him out of his trance.

'Sorry?' he says, looking around as if surprised to find himself here rather than in his own high-spec kitchen.

'You said the police had come to see you and you needed some advice. What did they want?' Ellie asks. She's clearly decided this is no time for niceties, and I'm surprised to hear her talking like this – she sounds more like Sandy than herself.

'They said... they said... Vanessa didn't kill herself. She was murdered.'

'Murdered?' Ellie's mug wobbles as she puts it down. 'But I thought they said it was suicide?'

'They did. But that was before they noticed there wasn't any blood on... on Vanessa. At least – not in the right places. They said if she'd done it herself, there'd be more blood on her arms or the floor or something... I can't remember it all. It was so unexpected. I couldn't take it all in. And there was something about the... the hole. It was too big. If she'd done it herself, it would have been smaller...' He pauses, trying to remember. 'Oh, and the residue, the gun residue. There wasn't any on her hands. There should have been. Yes, that was very important. The residue. They said...' Dean fumbles in a pocket for a handkerchief, the tears streaming down his face, and I can't help but feel sorry for him, even while my brain is trying to compute what he's just told us.

'Oh, Dean. I'm so sorry,' says Ellie. 'But... I suppose this means you were right after all. You said last night that you were sure Vanessa wouldn't have killed herself. I suppose it's good in a way that you were right?' She pats his hand gently in the hope that this might help, looking towards me for confirmation.

'Right,' I tell him, unable to think of anything more original to say. Dean nods soundlessly, over and over again, trying to regain control, and we find ourselves talking inanely, trying to cover our embarrassment.

'What are the police doing now?' Ellie asks. 'Is it a murder investigation now? Oh dear, that sounds awful.' She looks at me again, signalling that I should say something.

'It is awful,' I say, struggling to think of something to say that isn't just a repetition of Ellie's words. 'It's almost like something on the telly, isn't it?' Where on earth did that come from? Vanessa was filming for a TV series; it's the worst thing I could have said. I must be in shock too. 'Only this is a million times worse, of course,' I add hastily, hoping Dean's too upset to register my insensitivity.

'You're right,' he says, a hysterical half-laugh escaping from his lips. 'I feel like I'm in a dream, only it's not a dream, it's a nightmare, one I can't wake up from.' He takes a deep breath – he's probably telling himself to get a grip like I was yesterday – and pushes his mug towards Ellie, who fills it with more coffee.

'You know what they always say on the TV about the husband doing it?' Dean continues.

'Oh, Dean.' Ellie covers her mouth with her hand. 'They don't suspect you, do they?'

'Of course they do. They didn't say so, but why wouldn't they? There's a reason for it, you know – suspecting husbands. It's because it usually is them.' Ellie has no answer for this, and neither do I. We can hardly ask him if he did it.

'So what did they say, exactly?' I ask. He said he wanted to talk, after all.

'They said they'd opened a murder investigation, and they needed to ask a few questions but I wasn't under arrest.'

'I suppose that's good,' Ellie says doubtfully, and I reckon he might have been lucky there.

'They wanted to know what I was doing yesterday afternoon. And they took away the clothes I was wearing. The ones I was wearing yesterday. Not today.' Dean can hardly string his sentences together, and I'm not surprised.

'Of course,' says Ellie. 'But what did they want those for?' You can tell she doesn't watch much crime on TV. Maybe Dean would have been better off talking to Dad after all.

'To check for gun residue. They took a swab off my hand as well. Although surely it wouldn't still be there after so long.' His voice trails away, and he's staring into the middle distance. I can't imagine what he's seeing there – is it Vanessa and the hole, or a prison cell?

'So what happens next?' Ellie asks. 'They're not going to put you in a cell, are they?'

'No. Not yet, anyway.' Dean tries to smile, but it's not a joke. 'They said they'll be back once they've got the post-mortem results and the lab results on my clothes. It could be a few days.'

'A few days! That's terrible – how can they keep you hanging on like that?'

'They can do what they want, Ellie, they're the police.'

'I suppose so.' Ellie pauses, thinking. 'To be honest, Dean, I'm not sure Mike will be able to help you any more than I can. It's not as if he knows any criminal lawyers. You might be better off asking someone in your London production office.'

'I guess so,' says Dean. He's looking a bit calmer now, despite everything. Perhaps telling someone what's happened has helped him, like me talking to Jay last night. 'I suppose I should have thought of that before chasing round here.' He smiles ruefully at Ellie.

'Don't worry about it,' she says, but she takes the opportunity to stand up, signalling that it might be time for Dean to leave, and he follows suit. 'What will you do next?' she asks as they make their way out of the kitchen.

'I'm going to stay with Vanessa's parents – if they'll have me,' he says. 'I need to be with the kids and I can't bring them here, not with that crowd outside the house.'

'Good idea.' Their voices drift out of earshot as they walk down the hallway and I start to clear the table. The pot and matching mugs are Ellie's special ones and she doesn't like them to go in the dishwasher. I turn on the tap, squirt the washing-up liquid into the bowl, and that's when it hits me. Vanessa didn't kill herself. She was murdered. And I was in her room – how soon after? Soon enough for anyone who finds out to think it was me that did it. If it wasn't Dean, the number-one suspect could be me. I stand stock-still, my hands in the bowl, hardly noticing it fill, let alone overflow, as my thoughts race round my head trying to work out what it all means. Ellie returns to find me staring into space, up to my elbows in bubbles, but she doesn't question it, just turns off the taps and hands me a tea towel.

'Leave that for now, Billie,' she says, her voice brisk and tight. 'We need to talk. Before Alex comes asking for his lunch.' As I sit opposite her, still in a daze, I see her face has changed again. The smooth, calm features of the early morning have been replaced by the familiar wrinkles, and she looks as if she's seen a ghost. She was putting on a show of competence for Dean, but she can't put on a show for me, not for long. She's got to talk to someone; if Sandy were here, it would be her, but she's not. She'll have to make do with me.

'All right.' I sit down again and wait.

'Who do you think did it, Billie?' For one heart-stopping moment I think she knows everything and is about to accuse me. I'm about to deny it when I catch myself just in time, realising it's a genuine question, not a trap. Giddy with relief, albeit only temporary, I search for a more suitable response.

'Crikey, there's no beating about the bush with you, is there? Are you turning into Alex?'

'Be serious, Billie. We don't have much time.' I look at the clock behind me. She's right. Alex will come looking for his lunch at one o'clock sharp, and she needs to plan what to tell him.

'All right, but I don't know. Why would I? Isn't it the police's job to find that out?'

'Yes, but it's what Alex will ask, and I need to know what to tell him.'

'Tell him what I just told you. We don't know. The police will work it out. Do you have to tell him now, anyway? Can't you wait a bit? The situation's no different from his perspective, after all. Why don't you wait till Dad's home and discuss it with him?'

'No. I don't want to talk about it with him.' I'm surprised she's admitting this to me, but perhaps she's decided it's not worth pretending things aren't good between them. She seems to realise what she says and quickly adds, 'Well, maybe I should... I don't know... oh, my head's in a muddle – isn't yours? It was bad enough wondering why Vanessa would kill herself, but this is ten times worse.'

'Of course it is, but...' But what? We both know how these things work. Now it's murder, the police will be digging into every inch of Vanessa's life. And since coming to Beverley, she's hardly had time to make friends. All she's done is work and spend what little free time she has with the people in this house. How long will it be before they

36

coming knocking at our door, asking questions? But Ellie's barely listening to me anyway; she's almost talking to herself now, her hands twisting in her lap.

'I mean, I don't want to wait. I need to decide what to say to Alex now. Before he finds out another way.' I don't know why she's in such a hurry, but she's working herself up into a state and I need to calm her down. I put my hand on hers to stop the twisting and wait until she's looking at me again.

'Look, I get you want to tell him, that's fine. And I know he's going to ask who did it, but we can't sit here and make up an answer to that, can we? Just tell him someone was upset with her and killed her and it's all very sad. What else can you do?'

Ellie stares at me for a moment, pure panic in her eyes, and then she drops her head and rubs them hard, as if scrubbing her worries away. 'Of course. You're right. I'm sorry, Billie, I'm not thinking straight.' She gives me a crooked smile. 'I just need to stick to the facts. Alex can cope with facts, can't he? Vanessa's dead. We don't know who killed her. The police will find out who it was. Simple.'

* * *

Somehow, the rest of the day passes. There's not much opportunity for private contemplation when you're with Alex, and since Ellie's working and Dad's still out, entertaining him becomes my job. Alex has taken the latest news about Vanessa in his customary fashion, readily accepting the reassurance that the police will do their job and bring the culprit to justice. He's disappointed at the news that Heidi and George won't be coming over any time soon, so I suggest a baking session might be a good idea. Ellie's eyebrows raise at the idea of cooking in this heat, but the kitchen's cool at this time of day and Alex is delighted with the plan. My churning thoughts have to wait their turn while we bake and then decorate a vast number of biscuits, and it's strangely therapeutic. Ellie's still working when we take her a sample and I don't want to be around when Dad gets in, so I suggest a *Lord of the Rings* session, which both Alex and Ellie agree to with alacrity, Ellie because Alex will be out of her way, and Alex because he's not normally allowed to watch movies in the afternoon.

'All right, why not?' Ellie's halfway through a watercolour of the minster and barely gives her attention to us, let alone the biscuits.

'Awesome,' says Alex, already halfway out of the room and eager to get started before she changes her mind. 'Can we watch the extended version, Billie? You can choose which one we watch – there won't be time for more than one, will there?'

'Oh, I don't know… if we carry on after dinner, we might manage two – if we go for the originals, that is,' I say, thinking this might go down well with Ellie. I draw the curtains against the sun while Alex locates the DVDs. I'm sure we could find the films online somewhere, but Alex likes the old-fashioned way of watching. Maybe they'll be valuable antiques one day.

'Cool, let's start with number two.' I knew he'd say that. Alex hates stopping halfway through things, and he'll want to see Frodo at Mount Doom.

'All right, my precioussssss!' I rush up and grab him from behind, feeling a sense of relief in being able to act like a kid instead of an adult.

'Get off!' He likes it, though, I know, and we collapse in a sibling heap on the sofa. The film starts, and I tell my brain to give me a rest, immersing myself in the comforting world of Middle Earth.

* * *

It's late by the time we finish the movies and the pizza Alex has persuaded Ellie to let us eat in front of them. Dad joins us, happy to leave the 'women of the house' to discuss the day's events without him, and I manage to avoid the unwelcome thoughts in my head about Vanessa and who might or might not have killed her and whether I should go to the police after all by asking Alex daft questions about dwarves and elves and how much food orcs need to stay alive. I thought I'd want to call Jay again but I can't muster up the energy to go over it all again or to torment myself with the sounds of his holiday, and I go to straight to bed. Lying there in the dark, listening to the others moving around, my thoughts drift back to my conversation with Ellie this morning. I know she can get in a state, but that was something else – why on earth did she ask me who killed Vanessa? How was I supposed to know?

I turn over, trying to avoid the dodgy springs in the sofa bed, congratulating myself on doing such a good job of calming her down. And suddenly, as if in a rewind, I remember the last thing she said before Alex burst into the kitchen looking for his lunch. She'd just been talking about how it was simple after all, what she had to tell him. I remember her face suddenly clearing as she said the words. Then she looked around the kitchen for a moment as if waking up from a dream, got up and gave my shoulder a pat on her way to the sink. 'Vanessa's gone, that's all that matters.' She said it very quietly, as if talking to herself, but I heard her then and I can hear her again now. And there was something in her voice – a sort of cold satisfaction – that makes me shiver.

FIVE

Nora's in the kitchen. I want to turn around and leave but I can't. I've done well to avoid her for nearly a month, and I've managed to do it without actually being rude. Never mind Dad's expectations, my Granny Luci's always said rudeness and swearing were the only things Mum really hated, and I can't shake the feeling that they're both looking over my shoulder. Nora's sitting at the table, buttering a slice of toast with a cup of tea and a jar of posh marmalade in front of her. It's the one I gave her for Christmas. Before she moved in here and pinched my room.

'Morning, Billie,' she says, giving me a hesitant smile. 'The kettle's just boiled if you want some tea.'

'Thanks.' I switch it on again and start to make my own toast. 'D'you want another?'

'No, dear, but thank you for asking.' She carries on eating and I try to ignore her, keeping my back to her while I find the peanut butter and tea bags. I was hoping I'd left it late enough to have the kitchen to myself, but it looks like I'll have to eat in the study again. Breakfast made, I head for the door with my mug and plate, but Nora interrupts me.

'Why don't you stay here for your breakfast? It can't be much fun eating in that tiny room. And you might like to try some of this marmalade – it's very tasty, you know.' She twinkles her eyes at me and I know she's trying to butter me up, but I don't want to be accused of being impolite later on so I hide my sigh and sit down. We eat in silence for a minute or two, and then she puts down her cup and takes a deep breath, as if summoning up her courage.

'I'm sorry, Billie.' It comes out in a rush, and she's taken me by surprise, so I don't quite catch what she's saying.

'Sorry, Nora, what did you say?'

'I said I'm sorry. For taking your room. You were away when I moved in and I don't think Sandy and Ellie thought it through properly when they made their plans. I did ask if it was a good idea to take your room away from you, but they were so sure you wouldn't be needing it anymore, and I'm afraid I let them persuade me. It must be very difficult not having your own space in your own home, and I'm sorry it's because of me.'

'Oh.' She's taken me completely by surprise. Not just for what she's said but the way she's said it. Like a person with a mind of her own. A person who's got opinions and isn't afraid to share them. I've not heard her talk like that before.

'I know you've been avoiding me, and it makes me sad. I always felt it a shame we didn't get to know each other very well when you were younger. It wasn't easy for me to get away from York before William died – he needed a lot of looking after, of course – but I always enjoyed your company when we did spend time together.'

'I… I enjoyed your company too, Nora,' I say. It's true, even though this has to be the most awkward conversation I've had in my entire life.

'I don't blame you for being cross, dear. And I wanted to say thank you. For moving out for me, even though you didn't want to. When William died, I didn't know how I'd cope on my own, not with my hip being what it is. If it hadn't been for Sandy suggesting I come here, I don't know what I'd have done.' I feel awful. I've been so busy sulking about my room I've not thought for even a moment about what the reason might be for her living here in the first place.

'Nora… I'm sorry too. I…' I don't know what to say. Why shouldn't she move in? The house belongs to her daughters as well as my dad. And I had moved out, after all. It was only because I'm so rubbish at managing my money that I had to come back for the summer.

'I shouldn't have been mad at you, Nora. I don't need the room – I'm only home for a few weeks, what does it matter where I sleep?'

'Well, I know I'd rather not sleep on a sofa if I'm given the choice, but if you can manage it and we can be friends, it would make me very happy. I have a lovely grandson, but I've never had a granddaughter to call my own, and I wouldn't mind one if you're up for it?' A grandmother. I've not got one of those – at least not in this country. Dad's parents died ten years ago and Granny Luci's a very long way away. And the idea of making an old lady living in a strange town happy – corny though it sounds – isn't so bad.

'All right.' We give each other a tentative smile and she takes another sip of tea.

'Good. That's settled. And now you can put me out of my misery.'

'How?'

'Sandy and Ellie have got it into their heads that I'm a frail old woman who needs shielding from the harsher side of life. I want you to tell me all about this murder.'

* * *

It's not quite like one of those slushy movies where the disaffected teenager makes friends with the grumpy old person and it all ends happily ever after, but it is an improvement. Nora's dodgy hip means she needs a downstairs bedroom but there's nothing wrong with her mind. It helps to have something new to talk about, and by the time I've finished explaining about Vanessa my ideas about her have changed a lot. And as an added bonus, my mind's starting to believe the story of my first finding out about it at the barbecue. I always got the impression that Nora relied on William, but it looks like it was the other way around. And if her bank account is anything to judge him by, he did a rubbish job of providing for her in her old age. The way Sandy talks about her, you'd think she wasn't capable of making decisions about anything more than what to put on her toast, but she gets her head round the Vanessa situation in no time, telling me she's sure it won't be long before the police come knocking at our door to ask more questions.

'I've only been here a few months, but that's long enough to understand what's going on, especially when you're in the house as much as I am. And that woman didn't know anyone in Beverley except this family. They'll be here before the end of the day, you mark my words.'

'I expect you're right. We'd better get our stories straight, hadn't we?' I try to make a joke of it, but it's true. I need to decide, properly, what I'm going to say if – no, when – they come. I drain my mug, say I'd better be getting dressed and ask Nora if she'd like a hand getting back to her room.

* * *

We try to behave as if it's a normal day. I check my phone, and Vanessa's there, with varying amounts of coverage, depending on where you look. A single mention on the news, with links to pages about her career and personal life. Outpourings of gushing comments and grief on social media, most of it from people who never met her, of course. The inevitable sad messages from the world of film. It becomes repetitive in the end, and I put my phone in a drawer, not bothering to reply properly to any messages. I'd not mentioned Vanessa to many people, and I'm glad of it now. Jay, Gaby and a couple of others will have to make do with an emoji. I really don't have the energy to think of anything more to say. I can't be bothered going for a run, but the need for exercise of some sort is nagging at my brain, so I pull out my laptop and find a yoga session that Gaby's been raving about. I'm not normally into that sort of stuff, but it's surprisingly absorbing, and by the time I've finished, Alex is thumping on my door telling me he's back from his swim with Ellie and lunch is in the garden.

'What are your plans for this afternoon?' Nora asks as we sit down.

'It's the studio for me as soon as Mike gets back,' Ellie says. 'What about you, Billie?'

'I've got lines to learn,' I say. 'I thought I might sit in the garden to do it.'

'I think I'll join you,' says Nora. 'It's such a lovely day, it seems a shame to spend it indoors. I'll bring my book out, and if you want some help with those lines, you've only to ask.'

'Thanks, Nora, I might take you up on that.' I give her a smile, and I can't help noticing Ellie's not-so-well-concealed surprise to see us on such good terms. 'What will you be up to, Alex?' I ask, before Ellie has the chance to make a comment.

'Maths, chess and model building.' Alex counts them off on his fingers. 'You can help with the model if you like, although I expect you'd find it a bit hard.'

'I expect I would,' I say. 'What is it this time, or are you still working on the last one – a thunderstorm, wasn't it?'

'It's a Hurricane, silly!'

'Of course it is – silly me.' I can't resist teasing him, he's so funny when he tells me off. 'You can show me when it's finished, and I'm sure I'll be very impressed.'

'I will if there's time.' Alex considers the matter seriously. 'I've got piano practice as well, remember. You might have to wait until after dinner.'

'Okay, I'll bear that in mind. Keep me posted.' I push back my chair and start clearing the table, leaving Ellie to explain to Alex that a stamp and envelope won't be required.

* * *

We've done all right, considering our next-door neighbour's just been murdered, but it's a subdued evening meal nonetheless. Nora seems to have had a new lease of life now that we've made our peace and she chats away about her book and how she's enjoyed helping me with my lines.

'I've always thought of the *Dream* as one of Shakespeare's lesser works,' she says. 'But I think I may have been doing it a disservice. Just because it's a comedy doesn't mean it can't be clever too. What do you think, Sandy? Didn't you study it at school once?'

'I did study it, but I don't really have a view, Mother. It's a long time since I've seen it performed, I've not thought about it in years. Are you ready to go back to your room now? I've got some marking to do – I can take you before I go upstairs.'

'Not just yet, thank you. I'll have a chat to Ellie while she's clearing up. You don't mind, do you, dear?'

'Of course not. There's no rush, anyway. I won't be going back to the studio this evening. Maybe we can watch something together on the telly.' Nora looks pleased, and doesn't seem to notice the fleeting annoyance which crosses Sandy's face.

'Can I get down, please?' Alex interrupts. 'You said I could play on my Xbox after dinner. Can I go now?'

'Yes, as long as you've not got any homework to do?' Ellie looks across at Mike.

'No, we're good. All done and dusted this afternoon. Just an hour, mind you. I'll be up to check you've finished.'

Alex is already on his way, only pausing briefly to put his plate by the sink. 'Don't set the timer until I'm in my room,' he calls over his shoulder. We listen in anticipation as he thumps up the stairs to his room and slams his bedroom door. A few seconds later a muffled 'Now!' drifts down the stairs, and we all laugh.

'I've got work to do too,' Dad says. 'Can I borrow the study for an hour or two, Billie?' I'm just about to say, yes, no problem, I was planning on joining Ellie and Nora, when the doorbell rings. Alex will have his headphones on, and Dad's already half out of his chair so he goes to get it. The rest of us exchange glances. I think we've all got a good idea who it will be, and it's no surprise when we hear the detectives' voices, soft at first, but with increasing clarity as they make their way down the hall. There's a pause, and then Dad puts his head round the door.

'I've put them in the lounge. They want to talk to us,' he says in what I can only describe as a melodramatically loud whisper.

'All of us?' Sandy asks.

'Oh. I don't know. They just said the adults in the house. I didn't think to check which ones they meant.'

'If it's about Vanessa, I hardly suppose they'll need to talk to Mother. She barely knew the woman.' It's a reasonable statement, and Sandy no doubt thinks Nora needs protecting from the horrors of murder, but I can't think it matters much.

'We can't keep them waiting all evening while we try and decide who they do or don't want to see,' Nora says. 'Why don't we all go in and find out?'

'Good idea,' I say, before anyone has time to suggest an alternative. 'Come on, Nora, here's your frame.' I hand her the frame and give her a lift out of her chair before Sandy has a chance to protest, and Dad – an expression of amused surprise on his face – leads the way through to the lounge.

DI Twist and her sergeant have positioned themselves on the two armchairs, leaving the sofa for the rest of us. There's not room for all of us, and Nora can't get up again if she sits on it, so Dad pulls up the two chairs from Alex's worktable and Nora and I sit on those. Ellie and Sandy plonk themselves on the sofa, and Dad sits on the piano stool, no doubt thinking it a better option than being sandwiched between the two of them. We've been so busy sorting out who'll sit where, we've forgotten to ask if they need us all there, and by the time we're all settled it feel silly to ask. Fortunately it's not my job to do so.

'Um, do you actually need all of us?' Dad asks. 'I'm sorry, I should have asked before we all sat down. You said you needed the adults in the house, and well… this is us.'

'There are more people than I'd anticipated,' DI Twist says, although I'd already guessed that from the expression on her face as we all came in. 'For those of you we've not met before' – she looks across at first Sandy and then Nora – 'I'm Detective Inspector Ronnie Twist and this,' she indicates her partner, 'is my sergeant, Luke Carter. We're investigating the murder of Vanessa Forsyth, and we need to talk to anyone who knew her. I understand she had a limited number of friends in Beverley but that you knew the family, hence our visit. Perhaps you could let Sergeant Carter know your names before we start? For the record, you understand.' She's as cool as a cucumber, and I can almost see the cogs whirring behind her baby-blue eyes as she looks round the cramped room, taking in the old-fashioned TV, upright piano and self-assembled table, all squeezed into the room alongside the chairs and sofa.

'Of course,' says Dad. 'But we didn't all know her well. At least, some of us knew her better than others.' That's an understatement, I think, and I'm sure I'm not the only one. Dad must realise how this sounds, and hurries on. 'What I mean to say is, Nora – my mother-in-law – has only been living with us for a couple of months. She had very little to do with Vanessa, and I doubt she has much to tell you.'

'Thank you for that,' says DI Twist, turning to look at the table behind Dad. It's not very interesting, as it's kept immaculately tidy by Alex, who likes his books arranged in meticulous order. 'I think, if you don't mind, we'll start with everyone and assess the situation.' I can't work out exactly what this means, but it shuts Dad up. She looks at the sergeant, who turns to Ellie first, as she's sitting beside him, and asks for her full name and age, repeating the process with each of us in turn. It takes a while to get round us all, with explanations of who's related to who on the way.

'So, to confirm,' she says, once we're done, 'you, Mr Preston, live here with your wife, Ellie, her sister, Sandy, and their mother, Nora.' We nod. 'Billie is your daughter by your first wife, now deceased, and

Alex, who is upstairs, is your son.' We all nod again. She's not got notes to check against, but she's got the measure of us in a fraction of the time most people manage. I suppose it's part of her job to listen carefully. Satisfied with her understanding, she checks to see that the sergeant has got all the details before ploughing on.

'As you know, Vanessa Forsyth was found dead late on Saturday afternoon. Evidence gathered at the scene and at the post-mortem confirms that although suicide was indicated at first, she did not die at her own hand.' There's a pause, and it seems to occur to her that her language might not have been sufficiently clear. 'In other words, we are conducting a murder investigation.' There's a silence while we wonder what to say. We knew that, of course. Even if Dean hadn't been round yesterday morning, we'd have read or heard the news by now, but it feels rude to mention it so we keep quiet and wait for her to say more.

'We're at a very early stage of the investigation,' she says. 'But we are keen to speak to everyone who knew Miss Forsyth and who may have been in contact with her in the days leading up to her death. We may need to talk to you in more detail later in the next week or two, but in the first instance, please can each of you tell me when you last had contact with Miss Forsyth?' It's strange hearing her referred to like that, but I suppose she's not the only actress to avoid publicising her married status. Vanessa Westerby might have sounded okay, but I suppose she'd already picked her stage name before she met Dean. She turns to Dad first.

'Mr Preston?' Dad jumps, taken by surprise that she's starting with him.

'Yes?' His startled response has the unfortunate result of making him look like he has something to hide. But maybe that's not surprising.

'Can you tell us when your last point of contact was with Vanessa Forsyth? Did you see her on the day she died? On Saturday?' She's looking at him calmly but intently, a bit like a cat that you're not quite sure isn't going to jump at you.

'Um, Saturday, no, I didn't. I was working in the morning,

preparing lessons, marking, planning work for Alex.' She looks at him enquiringly.

'Work for Alex?'

'Yes. He's home-schooled. We share the teaching between us. I do maths, science and geography, and Sandy does English, history and classics. We both work part time so as to fit it in. Ellie takes care of the rest.' He gives her a quick grin, which she returns. They're still a team where Alex is concerned, whatever else might be going on between them.

'All right, so you were working in the morning. And cycling in the afternoon. When did you return home?'

'It was around five. I saw Dean on the pavement as I was approaching the house and asked him to join us for a meal.'

'So I understand. And the last time you saw Vanessa was...?'

'Let me think... it must have been sometime last week. Yes, Wednesday, that's it. George and Alex go to a local chess club together. I brought them home and took George over to the house. Vanessa was there, and she let him in.' It sounds plausible enough if you don't know any different. DI Twist doesn't know any different, so she doesn't challenge it.

'How did she seem?'

'Vanessa? Oh, she seemed fine. I only saw her for a minute. She said thanks for giving George a lift and she was sure she'd see me again soon.'

'Mrs Preston?' DI Twist has dropped Dad like a stone and he can't prevent a look of relief from crossing his face. I'm sure she'll have seen it but she's moved on to Ellie, who's quicker with her answer, having had more time to prepare.

'I saw Vanessa on Saturday,' she says, which is clearly of interest to the inspector. 'I was putting some rubbish in the bin and she came out of her house to get into her car. It was about seven thirty and I said something about it being an early start for her. She laughed and said not nearly as early as some of the film sets she'd been on, and that was it.'

'That fits with what we know about her timings for the day. Did you see her again after that?'

'No. I was at home doing housework in the morning and in my studio all afternoon.'

'You're an artist, is that correct?'

'Yes, that's right. You might have seen some of my work in the shops in Beverley. Quite a few stock them.' DI Twist smiles politely, not letting us into the secrets of her artistic tastes for now. She's been working her way round the room, so it's Sandy next.

'Miss Henderson? That's correct, isn't it?'

'Yes, that's me,' Sandy says, in a 'name, rank and number' kind of voice. She once told me that when she was training to be a teacher someone told her never to smile before Christmas, and she looks as if she's putting that advice into action right now.

'Can you recall the last time you saw Vanessa Forsyth?'

'I've been trying to think, and I believe it was quite some time ago. I'm not sure I can be exact. It must have been at the party. The one Vanessa and Dean held for George's birthday. It was quite a big affair, a lot of people were there, mostly from the film company, I think.'

'Do you remember how she was on that day?'

'The same as always, I suppose. I didn't really talk to her.'

'You weren't particularly friendly?'

'No, we had no reason to be. I don't have children, I'm not... creative in any way. We didn't have much in common.'

'But you attended the party?'

'Yes, they were kind enough to invite us all, and I thought it rude not to accept. It meant Mother had someone to help her, getting food and so on. And I thought I might be able to help with Alex. So that Ellie and Mike could enjoy themselves, you know.' She gives Ellie a little smile. Sandy's always looking for ways to help people, but I reckon looking after Nora and Alex will have given her a welcome excuse to avoid talking to Vanessa and her friends.

'So you didn't see her on Saturday?'

'No. I was working in the morning, like Mike. I went shopping in the afternoon and to change my library books.' DI Twist appears to mentally file Sandy in the 'not much to tell' category and moves on to Nora. 'Mrs Henderson. Your son-in-law seems to think you won't have much to tell us about Vanessa Forsyth. Is that correct?'

'I'm afraid so,' says Nora, apologetically. 'Although we had a nice chat at the party. She came and sat next to me and told me all about her children and the film she was making. It was set in the war, you know, and I was telling her about my mother and her experiences in the Blitz. She was very interested. A nice woman, I thought. Most people ignore you when you get to my time in life, but she didn't.'

We all turn to look at Nora in surprise. This is the first time anyone's described Vanessa as a 'nice woman' since I've been home, and none of us had any idea she'd talked to Nora at the party. If DI Twist notices our not-so-well-concealed shock, she's not letting it show, but she must be pleased to have a more detailed response from one of us at last.

'How did she seem to you?' she asks. 'I realise you didn't know her well, but did she seem stressed or unhappy, worried in any way?'

'Oh no. She was very happy. Full of life, she was. She really looked like a film star, didn't she?' Nora looks round the room for confirmation and we nod weakly. 'It was an afternoon party but she was all dressed up in a slinky blue dress. Aquamarine, it was, and shimmering in the sunlight. And thick makeup, of course. She needed that, mind, she was glamorous, but you couldn't call her beautiful...' Nora's in a world of her own, remembering the party, and she suddenly realises that perhaps this amount of detail isn't required. 'Oh. I'm sorry, you probably don't need to know all that, do you? You must forgive an old lady for letting her mind wander a little.'

'Not at all.' DI Twist smiles at her. 'We're trying to build up a picture of Vanessa, and everything we hear is useful.' She pauses. 'I don't suppose you saw her on Saturday?'

'No, I don't go out a great deal. I was at home all day, but I did hear Ellie calling to her. My window's at the front of the house and I like the fresh air, so I keep it open.'

'Thank you, Mrs Henderson, that's very helpful.' DI Twist turns, inevitably, in my direction, an enquiring look on her face. 'And Billie? What can you tell us?'

'I've only been home for a few weeks, so I didn't have much time to get to know Vanessa. I babysat for them a couple of times. And I saw her at the party, of course, but I never really spoke to her much.' It sounds reasonable enough, doesn't it? 'I wanted to get to know her better, of course. I was hoping she'd be able to help me, but I didn't want to look pushy, or to ask when she was busy with her filming.'

'How might she have been able to help you?' DI Twist asks.

'I'm an actress too. Not a successful one, of course. I've been working in a schools' touring production. I'm only home for the holidays – I'll be leaving in August to start rehearsing for the autumn show.'

'I see.' DI Twist nods understandingly. I think it came out all right, and I heave an internal sigh of relief, forgetting that I've not actually said anything about Vanessa. 'So was the party the last time you saw Miss Forsyth?'

'Yes, that's right.'

'And on Saturday?'

'I had a lie-in, washed some clothes, stuff like that. I was out shopping in the afternoon.'

'Like your aunt. Did you go together?' She's not my aunt, but I let it go.

'No, we're not really into the same shops.' Sandy grins at me, and it's easy enough to work out from my vintage Laura Ashley and her smart linen shift that I'm telling the truth. DI Twist turns to her sergeant, who is yet to speak, perhaps to check that he's kept up with what we've been saying. He certainly seems quick on the keyboard, so I can't imagine he's had a problem, and he gives her a nod in return.

'All right. I think we're done here. Thank you for your help.' Dad follows her lead in standing, ready to see her out.

'You're welcome, we're happy to help,' he says. 'Although I'm sorry we've not been able to tell you anything relevant.'

'On the contrary. Any information about Miss Forsyth, particularly in the past week or so, is relevant,' she says as they walk towards the front door. 'Good night.'

There's a stunned silence, no one knowing quite what to say until Dad comes back, uncertainty written all over his face.

'What do you suppose all that was about?' he says, moving the piano stool back into place and sinking into the chair vacated by Sergeant Carter.

'It's obvious, isn't it?' Ellie sounds uncharacteristically irritable. 'Vanessa was murdered and they're interviewing everyone who knew her.'

'And now they've done so, perhaps we can get on with our evening,' says Sandy. 'I don't know about anyone else, but I could do with a cup of tea.' She gets up and starts towards the door. 'Mother? Would you like one? I can bring you one before I go up.' Ellie and Dad stand up too and they head out of the room, talking about tea, washing-up, marking, anything but murder. Nora looks at me and raises her eyebrows.

'So that's it. No one's going to talk about it. Pretend it isn't happening and it's bound to go away. Oh well, they'll find out soon enough.'

'Find out what?'

'Those detectives will be back, you mark my words.'

'But why? They got what they wanted, didn't they? We told them everything we could about Vanessa, why would they come back?'

'We told them everything, did we? I don't think so, and I don't think that detective woman will think so either. But that's not the only reason they'll be back.'

'Isn't it?'

'No.' Nora reaches for her frame and manoeuvres herself into her favourite armchair. It takes a while, but she shakes off my hand when I try to help her and clearly expects me to wait for her to finish.

'No?'

'No. We're suspects.'

'Suspects?'

'Keep your voice down, Billie. We don't want Alex to hear.'

'What do you mean, suspects?' I move to sit closer to her and drop my voice.

'Vanessa didn't know many people in Beverley, did she?'

'No, she'd only been here a few months. She was busy filming. She didn't have time for socialising.'

'So how many people can there be on their list of suspects? Dean, of course. Maybe the film crew, people at the theatre. But they can't think it was a random stranger, can they?'

'I don't know what they're thinking, Nora. And I think you're putting two and two together and making about seventeen.'

'Maybe I am, but there's something else.'

'What?' This is starting to annoy me. I reckon Nora's been reading too many Agatha Christies, and I sincerely hope she's not thinking of sharing any of her bright ideas with anyone else.

'The alibis.'

'What alibis? They weren't asking about alibis.'

'Oh yes they were.' Nora leans back in her chair with an air of satisfaction. 'That detective with the funny name didn't just ask when we'd seen Vanessa. She asked if we'd seen her on Saturday. She was casting her net, finding out what we were doing at the time of the murder. Sneakily, hoping we wouldn't notice. But I did.' Is she right? Is that what they were doing? My stomach feels like someone's dropped a football into it, and I instinctively do what the others did – bury my head in the sand.

'Well, aren't you the clever one?' I say in my best jollying-along voice. 'But let's not tell the others just yet – we don't want to worry them, do we? Now, why don't I see what's happened to that cup of tea?' I take myself out of the room before she can reply and stand in the hall for a moment, telling my heart to stop thumping. Because I know she's right. We didn't tell them everything, and no one's got a proper alibi. Any one of us could have done it, and it's surely only a matter of time before they find out that our motives are in much less short supply.

***

If Nora isn't going to listen to my advice, I don't want to be in the room to hear it. Dad's on his way to the study to do his marking so I grab my bag first and take it outside. Ellie's in the kitchen, pouring tea for herself and Nora, and I tell her I fancy a bit of fresh air.

'And a smoke?' she says, giving me a conspiratorial smile.

'Maybe.'

'Well, better take this with you,' she says, handing me a saucer. 'I don't want you spoiling my nice lawn.'

'Thanks.'

'Billie?'

'Yes?' I turn, my hand on the door handle.

'Are you okay?'

'Yes. Sort of. It's all a bit weird, isn't it?'

'You can say that again. But it won't last forever. One day we'll look back on all this and say what a strange time it was.'

'I guess.' We both stand there, neither of us sure what to say. Time for more head-burying, I think. 'You'd better get that to Nora before it gets cold.'

'Yes, you're right. See you later, Billie.' She picks up the tea and leaves before it can get any more awkward. I sneak a lager out of the fridge and go out into the cool of the garden, where I roll a cigarette and call Jay. No reply. And no messages today. We've only been together a couple of months, but I didn't expect this, not after everything that happened on Saturday. A little support would be nice, even though I didn't answer his messages yesterday.

I need a distraction. From Vanessa, and from Jay too. Perhaps I need to get back on social media, at least just a little bit. I post a picture of Vanessa, saying how sad it is that she's gone before trying Jay again. Still no answer. I refuse to embarrass myself by leaving a desperate voicemail and call Gaby instead. She's not busy – do I want to meet up? Now? I look at my watch. Nine o'clock and nothing on the horizon except home improvement programmes with Ellie and Nora or a lonely evening out here on my own. I tell her I'll be with her in twenty minutes.

* * *

There's nothing like an evening with your best friend when you're feeling rubbish. Gaby gives me a huge hug, tells me off for being late, and it's as if we've never been apart. We start in Spoons, of course, sitting outside so we can smoke with our Aperol spritzes. Gaby's heard about Vanessa and it's good to talk about it to someone who didn't know her and isn't interested in acting anyway. She agrees it's a shame I didn't get around to asking Vanessa for a leg-up in the industry, and she's interested to hear about DI Twist coming to the house, but she doesn't seem to think there's anything for us to worry about.

'They always talk to everyone, don't they? At least that's what my mum says. She watches all those crime series on the telly and as soon as she found out about Vanessa and I told her you lived next door to her, she said, "They'll be questioned, Billie's lot, you wait and see. They talk to everyone, those detectives do." She'll be chuffed to know she was right.'

'Glad to be of service,' I say. And I am. I like Gaby's mum, and if she thinks it's normal to have the police in the house, maybe I shouldn't be worrying. I should never have listened to Nora. I let her wind me up much too easily. Who does she think she is anyway, Miss Marple? 'Drink up,' I tell her. 'Time for The Corner House. You can't have a night out in Beverley without going there.' It's easy to change the topic of conversation as we walk through town, and Gaby never needs any encouragement to talk. It's a running joke in the family, and I know Ellie will be asking how many words I managed to get in edgeways tomorrow morning.

I let Gaby rattle on about her girlfriend, her parents, her grandad, her new job and even her little nephew, although my brain can't help drifting back to the murder and the secrets hiding in our house. Will they come out now? Or will they just fade away with the passage of time? Do they even matter now that Vanessa's dead? I tell myself not to worry, the main thing is she's gone, and maybe life can get back to normal again. I make myself focus on Gaby's news and manage some appropriate responses. Gaby loves to talk but she's a good listener too. She asks about the tour and I tell her about Jay and my new part, and she says well done and asks questions, making me feel bad for not giving her my full attention. It's good to be back with her, and when she tells me I have to come bouldering with her soon so she can show off her new kit it's easy to agree. After a few drinks my worries about Jay don't seem so important – so what if he's hooked up with some French girl? I've got better friends than him. Gaby and me go back years, and I'm looking forward to getting back on a climbing wall with her. I upload a picture of our drinks and she tells me she loves my posts and asks how I manage to keep it up. We finish up at the Kings' Head, where Gaby's dad picks us up, refusing to let his daughter walk 'all the way back to Molescroft' on her own. By the time we say goodbye, I feel as if I've got a bit of me back again. Someone's made up the sofa bed for me, and I don't even bother to check my phone before falling into the best night's sleep I've had since it happened.

SIX

It didn't happen all at once, but now a few days have passed without the police coming back, it really feels as if things are back to normal. The house begins to feel like it did before I went away. And before Vanessa came to live next door. There's still something going on with Dad and Ellie, but Sandy's loosened up a bit, Alex is less twitchy, and I think it maybe wasn't entirely my fault that Nora was hiding in her room so much of the time before. She's spending much more time with the rest of us now, and she seems to be enjoying it. Now that it's gone, I can see there must have been tension in the house before I set foot in the door. Everyone – even Alex – seemed out of sorts. Sandy was short-tempered, shutting herself in her room every evening, pacing late at night, and not asking me in, even when I hinted that I could do with some advice. And there were the arguments, of course. Dad and Ellie sneaking off to the studio to fight where they thought no one would hear them, forgetting that I'd be in the garden with my roll-ups. They tried to keep their voices down, and I couldn't catch everything, but there was one word that came over loud and clear. Vanessa. Maybe Ellie was right. All that matters is that Vanessa's gone. There are plenty of unsolved murders, after all, and maybe this will be one of them.

I'm back from my run one morning, making coffee, when the doorbell rings. I forget for a moment that Alex has gone to his French class with Sandy and after a minute it rings again.

'Doorbell!' calls Nora from her room.

'Got it,' I shout back, already on my way down the corridor. There's a tall shape outlined on the other side of the frosted glass, and I wonder if Ellie's expecting a delivery today. But it's not a delivery. It's Dean.

'Hey, Billie.' He doesn't look quite so awful as the last time I saw him, but he's not far off. And there's a shifty look about him, as if he'd rather not be here.

'Hey, Dean. How are you? I thought you were away – with Vanessa's parents.'

'Yeah, I was. It… it wasn't working out so well for me there. They told me the reporters have gone away, so I figured I'd come back.'

'Oh, okay.' It's true. It didn't take the newshounds long to realise they were wasting their time. And after all, Vanessa wasn't an A-lister, even though she liked to talk as though she was. I struggled to find any mention of her online this morning; they've all moved on to other things.

'Did you want to see Dad?'

'No, I didn't.' He's still looking awkward.

'Well, Ellie's here. She's in the studio but I was just about to take her a coffee. You'd better come in.'

'Okay… actually, Billie…' He starts speaking again, but I've already turned towards the kitchen, leaving him to shut the door behind himself. He takes a seat while I go on through the back door and tell Ellie he's here.

'Oh dear, what do you suppose he wants now?' she says, putting her brush in a pot of water and removing her smock. 'I know he's having a terrible time, but I really didn't see myself being cast as his personal counsellor. Stay with me, will you? I might need some moral support.'

'No problem,' I say, and she manages to keep the conversation in small-talk territory while I take Nora her coffee.

'So, you're back in the house?' she's saying as I walk back in. 'How long will you be here?'

'I don't know.' Dean takes a sip of coffee. 'The production company say I can stay as long I need to, although they won't want to pay the rent for long. I guess I'll move out soon. The London house is empty right now, so that's not a problem, but I'll need to arrange for some help with the kids.'

'I suppose they can stay with Vanessa's parents for a while, with it being the summer holidays. They'd already broken up, hadn't they? Mike and Sandy have another week at school, but I suppose George and Heidi have already been off for a week or so?'

'Yes, that's right.' Dean sounds vague on this count, and I don't suppose he's had much involvement in the children's social arrangements.

'How are the children? And Vanessa's parents? She talked about them a lot when you first moved in, before she…' Ellie hesitates, not wanting to say the wrong thing. 'Before she got busy with her filming,' she finishes, covering her embarrassment with a sip of coffee.

'I remember. You two used to spend a lot of time together, didn't you?' Dean hasn't noticed anything amiss. 'I remember her saying how welcoming you were. A lot of people don't know how to talk to people like her. You know, actors they've seen on the screen. She always felt relaxed with you, normal, you know?' Ellie clearly doesn't know what to say to this. It was true at one time, I'm sure. Ellie's lovely to everyone, and I bet she was the nicest neighbour ever to Vanessa before she saw what was going on between her and Dad.

'I don't suppose she had much time to see her parents while she was filming?' I ask, bringing him back to the question before he starts reminiscing about the good old days when Ellie and Vanessa were best mates.

'No, she didn't. They're devastated, of course. But looking after the kids seems to be helping them. It's giving them something to do, I guess. They want to start arranging a funeral, but the police say we can't fix a date yet. Not before…' None of us want to finish the sentence, even though we all have a good idea what he's talking about.

'Didn't you want to stay with them?' Ellie asks. 'Won't you be lonely in that big house on your own?'

'Maybe. But the police wanted to talk to me again and Vanessa's parents weren't acting too friendly. It feels like they blame me. For Vanessa's death, you know?'

'How can they do that?' asks Ellie. 'They don't think you killed her, do they?'

'I don't know what they think. I don't think they know themselves. One minute they were telling me it was all my fault, I must have made her miserable and that's why she killed herself, and the next they were suggesting I shot her myself. I couldn't stand it any longer. I had to get away.'

'Oh, Dean. How awful.' I expect Ellie's thinking that it was more likely Vanessa making Dean miserable, not the other way around, but she can hardly say so, and fortunately he doesn't seem to need a more detailed response.

'The thing is, I did make her miserable. I know I did.'

'I'm sure you didn't, Dean.' I can't let him carry on beating himself up like this, not having seen the way she flirted with Dad, and who knows who else.

'Oh, it worked both ways. We both knew it wasn't working, but I didn't love her like I should have done. Perhaps if I'd tried a bit harder, we could have made things work. And now… I've been such a fool, and now look where I am, number-one suspect for my own wife's murder.' Ellie isn't looking as surprised as I'm feeling, and it's starting to dawn on me that there's something going on that they both know about and I don't. Dean heaves a sigh.

'Look, I didn't come over here to dump my problems on you. At least, I did, but it's not the only reason I'm here.' He pauses.

'Go on,' says Ellie.

'It was actually Billie I came to see. To... well, to apologise, I guess. And... to warn you.'

'Warn me?' My stomach's got the football feeling again and my legs turn to jelly, even though I'm already sitting down. How can he know? Was he at the theatre too that afternoon? What did he see?

'I'm sorry, Billie. They were at me and at me, going on and on, and I didn't know what to say, and they'd found out so much other stuff I didn't dare not tell them everything in case they found out later and made it all look worse and...' He's losing control now and it's not making me feel any better. What does he know and what has he told the police? I open my mouth to ask what he's talking about, but Ellie gets there first.

'Hold on, Dean. Calm down.' Ellie's voice has hardened into the tone I've only heard her use when she's arguing with Dad. 'Tell us exactly what's been going on. From the beginning.' She shoots me a look that says 'leave this to me', and I take the hint and shut up. Ellie tops up Dean's mug, giving him a moment to take a deep breath and pull himself together.

'Okay. From the beginning. I'm sorry, There's no need to panic, I've been bottling it up for a long time, I guess. All right. So I came back last night. I'd had a fight with Vanessa's parents and I couldn't stand to stay another night in that house, so I packed a bag and drove back here. There was a message on my phone as soon as I checked it this morning, saying that detective – Twist, you know?' We nod. 'Saying she needed to see me. I called back and they came right away. I'd barely had time to shower.'

'They?' I ask.

'Sure, the Twist woman and her sergeant. Big guy, doesn't say much, types real fast... Carter, that's it.'

'And what did they want?' I know Ellie wants me to shut up but I can't help myself. I need him to get on and tell me what it's all about.

'They'd been finding out stuff. Stuff about me. She said they'd talked to everyone on the set, all the theatre staff, everyone, and there was no way Vanessa took that gun in. They practically strip-search everyone who walks through the theatre door while they're filming in there, and they checked her over as well as anyone. So no matter what anyone thinks, she didn't take the gun in herself. Someone else did.'

'So it can't have been suicide,' says Ellie. 'Although I suppose we already knew that.'

'Yeah, we did. I told them from the get-go, didn't I?'

'But surely everyone going in would be searched, not just Vanessa?' Ellie asks. 'How did someone else get a gun in there?'

'Through the fire door. Nuts, isn't it? All that security going on, metal detectors, scanners, the lot, and some idiot thinks it's okay to leave a fire door open to let in some air. Can you believe it?' It's a fair point, even though it's not something I'd have thought of myself.

'And that's how they think the... the person who shot her, got in?'

'Yup. It opens out onto the car park, and that's open to the public at the weekend. Anyone could get in that way. It's only the front entrances to the theatre that have the security. Whoever's in charge of that's got something to answer for. I'll be getting my lawyer onto it as soon as they stop trying to pin the murder on me.' Directing his emotions into anger rather than panic has helped him calm down a bit, but he still hasn't told me what he's here to warn me about, and I can't stay quiet any longer.

'Dean,' I say. 'What did you need to warn me about?' But he's got into his stride now, and barely registers the interruption.

'So they tell me they're sure it's murder. Everyone on the crew has an alibi. They even sent two people to look for her when she didn't come for her call. So it must be someone else who killed her. And how many people would know about the open fire door? Very few, they reckon. So few, they tell me, that she must have invited someone in herself. Told them to sneak in round the back where no one could see them.'

'Really?' says Ellie. 'Why on earth would she do that?'

'Oh, they had ideas about that, don't you worry. Drugs.'

'Drugs?' Ellie's looking bemused. She always has been naïve about these things. I haven't dared tell her half of what I got up to when I was in London.

'Drugs.' Dean nods, gratified despite himself by Ellie's rapt attention. 'They asked me if she took drugs. Can you believe it? They said there's a story going round the around the set about actors and drugs. They reckon she asked someone to bring her pills or whatever it is they use these days, and told them to come round the back so as to keep it quiet. Drugs? Vanessa? What are they thinking?' Something close to the truth, I want to tell him, but I can't. What's going on? Did Vanessa tell him about our meeting? Surely not – he wouldn't have taken this long to work up to it, unless he's more manipulative than I've given him credit for. I cover my mouth with my hand to stop myself saying something I shouldn't, knowing it will look like shock.

'I can't believe it,' says Ellie. But Dean hasn't stopped for encouragement, only to swig back his coffee. All this talking must be making him thirsty.

'I told them, I *really* told them. Vanessa. Doesn't. Do. Drugs. End of. She tried it once back in the day and had a bad trip. She'd never take anything now. I told them straight, it's a vicious rumour. If someone was there, they need to look for another reason.'

'Well done, Dean. It must have been so hard for you,' Ellie says soothingly.

'That was just the start. What do they say next? They ask did we have a happy marriage? Well, I knew where that was leading, so I said yes, of course, at least as happy as anyone else I know. And then they said…' He's been on a roll while he's been in self-righteous mode, but now he deflates a little. 'They said they'd been digging around – that's not what they said, but it's what they meant – and they thought maybe it hadn't been all that happy after all.'

'What did they mean by that?' I ask. I knew Vanessa was fooling around with my idiot of a father, but was it really that serious? And what does it have to do with me? It's Dad he should be warning if that's what they think.

64

'I…' He takes a breath. 'I've been seeing someone.' He lets it out again and stares at the floor, his shoulders slumped.

'You've been seeing someone?' I say, only managing at the last minute to avoid emphasising the first word of the question.

'I'm not proud of it, Billie. It didn't mean anything. Vanessa didn't know. That is, I don't think she knew. Maybe she did, maybe she told her parents, maybe that's what they meant…' He breaks off, apparently not having considered this possibility before.

'And they think you…' I can't make myself say the word, but fortunately I don't have to. Dean's always been happy to hold forth, and his current predicament doesn't seem to have changed this.

'Yup. They think I wanted to get rid of my wife. They think I killed Vanessa.'

'That sounds a bit far-fetched,' says Ellie, and it's hard not to laugh at the understatement, despite everything.

'That's what I said. Although perhaps not so politely.' Dean gives her a wry grin. 'But no, they were very sure of themselves. I said if I'd wanted to shack up with Miranda, all I had to do was ask Vanessa for a divorce. It wouldn't be the first time, after all, at least not for me. But no, they had an answer for that too. What about the insurance policy? The one we took out when we got married. I mean, everyone does that, right? Prenup, insurance, it's what you do when you get married, right?'

'Er… right,' says Ellie, although I don't think there was a prenup involved when she and Dad got together.

'Well, I told them, these policies don't pay out if it's suicide, so if it was me, why would I try to make it look like one? They didn't have an answer for that, but it didn't seem to bother them. I suppose they'll say it was me trying to make it look like someone else, a kind of double-bluff, you know?'

'Yes, I suppose so…' says Ellie. She sounds as if she's losing the will to live; it's like being battered, listening to Dean. He always talks just a little too loudly, he's leaning across the table, talking right at her, and his anger is only making it worse.

'So that brings them to the gun. They want to know how come Vanessa's got a gun. They don't have a record of a permit in her name, or in mine for that matter, so it must be illegal. And while we're at it, is it even her gun? How do they know it isn't mine? I told them again – it's her gun. She smuggled it off a film set when she was starting out in America and snuck it into this country in her suitcase.'

'Did she really?' I can see Ellie holding back a giggle, and I can understand why. It's just the sort of outrageous thing Vanessa would do.

'Sure she did, you know what she was like. Rules were for other people as far as she was concerned. As soon as she showed it to me I told her she should get it licensed but she wouldn't listen. So they're saying they need proof it was hers. Is there someone who'll remember it, someone who was on the set when she took it?' He looks at Ellie, as if expecting a reaction, and she's able to oblige with a genuine one this time.

'That's ridiculous! How could anyone be expected to remember that far back, even if you could find them?'

'That's what I said to them. So they were going on and on at me, about Miranda, the insurance, the gun, saying there's no proof it wasn't mine in the first place, and then I remembered.' I knew it, here it comes. 'She showed it to you, didn't she, Billie?' There's a silence. Ellie's mouth has dropped open. She must have thought she was the only one with secrets. I only wish she were.

'She did what?' Ellie hates guns more than anything. She's always said she'd never visit America even if you paid her, just for that reason. She never let Alex play with them when he was little, and I have a feeling the time will come when she'll point to this as proof that she's always been right about them.

'She showed me her gun,' I say, looking at Dean, thankful to have a good reason to avoid Ellie's gaze. 'And you told them, right?'

'I'm sorry, Billie. I came round as soon as I could to warn you. I didn't think I'd have the chance. I thought they might come straight over here, but a call came through on the sergeant's phone and they drove off in a hurry. I took my chance and came right away to warn you. Billie, I'm sorry to drag you into it, but you'll back me up, won't you? You'll tell them it's hers?'

'Of course I will.' I'm so relieved he's not found out I was at the theatre, I'll do anything he asks right now. 'Although… I've not seen it. They showed you a photo, didn't they, but they didn't show it to the rest of us.'

'That's not a problem,' he says, reassured. 'It's hers. And if you can back me up, it would be awesome. Thanks, Billie, you're a star.'

'But Dean,' says Ellie, 'how will that help? Surely you're still a suspect, whoever the gun belonged to?'

'Oh, sure I am,' he says, apparently much less disturbed by this now. 'But don't you see, Ellie? If I can prove it was Vanessa's gun it means I'm not the only one who could have done it. Anyone could have stolen it from her and used it against her. She could have taken it to the theatre herself to show off to someone. Hell, she might have done just that and then it went off by accident. I bet they've not thought of that.' He jumps up, his customary vigour fully restored. 'Thanks again, Billie. And thanks for the coffee, Ellie. I'll… I'll see you around, okay?' He's suddenly eager to leave, perhaps realising the police could be here at any moment and it mightn't look too good if he's still with us. Ellie sees him out and comes back into the kitchen before I have a chance to leave.

'So. Billie. Tell me about this gun.' Ellie's wearing the face she uses when Alex is trying to hide something from her. Only I'm not ten years old and she's not my mother.

'I'd rather not talk about it, if you don't mind. Not now. I've got stuff to do and Dean's already taken up half the morning.' I start to make my way towards the door, but she blocks my way.

'I'm sorry, Billie, but I don't think this can wait. Tell me about the gun. Now.' I heave a pointed sigh and sit down again. She positions herself across the table, Spanish inquisition-style.

'Honestly, Ellie, there's nothing to tell. Vanessa had a gun. She showed it to me once. End of story.'

'When?'

'I don't know, a couple of weeks ago. Does it matter?'

'It matters to me. Where did she keep it?'

'In a drawer in her desk. In the snug.'

'In the snug? Ready for the children to find?' Ellie's voice has risen about an octave in alarm. Of course. She thinks Heidi or George, or even worse, Alex, could have found it and messed around with it and done who knows what else with it.

'No, not ready for the children to find. Even Vanessa wasn't that stupid. It was in one of those special books they make for hiding things in. You know, where they cut the pages out and you can put something inside.'

'Really?' Ellie's panic shows signs of receding.

'It looked really boring, Ellie. I can't remember the title, but there's no way a child would think it looked interesting. And that's if they opened the drawer in the first place, which they really wouldn't. Vanessa told me it's an "adults-only" room, and they're good kids, I'm sure they wouldn't go in.' That bit's not quite true, but it doesn't matter now, and I need her to calm down.

'Oh. Okay.' She pauses. 'But you see why I was worried?'

'Yeah. I see.' I give her a smile and think we could do with another coffee, but before I can suggest it the doorbell rings again and there's no need to wonder who it is this time.

SEVEN

'Can I offer you something to drink?' Ellie's asking as they come into the room. 'We were just thinking about having another one,' she adds, catching DI Twist looking at the mugs in my hand. I've managed to pop Dean's into the sink, thinking it might be just as well not to let them know he's been here already.

'Thank you, that would be lovely,' says DI Twist, looking at her sergeant for confirmation.

'Yes, please,' he says. 'We're both milk and no sugar.'

'No problem.' Ellie and I both head for the kettle at the same time. I can tell she's flustered, and so am I, but I'm better at not letting it show than she is, so I let her make the coffee and turn to the detectives.

'I didn't catch who you've come to see?'

'Sorry, didn't I say? We've got a few questions for you, Billie. About a conversation you had with Vanessa a couple of weeks ago. It shouldn't take long.'

'All right.' I put on my best 'I don't know what I can possibly help you with' face, and suggest they might be more comfortable in the lounge.

'We're fine in here, thanks,' she says, and they take seats at the table. I wait for them to say that Ellie can stay, but she doesn't give them a chance, putting the drinks in front of them as quickly as she can and saying she'll check on Nora. I suppose she thinks she knows what it's about and reckons I can cope on my own. It would look odd to ask her to stay, so I don't. DI Twist watches Ellie leave while Sergeant Carter gets out his tablet. I don't have the energy for polite conversation so I sip my coffee and wait.

'We're looking into the gun found with Vanessa Forsyth's body,' says DI Twist, and I feel very grateful to Dean for warning me about this. It would have been a huge shock otherwise. I don't want to get him into trouble, though, and I remember to look surprised.

'Oh?'

'Yes. Unfortunately, Miss Forsyth hadn't registered or obtained a permit for the weapon, so we're having trouble confirming its ownership.'

'I see.'

'Mr Westerby tells us you're familiar with Miss Forsyth's gun. Is that right?' She's talking calmly, as if it's just a matter of ticking boxes, working through a prescribed sequence of events, and perhaps it is. I remind myself that this isn't about my being at the theatre, and I can't be accused of anything simply because Vanessa took it into her head to show off her firearm to me.

'Yes, she showed it to me once. But hasn't Dean already identified it for you?'

'Yes, I think you were here with him at the time. However, an independent identification would be helpful.'

'Oh. Yes, I see. Do you need me to look at the photograph? The one you showed to Dean?'

'Not just yet. We'd like you to describe the weapon you saw first. We can take a look at the photograph afterwards.'

'All right. Um…' I hadn't expected this, but I can see what she's doing. She knows Dean could have asked me to back him up, and showing me the photo would make it too easy. I suppose he could have told me what it looked like, but that would be much harder to pull off.

'Sorry,' I say. 'It's hard to remember, exactly... she didn't have it out for very long.' And thinking about the gun has made me think about the dressing room again. I'd managed to bury it over the past couple of days, hoping I wouldn't have to think about it again, but it's all flooding back now. Vanessa slumped in her chair, the hole in her head, the weird smell of eggs mixed with something floral... The image is so clear, there's no chance of me remembering what the gun looks like. My brain's completely frozen, and I know the shock must be written all over my face.

'Shut your eyes,' Sergeant Carter advises. His boss doesn't look surprised at the interruption. Perhaps coaxing information out of nervous people is his speciality.

'Okay.'

'Now visualise the room where you were. Vanessa's snug, perhaps?' I suppose Dean must have told them where she kept it. He's got a nice voice, low but not growly, and warm around the edges.

'Yes. That's right, it was the snug.'

'Good. Now, I want you to imagine you're in there now, Billie, with Vanessa, on that evening.'

'Okay.' It's a weird thing to ask, but I suppose it can't hurt to try. He waits a while, giving me time to remember.

'All right, where are you sitting?'

'On the sofa. I'm sitting on the sofa.'

'Good. Now, she's getting the gun out. Where was it?'

'In book. A hollowed-out one. In the desk. Top drawer. Silly place to hide something.'

'That's really good, Billie. Where's Vanessa? Is she on the sofa too?'

'No. She's on a stool. Opposite me. She's opening the book. *Sense and Sensibility*. She's making a joke about it being a sensible place to put it.'

'I suppose it might have been. So, she's opening the book. What can you see?'

71

'A piece of cloth, it's black and it looks soft, like velvet. And a silencer too, it only just fits in the space. She's taking out the cloth and unwrapping it. The gun's inside.'

'What does the gun look like, Billie?' It's easier now. Closing my eyes has helped me relax, and by focusing on other things, I've been able to come back to the gun without panicking.

'Small. I never saw a gun in real life before and I thought it would be bigger. And it's… almost pretty. The barrel's black, but the rest's a sort of creamy colour.'

'Is she letting you hold it? Is it heavy?'

'Yes. Heavier than I expected. And it feels rough. Bumpy. There's a sort of lacy pattern cut into it. Maybe it's ivory. I'm giving it back to her now. I don't like guns.' I open my eyes and blink a couple of times in the bright light of the kitchen. 'Wow. I didn't expect to remember it that well.'

'You did really well, Billie. Thank you.' Sergeant Carter smiles at me, and I almost forget I'm talking to detectives. He must be the good cop, because it's DI Twist's turn again and she's not so friendly.

'Thank you, Billie,' she echoes, but it sounds more of a formality when she says it. 'Your description matches the gun we found, but it's always best to check – can you confirm that this gun was Vanessa's?' There's a sheet of paper on the table – she must have put it there while I had my eyes shut – and she turns it over and places it in front of me. I lean forward a little, trying not to notice that the gun's lying on what I can see is the floor of Vanessa's dressing room.

'Yes. That's it.' I lean back in my chair, relieved it's over at last and hoping this means they'll go now, but she barely breaks eye contact as she passes the photo to Sergeant Carter.

'Why was Vanessa showing you her gun?' she asks. Her tone's conversational rather than questioning, and she might as well be asking why I put sugar in my tea.

'I… I don't know, really.' I pause and think. Careful, Billie. Keep it simple. If they ask about it again you'll need to be ready with the exact same story.

'All right, let's approach it another way. When did she show it to you?'

'I'd been babysitting. For her and Dean. It was two weeks ago. It was a Saturday, they went out for dinner.'

DI Twist nods and looks out of the window as if trying to remember something. 'Before the party?'

'Yes, that's right. A week before.'

'So not the last time you saw her, but a fairly significant event, don't you think? Considering what happened afterwards?'

'I… I suppose so.'

'When we came to see you before, Billie, you said – please check your notes, Luke, in case I'm wrong – you said that you didn't know Vanessa well and had never talked to her much.'

'Um… yes. I did say that.' A silence hangs in the air. I don't know what else to say.

'So how is that accurate in the light of her having invited you into her private room to show you her gun?' Her voice is quiet but pure steel.

'I…' I'm thinking furiously. How could I have been so stupid? Why didn't I tell them about the conversation in the first place? I was so busy worrying about them finding out about my being at the theatre I forgot how bad it would look that I'd not mentioned this earlier.

'Please don't tell me you forgot,' says DI Twist.

'I didn't forget,' I say, sitting up a little straighter now that I've got a plan. 'I didn't tell you because I thought it would look bad. I thought if you knew I'd seen the gun that I'd be a suspect.'

A tiny smile mouth curls at the corner of her mouth, unwillingly, but it's there. 'I suppose that's a fair supposition,' she says. 'But it's out now, it doesn't look good, and since you're already on our suspects list, you may as well do your best to cooperate, don't you think?'

'I suppose so.' She's made me feel pretty stupid, but I'm an actress not a spy, so I suppose it's inevitable. I'll have to do a lot better if the question of my being at the theatre comes up, that would look way worse.

'So, tell us about that night. Am I right, perhaps, in thinking it wasn't Dean who paid you, but Vanessa?'

'Yes.'

'And how did the two of them seem when they came back? Happy? Tense? Drunk?'

'Something was definitely off between them, as if they'd been arguing. Dean went straight upstairs. He said he was tired. Vanessa said she would pay me and to come into the kitchen to get the money. She said something about not using cash anymore, and I said I didn't mind waiting, or she could pay me electronically if she wanted, but she said no, Dean would be on her case in the morning if she didn't do it straight away.'

'You went into the kitchen? Not the snug?'

'No, the kitchen first. She found some cash and then she said she didn't want to go to bed yet and did I want a nightcap?'

'Was that something you'd done before? I thought you said you didn't know her very well?'

'I didn't. But, like I said, I wanted to get to know her better. I was hoping she might be able to help me. You know, in my career. She couldn't get me a part or anything, but she might have helped me get a meeting with her agent, or a casting director. Dean might have been able to help me too, but he's away a lot and he's not got to know my parents as well as Vanessa.' Oops, shouldn't have said that. No one said they knew Vanessa well, did they? I rush on, trying to cover my slip. 'So I said yes, and she said why didn't we go into the snug, it was more comfortable there. She got a bottle of wine from the fridge and some glasses and we took them in with us.'

'All right. You were in the snug, having a nice chat with her about her career and how she might help you with yours. Where did the gun come in?'

'She was telling me about the time she went to America. It was early on in her career. She made a few pilots out there.' DI Twist looks puzzled. 'Sort of try-outs for TV series,' I explain. 'Lots of people make them and show them to production companies, but most of them don't get made. Vanessa was in a few but they weren't picked up. But she did get spotted in one of them and she was cast in a film on the back of it. It was her big break, I guess.'

'And the gun?' DI Twist doesn't seem to mind hearing a potted history of Vanessa's early career and a lesson on the American TV industry at the same time, but I don't blame her for wanting to get to the point.

'She took it. From the film set. It was a spoof Western, *Up West*, it was called. She was playing a cowgirl, I don't suppose you've seen it?' They both smile and shake their heads. Even if they were big movie buffs, it's hardly a mainstream film; I had to spend ages searching for it online so I could talk about it to Vanessa without looking like an idiot.

'Anyway, she pinched the gun on her last day. She said she wanted a souvenir and she just loved the gun they gave her to use in the film. You could never get away with it these days, they're way more careful about props, but she said she bribed the prop boy.' I can't help smiling. Vanessa might have been a pain, but she was a good actress, and she told the story really well.

'But surely they don't use real guns in films?' asks DI Twist.

'They do in America,' I tell her. 'It's all very different over there.'

'I see,' she says. 'And I suppose she offered to show you the gun?'

'Yes, and after hearing the story, I thought, why not? It was late by then and I wanted to go home, but she was desperate to show me, and I thought if she did then I might be able to leave.'

'And after she'd shown it to you? Did she put it back in the book? And in the drawer?'

'Yes. I remember her showing me a little velvet bag. She said it was full of bullets. She said she'd had to smuggle them back in her suitcase when she came back to England. And she said not to tell anyone, she didn't want to get into trouble for not having registered it.'

'I see.' DI Twist clearly isn't impressed with this, but it's hardly my fault. 'And did you tell anyone? About your chat? About Vanessa showing you the weapon?'

'No. I thought it was a bit weird to be honest. I tried to forget about it.'

'Hmm.' She looks around the room, as if searching for something, and her gaze fixes on the basil plant on the windowsill. 'What else did you talk about? Apart from acting, films and so on?'

'Um…' Why does my brain insist on thinking about stuff I don't want to tell her about? 'I don't know, not much else.'

'Did she talk about her husband at all? Perhaps something about their argument earlier on?'

'No.' It comes out much too quickly. 'I mean, no, she didn't. I didn't want her to. I didn't want to get involved in her marital problems.'

'So you knew they were having problems?'

'No! It was just a phrase. I don't know what was going on in their marriage. I hardly knew them at all, I'd only been home for a week. What could I possibly know about their marriage?'

'Fair enough. I'm sorry if I misunderstood you. We're trying to find out as much as possible about the last few weeks of Miss Forsyth's life, and any insight into her personal life is helpful.'

'All right,' I say. I find I've been sitting on the edge of my seat, and I relax a little now that it sounds as if it's over. 'Is that it? I've told you everything about that day now.'

'Yes, that's it for now. Thanks, Billie, you've been very helpful.' She stands and nods to Sergeant Carter, who puts his tablet and the photo into a slim briefcase.

'Well done, Billie,' he says. 'You did a great job remembering about the gun.' His voice is perfectly normal, but the words sound as if he's talking to a child. I'm tempted to remind him that I'm an adult but decide it might be better in the long run if they don't take me too seriously. The house is quiet as I walk them to the door. Ellie must have stayed in Nora's room, wanting to avoid gate-crashing our conversation in the kitchen, and I have to admit to being grateful for this.

'Goodbye,' says DI Twist as they go out of the door. 'I hope we won't need to talk to you again, but please do stay in the area, or let us know if you leave, just in case.'

'Okay.' I was just starting to feel better, but this makes my knees turn to jelly all over again. And she's not finished.

'And Billie?'

'Yes?'

'If you know anything else about Vanessa, please don't keep it from us. Think about it. Think hard. And let us know when you're ready to talk again.' They're both looking at me now, and whilst I expected to see steel in their eyes, there's only kindness. As if they know what I'm hiding and about the impossible position I'm in. I almost tell them. Not everything, not about the theatre, but about what Vanessa really said that night. About having done whatever it took to get to the top. About being ruthless. About getting the man she wanted. And about how lucky Ellie was to have my dad.

'There's nothing else,' I say, but she's already handing me her card. 'DI Sharon Twist', it says. I almost laugh – she's so unlike a Sharon it's not true, and I have to admire her for turning it into a cool name like Ronnie – but I know that won't go down well. It doesn't matter anyway: by the time I look up, they've gone.

EIGHT

I'm desperate for a smoke and I know Sandy and Alex will be back any minute now for lunch, so I grab my pouch from the study and go into the garden. I find the saucer Ellie gave me behind a flowerpot and sit on one of the plastic chairs to roll a cigarette at the table. My hands are shaking as I lick the thin paper and place the filter at the end of the line of tobacco. I don't want to make a mess of it, so I make myself take a few deep breaths before I attempt to roll and light it. That first pull is always the best, and by the time I exhale I'm already feeling better. I don't know whether Ellie's more likely to want to know what the detectives have been asking me or to do everything she can to avoid finding out, but either way, I need some time to work out what the interview has done to change things.

They know I saw the gun, and they know I lied about it. That's not great, but it would be far worse if they knew about me being at the theatre. Always look on the bright side of life, isn't that what they say? It was good of Dean to warn me they were coming, but it wasn't too clever of me to let slip that Dad and Ellie knew Vanessa well. Did I actually say that? Or did I just say they knew her better than I did? Whichever it was, I'm sure they'll have noticed. I reckon it will be them being asked awkward questions next. Well, so what? Let them deal with their own problems – I've got enough of my own to worry about, not least of all the fact that I'm one of only two people known to have seen the gun. That must put me right at the top – or near the top – of their list of suspects. Along with Dean. Who was having an affair with another woman, who knew where the gun was and who was arguing with Vanessa only a few weeks before she died. I reckon he did it.

* * *

I tell them in the end. Not Alex, of course, but the others. It would look odd if I tried to hide it and I need to talk to someone. There's no point trying to contact Jay, and Gaby will be working. We send Alex inside to practise the piano, and I sit with Ellie, Sandy and Nora in the garden, explaining why the police needed to talk to me.

'I don't know what to think,' says Ellie. 'It seems such a strange thing to do.'

'What seems strange?' Sandy asks. 'To steal a gun, smuggle it home in your suitcase or show it to someone you've barely known for two minutes? It all seems pretty strange to me. But then, Vanessa wasn't like the rest of us, was she?'

'That's certainly true,' says Ellie. 'I suppose the strangest thing to me is getting it out and showing it to you, Billie. I can't help it – it makes me feel very uncomfortable knowing it's been sitting there all this time, when Alex has been over there so often. I can't believe she'd be so irresponsible. Leaving it lying around like that for anyone to pick up – it's unbelievable.'

'Strictly speaking, it wasn't lying around,' Nora says. 'It was in a drawer. In a book in a drawer. In a room the children weren't allowed in.'

'So Billie says.' Ellie sounds scornful, and there's no mistaking the anger in her voice. 'Vanessa never said anything of the sort to me. It wouldn't surprise me if she made that up so as to look like a responsible parent in front of Billie. That would be just like her.'

'Would it?' Nora asks. 'I didn't know her as well as you did, and I gather you were quite close at one point. That's what Dean said, wasn't it? But you don't seem to feel friendly towards her now. Did something happen to make you fall out?'

'No, not really,' Ellie sighs. 'I was nice to her when they arrived. Like I would be to anyone new moving in. I took some home-made brownies round, a copy of the bin calendar, you know, that sort of thing.' My mind boggles at the thought of Vanessa's reaction to being provided with details of dustbin collections, and I can't help laughing.

'Ellie, you didn't! Please tell me you didn't take a famous movie star a plate of calorie-laden cake and advice about when to put her rubbish out.'

Ellie looks surprised. 'I suppose it does sound silly when you put it like that, but Dean and the children loved the brownies.' She pauses. 'I'm not so sure about the bins, but they did keep the calendar. And anyway, she wasn't all that famous. She was only in one or two movies ten years ago and some stuff on the telly.'

'I think you'll find it was rather more than that,' says Sandy. 'I'm sure Billie will agree that Vanessa had a considerably more successful career than most people in her profession. She had the lucky break that everyone's hoping for and made the most of it, isn't that right, Billie?'

'Yes, it is,' I say, surprised that Sandy knows so much about Vanessa's career. But then, Sandy loves Google with a passion. She's always the one to rush to her phone to find out the answers to obscure questions.

'I'm sure they were very grateful,' says Nora soothingly. 'And you became friends, did you? You and Vanessa?'

'Yes, I suppose we did,' Ellie agrees. 'They moved in a few weeks before filming started. They already had a school lined up for the children, but I helped them out with other things as well as bins.' She gives me a reproving look. 'Like where the supermarkets are and nice places to eat. And we invited the children over to play. They're a bit younger than Alex but he doesn't mind that. He and George both love model-making, and Heidi's a sweet little girl. She tags along with them and they don't seem to mind.'

'And you and Vanessa? What did you like to do together?' Nora asks. It's a good question – I still don't understand what brought the two of them together in the first place. It seems a very unlikely friendship to me.

'Oh, I don't know. Not a lot, really. We had them over for drinks, and then dinner. They took us out once or twice – Vanessa didn't like cooking much. Dean and Mike got on well, they both like sport. Mike suggested Dean join the golf club. He's often away in London, but he likes his golf.'

'What about you and Vanessa? What did you talk about?'

'The children, mostly. I told her about Billie, and she said she'd like to meet her. Although once Billie got here, Vanessa was tied up with filming and didn't have so much time.'

'Is that why you drifted apart?' Nora asks. 'She was too busy?'

'Yes, I suppose so. And…' Ellie hesitates.

'And the shine wore off,' Sandy finishes for her.

'For Vanessa? Or for you?' Nora's not daft. I'm sure she's already read enough between the lines to have an idea as to how this particular friendship panned out.

'For both of us, I guess. She seemed to enjoy a bit of "normal" life, as she was always calling it. I'd expected her to have more people to help her, you know, a housekeeper, a nanny, that sort of thing. But they didn't, just a part-time home help, I suppose you'd call it, Tess, to do the cleaning and pick the children up from school. She said they were trying to live a simpler sort of life, but I did wonder if they were short of money.'

'Quite possibly,' Sandy chips in. 'I don't think she'd worked much recently. Not enough to keep up a film-star lifestyle, at any rate.'

'I think the novelty soon wore off,' Ellie continues. 'And I was part of that novelty. You know – a "normal" friend for a "normal" life. I'm not sure there ever was much of a shine for me in the first place. I don't know much about films, and Vanessa knew nothing about art.

It was nice for Alex to have someone nearby to play with – I probably kept the friendship going for his sake as much as for mine. And in the end, he didn't need me to be friends with Vanessa, he's quite capable of asking George round to play without my help.'

'And Mike? Did he keep up with Dean? He asked him over last weekend, didn't he?'

'Oh, you know how it is with couples. If the wives don't make the arrangements, the husbands soon drift apart. He didn't fall out with Dean; their paths didn't cross much, that's all.' Nora seems to accept this explanation.

'I suppose it would have looked rude not to accept the invitation to the party. Not with you living so close,' she says, looking at Sandy.

'Mmm,' she says. 'No point in upsetting people, is there? And it was a nice afternoon. You seem to have enjoyed yourself chatting to Vanessa.' She stands and begins to gather our coffee mugs together, and Ellie pushes her chair back, ready to get back to work. Nora and I sit a while longer, enjoying the sunshine and the peace and quiet.

'She doesn't want to tell me, does she?' Nora says.

'Sorry? Who doesn't want to tell you what?' My mind's been busy thinking about the gun, imagining a younger version of Vanessa wrapping it up in her swimsuit and hiding it in her suitcase. Although why it's a swimsuit, I'm not sure.

'Ellie doesn't want to tell me why she fell out with Vanessa.'

'Did she? Fall out with her?' I'm pretty sure she did, but I don't want to admit it. It might lead to some awkward questions if I do.

'Of course she did.' Nora seems completely confident in her assessment. 'The way she talked about her. Irresponsible parent, superficial lifestyle, lying to look good in front of you. She doesn't have a single good thing to say about her. She even managed to tell us that she was short of money and couldn't cook.'

'I suppose she did. I hadn't thought of it like that.'

'I won't push it. She doesn't want to talk about it, and there's no need now the woman's dead. But she'd better be careful. If she carries on talking that way, people may start to wonder if she disliked her enough to murder her.'

'Nora! That's ridiculous. Ellie's your own daughter – how can you think such a thing about her?'

'I'm not saying I think it, Billie. I'm saying other people might. And I'm worried about Ellie. It's not like her to speak about anyone like that, never mind someone who's been a friend, and certainly not someone who's dead. She's always been so understanding of people, so forgiving. I can't understand it. Something's upset her badly. I'd like to help her, but I'm not sure she'll let me.'

'Nora…' I want to tell her she's amazing, she's right, she knows her daughter better than anyone, but I can't. It's not my place to say what I think's going wrong for Ellie; it's her own story to tell.

'Yes, dear?'

'I think you're right. Vanessa wasn't perfect, that's for sure, even I could see that. But Ellie doesn't sound like herself. And she doesn't normally get mad at people. Maybe it's worth trying again. Talking to her, I mean. Only perhaps not when there are so many of us around. Perhaps there's stuff she wants to say that she'd rather Sandy and I didn't hear?'

'Perhaps there is.' Nora nods thoughtfully. 'We had a nice chat this morning, while you were with the police, you know. But not about Vanessa. I had the feeling she was trying to avoid the subject. And maybe she was. It's much harder to lose a person you don't love than one you do. Maybe she's feeling Vanessa's loss more than she even realises herself.'

'What do you mean? Surely losing someone you love is the hardest thing in the world?' I say.

'Oh no, dear. When we've loved, we mourn, of course, we do. But eventually – your father will tell you this, I'm sure – we remember the good times too, and we've nothing to blame ourselves for. All that's left is memory, sadness, grief. When someone dies with whom we have a difficult relationship, we lose so much more. We lose hope, the possibility of better times, the chance of reconciliation, of resolution.

83

When someone we don't love – or like – dies, we've lost any last chance of making it better. And we're left with regret – even guilt.'

Neither of us speak for a few minutes. I don't know what Nora's thinking, but I'm turning over what she's said in my head and realising that she's right. I can hardly remember my mum dying, I was very small, but Dad's face still lights up when he talks about her. He used to be smiling through tears, but that doesn't happen so much now. They're more likely to glisten in his eyes than run down his cheeks. And Grannie Luci's the same. She'd not seen Mum for over a year when she died, and she couldn't afford a flight to come over from St Lucia for the funeral. One of my earliest memories is of her scooping me up at the airport and squeezing me so hard I could hardly breathe. Years later she said it was knowing I was there, a piece of Mum, that kept her going. And knowing that they'd loved each other as much as a mother and daughter ever could. She said Mum lived an amazing life, she was a wonderful daughter, and I was a gift from God to help her carry on when Mum went. And her face shone through the tears too, just like Dad's. Suddenly, fiercely, I really want to see Grannie Luci again. I'll save this time. I won't buy clothes or anything else until I've saved enough to buy a plane ticket and visit her again.

'Billie?' Nora's voice interrupts my thoughts. 'Are you all right?'

'Yes…' I clear my throat. 'I think you're right. And I think Ellie does need to talk, only she might not be ready just yet.'

'Maybe not. Or perhaps it's Sandy she needs to talk to, not me. They've lived together for so long, since Ellie was only sixteen. Sandy's been like a second mother to her in many ways. And to you as well, perhaps? It always seems to me that you and Ellie are more like sisters than anything else.'

'Nothing gets past you, does it?' I smile at her. 'You've got us all sorted out. And how long have you been here? Two months? Three?'

'Two and a half if you want to be exact. And I like to think I'm a good listener. It's how you find out about people, not through talking, you know.'

'Is that a hint?' I give her a gentle poke in the arm. 'Well, you can do some more listening if you like. I've still got three quarters of a play to learn and those lines won't learn themselves. How about it?'

'I'd be delighted,' she says, and I go inside to find my script. It feels like it's time for a cup of tea and I look out of the window at Nora while I wait for the kettle to boil. I can't believe how quickly my feelings about her have changed. A few weeks ago she was just a nuisance of an old woman who'd stolen my room, and now she's as close to a grandparent as I've had in a long time – at least one who's in the same country as me. And it's amazing the way she seems to know exactly what's going on inside everyone's head.

Only she doesn't really, does she? She doesn't know about me being at the theatre, and she definitely doesn't know why Ellie was mad at Vanessa. Mad at Dad as well, come to that, although perhaps she'll forgive him now that Vanessa's gone. It all comes back to that, doesn't it? We're all better off, it seems, now she's dead. I just wish it wasn't only me who knew about the gun apart from Dean. The kettle boils and I pour water into the teapot that I know Nora likes. I remember Sandy telling me, my first day back, how she likes her tea made, although I didn't pay much attention at the time. She likes showing people things, Sandy does, a bit like Vanessa, come to that, showing me her…

The thought clicks into place in my brain. How could I be so stupid – again? If Vanessa loved showing off her gun so much, how do I know I was the only one who saw it? She told Dean about me seeing it, but he was obviously annoyed by her keeping it in the first place. She probably only told him that time because she'd been drinking too much and they'd been arguing. How many other people saw it? How many other people knew exactly where it was? And how many other people might have thought that the world would be a better place without Vanessa in it?

NINE

It's a week now. Since it happened. In some ways it feels like only a few hours, but in others it's more like a century. When I wake up on Saturday morning, I realise it's just two weeks before I'll be leaving to begin rehearsals in London and I ought to start looking for a place to stay while I'm there. It's only for a fortnight, before we start touring, and if I'm lucky I'll be able to find someone who's out of town and happy to let me borrow their room. I put a post on Facebook asking anyone who can help to message me and upload a photo on Instagram before getting up. It's one I took yesterday in the garden, matching the flowers in one of Ellie's containers to my dress. I check a few feeds, add some comments and check the news again for anything about Vanessa. Nothing – good.

Despite Nora's predictions, we've not seen the police again. Not yet, anyway. Perhaps it's too soon to relax, but the image of Vanessa in her dressing room isn't popping into my brain so often now, and I've managed to learn nearly half my lines, thanks to Nora's help. The sun's shining, I'm going bouldering with Gaby this afternoon and it's our annual end-of-term celebratory meal this evening. Now that he doesn't go to school anymore, Alex has decided he should be in charge of the preparations, with me and Ellie as his willing servants.

He's delegated table-decorating to me, so I'll pick up some bits in the market this morning. A sudden surge of energy propels me out of bed and into my running gear. I'll go out early, while it's still cool.

* * *

Feeling pleased with myself for having completed five miles in record time, I come into the kitchen for breakfast just as everyone else seems to be leaving.

'Where're you off to?' I ask Alex. He's cutting sandwiches, marking them out around the lid of a plastic box so that they fit inside perfectly. 'Mmm, peanut butter.' I sneak a crust from him on my way to the fridge.

'Chess tournament,' he says. 'Mum's taking me. It's in Leeds.'

'Oooh, very nice,' I say. 'How long will you be gone?'

'Most of the day,' says Ellie. 'Sandy and Mother are coming too. They've got some secret shopping to do for this evening, I believe.'

'Sandy's not supposed to be helping,' Alex says, outraged. 'It's her celebration meal, it's supposed to be a surprise!'

'It's all right. Your gran's doing the shopping, Sandy's just helping. She'll stand outside the door, she won't see what Gran's buying.' Ellie gives me a wink which Alex doesn't see, having returned to his task.

'She should be having a rest,' he grumbles. 'She's been working very hard, you know.'

'Don't worry, Alex. I've got six whole weeks to have a rest in.' Sandy's on her way in with Nora's breakfast tray. 'I'll enjoy looking round the shops – it's ages since I've been to Leeds. And I promise not to peek at whatever it is Gran buys.'

'All right.' Mollified, Alex packs his sandwich box and begins the serious business of negotiating the addition of crisps and chocolate to his packed lunch.

* * *

There's too much hustle in the kitchen, so I take my breakfast outside while they get themselves out of the house. By the time I return it's quiet and tidy. Despite Alex's best efforts at causing chaos in the kitchen, Sandy refuses to let even a teaspoon sit unwashed for more than a minute, and the place is spotless. I do my bit, putting my dishes into the dishwasher, and wonder where Dad is. I fancy another coffee before hitting the market, and think he might like one too. Term might be over, but if I know Dad, he'll have found some work to do – probably planning for September, he's a total workaholic. He's been careful not to use the study without asking while I'm home, and I find him, as expected, in the lounge, with papers and textbooks spread out over Alex's worktable.

'You'd better be sure to put it all back where you found it,' I tell him. 'You don't want to get into trouble with Alex.'

'I will.' He turns round and gives me a smile. 'Have they gone?'

'Yes. The Leeds contingent has left the building. Do you want a coffee?'

'Yes, please. Aren't you off to the market this morning?'

'It can wait. I'm making one for myself before I go. I'll bring it through if you like.'

'Thanks, Billie.' He turns back to his laptop, keen, no doubt, to make the most of a quiet day at home. I go back to the kitchen and put the kettle on. I'm spooning coffee granules into mugs when the doorbell rings. Dad will be too immersed in his work to remember Alex is out, so I answer it myself, expecting it to be the postman. It's not the postman. It's them.

'Good morning,' says DI Twist. 'I hope we've not called at an inconvenient time?'

'It depends who you've come to see,' I say. 'Sorry, that came out wrong, I didn't mean to be rude. No, it's not inconvenient, but there's only me and Dad in.'

'That's fine,' she says. 'It's your father we need to talk to. Can we come in?'

'Sure. He's in here.' I stand back to let them through and shut the

88

door behind them while they stand by the shoe rack. It's a narrow hall and it's a bit of squeeze to get past them to the lounge door.

'I'll let him know you're here,' I say, and put my head around the door. 'Dad. The police are back. They want to talk to you.'

'What?' He was expecting coffee not coppers, and he does a double-take, but he's quick to recover and I let them in. They sit in the same chairs as last time, and Dad takes a seat on the sofa. I hover by the door, not sure what to do.

'Would you like some coffee, Inspector?' Dad asks. 'Billie was just making some.'

'That would be very nice,' DI Twist says, not waiting to see if her sergeant wants one or not. She opens her mouth to tell me how they like it, but it's with a sense of satisfaction that I beat her to it.

'White with no sugar, right?' I say, and leave before they have time to decide they want to talk to me too. I make the coffee quickly, putting the mugs on a tray and adding a plate of Alex's biscuits. DI Twist doesn't seem the sort to be softened up by sugary treats, but it's got to be worth a try. I leave my own mug on the kitchen table and carry the tray through to the lounge. They're making polite conversation while they wait, clearly not wanting me to listen to anything they've got to say.

'I trained at Manchester and Sandy was at Hull,' Dad's saying. 'So no, our paths didn't cross. I was a mature student, anyway. I was an accountant before my wife died. I took up teaching so as to be able to spend more time…'

'With me,' I say with a smile. 'And he's an excellent teacher, even though I say it myself.'

'I'm sure he is,' says Sergeant Carter. 'And someone's an excellent baker, by the look of things.' He's doing it again, talking to me as if I were twelve years old rather than nearly twice that age. It's great for getting work playing children, but being five feet nothing can be very infuriating at times.

'You'll have to blame Alex for the decorations,' I say. 'Spiders are really not my thing.' It gets a laugh, and Dad shoots me a grateful look, knowing that I've bitten back a short reply about being a grown-up.

'I'll leave you to it, then,' I say, and no one stops me from making a swift and grateful exit. I close the door quietly behind me and go back to the kitchen for my coffee. As I pick it up, an almost uncontrollable urge comes over me to tiptoe back into the hall to hear what's going on. I can only hear the mumble of voices from here, but I know from past experience that I'd hear every word if I was in the hallway. Now that the relief of it not being me they want to question has subsided, I'm overwhelmed with curiosity. I think I know what they'll be asking, but how can I be sure? And what will Dad be saying? It's no good, I can't resist it. I put my mug back down, slip out of my sliders and creep along the hallway. Some of our stairs are creaky, but not the bottom one, and that's where I sit, only a metre or so from the lounge door. I can hear everything.

'So how soon after their moving in did you become friendly with Miss Forsyth and her husband?' It's a man's voice this time. It must be Sergeant Carter's turn to ask the questions for a change.

'I wasn't friendly with them, exactly,' says Dad. 'It was more my wife and Vanessa who knew each other than me and Dean.' Wow, he's dropped Ellie in it there. Has he forgotten they both claimed not to know Vanessa well?

'But you all spent time together? As a foursome?' the sergeant continues. 'We've established this much from our conversations with Mr Westerby.'

'Well, yes, we did. But not many times. That's why we said what we did. We weren't trying to hide anything. We were friendly for a while, after they moved in. Ellie likes to make new neighbours welcome when they arrive. I mean, it doesn't happen often, but when it does, she's nice to them. Takes them cakes, that sort of thing. And she did the same for Vanessa and Dean. It doesn't mean we're best friends with everyone.'

'Of course not. But more than one other person has mentioned that you and your wife knew the Westerbys better than most.'

'Really? Who?' There's an awkward silence and I hold my breath. *Please don't mention my name*, I say in my head, *it would cause so much trouble.*

'That's not important right now,' says the sergeant calmly. 'Please just answer the question.'

'What question?'

'I was asking about your friendship with Vanessa Forsyth and her husband.'

'Oh, yes, sorry. Let me see. We had them over for dinner… twice. They took us out for a meal a couple of times – Vanessa didn't like to cook much, and neither did Dean, I suppose – and we all went to George's birthday party, as you know. Alex played with their children quite a lot. And Ellie had coffee with Vanessa a few times in the early days.'

'But not more recently?'

'No. Vanessa got busy with her filming and Dean's always been away a lot for work. It had more or less tailed off completely by the time George's birthday came around. We were seeing very little of them by then. To be honest, I think they only invited us to make up the numbers. They didn't know many people in Beverley, but Vanessa liked a crowd.'

'Did she?' DI Twist's voice breaks through like a sharp knife slicing through an apple, crisp and clear. 'How do you know that?'

'I don't know. It must have been something she said. Does it matter?' Dad sounds flustered now, and I don't blame him. Flitting between his professed distant dealings with Vanessa and intimate knowledge of what she did and didn't like isn't doing him any favours.

'Everything you can tell us about Vanessa matters,' says DI Twist. 'That's how it is in a murder investigation. And we'd appreciate it if you could be completely honest with us regarding your relationship with Miss Forsyth. Hiding things now won't help your credibility in the future, you know.'

'What do you mean?' Dad's panicking now, I can tell. 'Why are you talking about my credibility? What are all these questions about? Should I be asking for a lawyer?'

'Please calm down, Mr Preston.' Sergeant Carter's soothing tones return on the other side of the door, and I can feel my fingers relaxing, even though I didn't know I'd clenched my fists. 'There's no need for a lawyer. If there were we'd be down at the station talking to you under caution, and we're a long way off from that.'

'Good,' says Dad.

'However,' he continues, 'we have spoken to a great many people over the past few days. Other neighbours, people on the film set and so on. And one of them says that she told them the two of you were… intimate.'

'Intimate?'

'Miss Forsyth confided in this person about your relationship with her. She said the two of you had fallen in love and you were preparing to leave your wife and Mr Westerby in order to be together.' His words land like a bomb, and I have to clap my hand over my mouth to stop myself gasping in shock. I'd guessed something was going on, but I never thought it was more than Vanessa boasting and perhaps a bit of flirting. That would be enough to upset Ellie, especially given her history and Vanessa's film-star looks, but this…

'She said *what*?' Dad's disbelief comes through the door loud and clear. So he wasn't having an affair with her. Or was he? Wouldn't he deny it anyway?

'She said the two of you were having an affair and were planning to move in together.' Sergeant Carter puts it more bluntly this time, and he's slowed his speech a little, as if explaining something complicated to a small child.

'Well, we weren't.' Dad's recovering himself now, and I can picture him pulling himself up in his chair, ready to take on all comers.

'This witness is very clear about what was said to them. Are you saying they lied to us?' DI Twist is back in the conversation, making it sound as if Dad's about to be accused of slander, or is it libel?

'I'm saying we weren't having an affair. I'm saying that Vanessa liked attention and she liked… me. She flirted with me. She flirted a lot – it was embarrassing, to be honest – but we weren't having an affair.' I can hear a ring of truth in his voice, but the detectives don't know him, and I doubt a denial will be enough to change their minds. It's what they'd expect him to say, after all.

'So you didn't visit Vanessa, on your own, at night, when her husband was away, on multiple occasions?' asks DI Twist.

'I…' Dad's faltering now.

'Please be careful with what you say, Mr Preston. We've already established once that you haven't been completely honest with us. It would be better to tell us the truth from the start, don't you think, however difficult it might be?' There's a pause, and I can almost hear Dad thinking at the speed of light, working out what he should and shouldn't say.

'I did see Vanessa on my own. More than once.' What is he saying? Despite Vanessa's boasts, I never for a minute thought that Dad was guilty of anything more than failing to stop her flirting. Could there have been more to it than that?

'Thank you, Mr Preston. This tallies with information obtained in our investigation.' What can that mean? Has some neighbour seen Dad sneaking into Vanessa's house? 'Can you tell us the nature of these meetings?'

'The nature?'

'Why were you visiting Miss Forsyth?'

'I was helping her. With her finances.'

'Really?' DI Twist manages to sound polite at the same time as conveying total disbelief. It's very clever, and I think I should try it out myself some time. Dad's not fazed, though, he's on his high horse now, full of self-righteous indignation.

'Yes, really. She told me that Dean was having an affair with a younger woman. In London. She said she'd had enough of him, that he was a bully, violent even, and she wanted to divorce him.' Dad pauses.

'And she asked for your help? What sort of help? You're not a divorce lawyer, are you?'

93

'No, but I used to be an accountant. I do know about money, and she thought I could help her make some decisions about what to ask for when the time came.'

'So your meetings were purely… shall we say, business meetings?' DI Twist's talking calmly, but there's still an unmistakeable incredulity in her tone.

'Yes. That is…' Oh dear, Dad's never been very good at keeping secrets, not in the face of direct questioning, and you don't get more direct than Ronnie Twist.

'That is…?'

'She did try it on. She was a terrible flirt, she couldn't help it. It didn't mean anything, at least I thought it didn't. That is, it didn't mean anything to me…'

'But it did mean something to her? To Vanessa?' Sergeant Carter's voice drifts through the door again. Perhaps he's trying the man-to-man approach.

'Yes. And to Ellie. She was right all along.'

'About what?'

'Ellie knew I was helping Vanessa, she felt sorry for her. But then she saw Vanessa flirting with me. She was very upset. I told her it was nothing, it was just Vanessa's way. But she was right.'

'Because of what Vanessa told her friend?'

'Not just that. Because of what she told me. I can't believe I was such a fool. I nearly let that woman ruin everything, and now…' I don't know if he's crying or just frightened, but there's a pause, and I reckon they're giving him time to pull himself together.

'What did she tell you, Mike?' asks the sergeant, quietly but clearly.

'She told me she was in love with me. She said it was obvious I loved her too, but it wasn't, I promise you it wasn't.'

'Okay, it wasn't. What else did she say?'

'She said she was ready to leave Dean and I had to leave Ellie and we'd move in together. I tried to tell her she'd got it wrong but she wouldn't listen. The only way I could get away was to say yes, I loved her, but I needed some time to sort things out before I told Ellie. I said it would be our romantic secret. She liked that idea; she said she'd wait for a month, then we'd tell them both – Ellie and Dean, that is – and start to make plans.'

'When was this? When did this conversation happen?'

'It was… um… before the party. Yes, the day before. I tried to avoid her at the party, but I couldn't. She was all over me at one point and… Ellie saw.'

'Your wife saw you with Vanessa.'

'Yes, she was kissing me. I couldn't stop her. We were behind a big bush in their garden, but it wasn't enough. Ellie saw us.'

'What did she do? Ellie?'

'She waited till the next day. She got me to go into her studio so we'd have some privacy, and she asked me if I was having an affair with Vanessa. I told her no, of course not, but she got very upset. I explained what had happened, told her everything, and…' I can tell from his voice that Dad's near to tears, and as he breaks off, DI Twist suggests he might like a drink of water. I'm lucky it takes Dad a few seconds to splutter out a reply, and it's just enough time for me to sprint into the kitchen and open the fridge before Sergeant Carter walks in.

'Oh. Hello, did you want more coffee?' I pull out a can of Alex's horrible orange fizz and pop the tab for good measure.

'No, just a glass for water for your father,' he says.

'I'll get you one,' I say, reaching for a glass. I fill it from the tap and he leaves without further comment. I don't actually care if he's seen my full coffee mug sitting on the table. I'm too busy wondering if Dad was telling the truth and what Ellie said to him. I was sure there was something up between them, and now I know what it was. And it explains why, despite everything, they're both happier now that Vanessa's gone. Much happier. How much damage could she have done to them? Could she have wrecked their marriage? And how far would either – or both – of them have been prepared to go to protect it?

TEN

Dad will expect me to be in the garden, and you can't hear what's happening at the front door from there, so I decide it's best to go outside. I roll another smoke, needing something to help me calm down and think straight. How did this happen? How is it even possible that I'm sitting here wondering if my father could be a murderer? Or Ellie, of all people?

Something Vanessa said to me that night, the time she showed me the gun, comes back to me. She said a lot, she was on a roll, and the shock of seeing a real gun blotted most of it out, but I remember now. She told me the production company had commissioned another three seasons of her TV series. She was supposed to keep it a secret, but she couldn't resist telling me – she said she had to tell someone, and she couldn't hold it in any longer. Did she tell Dad as well? Did he and Ellie know that she wouldn't be leaving at the end of the shoot? She was so happy about it, saying how thrilled she was to be staying in Beverley; she loved the house and was thinking of asking the owners to sell it to her. She would make them an offer they couldn't refuse. And then she started going on about Dad. She began by saying how great the neighbours were, but it wasn't long before she was busy telling me how great he was and how lucky Ellie was to have him. She seemed to forget she was talking to his daughter, but maybe she didn't care who she was talking to, as long as she had a captive audience.

'Billie?' I've been so lost in thought I didn't notice Dad coming outside. I jump, dislodging the dead end of my roll-up that's been growing unnoticed in my hand. It falls on the ground, and I get up quickly to kick the ash out of sight.

'Dad! You gave me a shock. You've been ages, is everything okay?' Dad's as pale as a sheet so I have to ask, but there's no way he's going to tell me what they've been grilling him about, and although my head is bursting with furious questions, I'm not ready to ask them yet.

'Everything's fine. They wanted to check some details about Vanessa and Dean, how well we knew them, when they moved in, that sort of thing.' It's a poor attempt but I let it go. It won't help him to have me quiz him. 'I thought you'd be gone by now. Didn't you say you were going to the market?'

'Yes, I did. And I'm going now.' I head inside, not wanting to have to think of an explanation for not having left already. 'Do you need anything? Something nice for lunch, perhaps?'

'Why not? Surprise me,' he says, looking better now that I've accepted his explanation. 'Billie…'

'Yes?'

'Um… nothing, I forgot what I was going to say.' Was he going to tell me everything? Or was he about to ask me to keep quiet about the police being here? And did he change his mind, thinking it would look suspicious? It won't help to ask, and I hate myself for even thinking it.

'You must be getting old,' I tease him, and he smiles as he starts to clear away the coffee mugs. But the creases on his forehead give him away. There won't be much planning done now; he'll be too busy working out what to tell Ellie when she gets home.

∗ ∗ ∗

97

Lunch with Dad is – not surprisingly – a bit awkward, and it's a relief to get away and join Gaby for our bouldering session. I'm out of practice after so much time on tour, and I have to warm up on the easier climbs, but I'm soon back in my stride and it's a wonderful distraction. We stay until the end of the session and then go to the park next door, where we lie in the late afternoon sun, a packet of Haribo between us.

'We'll have to do that again before you leave,' Gaby says. 'We should go midweek next time, when it's cheaper. I can just get here in time if I leave work on the dot.'

'Sure,' I say. 'It'll have to be soon, mind. I'm leaving in two weeks.'

'That came round quick, didn't it? Although I guess you'll be glad to move out of that teeny room.'

'You bet.'

'It must have been nice to be home for a while. Don't you miss your family when you're away?' Gaby's the biggest home bird I know. Even meeting Katie, whom she's already calling the love of her life, hasn't tempted her to move out, although I know Katie wants her to.

'A bit… well, not much to be honest. I'm too busy most of the time. And it's been weird this time. With everything that's happened.' I don't want to talk about Vanessa, and I'm definitely not ready to tell her about this morning's police visit, but I can't pretend her death hasn't made for a disturbing visit home. And it's not over yet. I'm on the verge of being distracted by it all over again when Gaby comes to my rescue.

'I saw an article the other day about families,' she says. 'This woman reckoned that some families have what she called a secret centre.'

'A what?'

'A secret centre. She said most people, if you ask them, can name the most important person in their family. In the house, that is – it's different if you all live in different places.'

'Yeah, so what?'

'Well, she said the person people *say* is the most important often isn't. The most important, that is.'

'Gaby, you're really not making sense.' I can't help laughing. She's always doing this, reading weird stuff online and believing it.

'No, it's true,' she says, sitting up to make her point. 'If you ask anyone in our house who's the most important person in the family, they'd say...' She looks at me expectantly.

'Your mum.' Everyone in Gaby's house adores her mum. She manages everything from packed lunches to car maintenance, and they all do exactly what she says.

'No!' she says, triumphantly.

'What d'you mean? Your mum rules your house with a rod of iron, even I know that.'

'But does she?' Gaby's putting on her 'face of mystery' now, which only makes me laugh even more. 'No, I'm serious,' she says. 'Shut up a minute and I'll explain.'

'All right. Explain.' I sit up too, facing her with our legs crossed as if we were back in school, my brown knees opposite her white, freckly ones.

'Okay. It *looks* like Mum's in charge of everything, but it's actually Dad who's the centre.'

'How d'you work that one out? Your dad's at work all day. And he's working half the time he's at home too from what I've seen.'

'Ah, that's the thing. What you've seen. What *haven't* you seen? When I met Katie and things started to get serious, Mum said she was really happy for me and she hoped Katie would be a rock for me like Dad is for her.'

'Did she?'

'Yes. And I said surely it was her being Dad's rock and she said no, just because she does all the practical stuff in our house doesn't mean she makes all the decisions. She said you can't know what's going on behind the scenes if you're not there yourself. And that the person who'd made all the real decisions in our house, the important ones, was Dad. She said it was him who said we'd help Jenna bring up

Harry if her rubbish boyfriend wouldn't stick by her. And it was Dad who came up with the idea of me doing an apprenticeship instead of going to college. I never knew. I thought it was all her.'

'Wow.'

'I know. You spend your whole life living with your family thinking you know how it works, and then – bam! – you realise you had it wrong the whole time.' Gaby uncrosses her legs, pops a yellow ring in her mouth and lies down on the grass again, squinting up at me. 'So what d'you reckon?'

'About what?'

'Who's the secret centre in your house?'

'Um… I don't know. I'm not even sure I know who the un-secret one is. Ellie does lots of stuff, especially for Alex, but so does Sandy. And Dad too, come to that.' I pause, feeling weirdly unsettled by the thought. Who *does* make the decisions – the big ones, that is? 'Oh, it's all a load of rubbish, Gaby, just like most stuff you read on the internet. It'll be little green men from Mars next.'

'*You're* a little green man from Mars,' she says, resorting to our favourite childhood response. 'And isn't it time you took a photo or something? It's at least – ooh – twenty minutes since you posted, your followers will be wondering if you've died.'

'Shut up!' But I pull my phone out anyway and pull her up so I can take a picture of our shadows, our bare feet sticking out at the bottom of the photo below the caption 'Best friends'.

* * *

I stay out with Gaby as long as I can and by the time I return, the house is full. I half expected to find the police back again, talking to Ellie, finding out what she thought about Vanessa and her stories about Dad, but there's no sign of them. I suppose they have other cases to solve too, and Ellie's hardly likely to be categorised as a flight risk. It does surprise me that they're not keen to talk to her before she and Dad have time to cook up a matching story together, but perhaps they think there's no point, there's been plenty of time for them to do that already. Ellie and Dad seem relaxed, and I wonder if he's even told her about the police visit. It's not my job to tell her, so I stay out of it. Maybe he's waiting until tomorrow morning. As far as I know, they could have already told him they're coming back then. It's all too much to think about and I take the easy option, focusing on helping Alex with the dinner preparations.

The meal's a success, Alex approves of my decorations and his first attempt at prawn linguine is a triumph. We finish with the traditional dessert for these occasions, Ellie's excellent tiramisu, and finish with coffee and chocolates in the garden. It's Nora's first end-of-term meal with us and she's enjoyed herself hugely.

'Thank you for a wonderful evening,' she says. 'I can't remember the last time I had such a delicious meal, and in such convivial company.' She beams round at us all, and Alex glows with pride.

'You're most welcome, Gran,' he says. 'But what's convivial?'

'It means friendly, enjoyable, that sort of thing,' Ellie says, at the same time as Sandy says, 'Look it up in the dictionary.'

'Typical teacher,' says Dad. 'Come on, Alex, time for bed. You're late already.'

'Will you come up with me, Sandy?' Alex asks. 'It's *ages* since you read to me.'

'Aren't you a bit old for that now?' says Dad. 'Surely you're capable of reading anything you like now.'

'You're never too old for a bedtime story,' says Sandy. 'But it's Mother's bedtime too, and she needs my help.'

'Oh, get along with you,' says Nora. 'I can stay up a while longer, or Ellie can help me. It's not that hard.' Sandy gives her a frown, but it passes quickly and she gets up with Alex.

'All right,' she says. 'Did you have anything particular in mind?'

'*The Hobbit!*' Alex is leading her inside with a spring in his step. 'With your special Gandalf voice. No one does the voices like you, Sandy!' It's true, Sandy is the best storyteller I know, especially when it comes to the voices. No wonder she's such a good English teacher;

I bet she has entire classes spellbound when she reads to them. It was Sandy who first made sense of Shakespeare for me, and I've never looked back.

'She's a wonderful aunt, isn't she?' Nora says, watching them go. 'And she's done her share of looking after you too, I suppose, Billie?'

'We've all had a share of that terrible burden.' Dad smiles. He's made a joke of it but I notice he's not actually agreed with Nora.

'Sandy's always been a great help,' Ellie says firmly, gathering up coffee cups and putting them on the tray. 'She's got us through some very difficult times.' Dad opens his mouth to say something more, but Ellie gives him an uncharacteristically sharp look and he shuts it. Perhaps she's thinking that he's been the one to cause the difficult times, at least the most recent ones. Nora's busy helping Ellie and doesn't see the look on her face, and I get up too before she can say anything more of an inflammatory nature.

'Here, Nora, let me give you a hand,' I say, handing her frame across to her. 'Let's see what's on the news before you go to bed.' Nora loves her news, and quickly welcomes the suggestion. Ellie looks relieved, and Dad says he'll join us. We manage to keep talking about Alex and his cooking until we reach the lounge, where national affairs and the weather forecast fill Nora's attention. My brain is less easily distracted, though. No one – no one at all – has mentioned the police coming earlier. Dad hasn't told Ellie, he can't have done. But why not? What, exactly, is he hiding?

ELEVEN

'Dad's taking you to the minster this morning,' Ellie says as I come into the kitchen.

'Dad?' Alex stares at her.

'Yes, Dad. He does know how to get there, you know.' Ellie tries to inject some humour into her voice, but I can tell it's a struggle.

'But you always take me. Dad goes cycling on Sunday mornings.'

'He's going cycling after he's taken you. I'll be picking you up.'

Alex's mouth opens and shuts as she answers his question before he manages to ask it, and I exchange smiles with Ellie.

'Nice one, Ellie.'

'Nice one what?' Alex asks, his mouth full of breakfast.

'It looks like being another nice day,' I say, knowing Alex has to have an answer, no matter how trivial the question.

'Oh. Okay.' His arrangements for the morning settled to his satisfaction, Alex returns to his Weetabix. 'Can I have a boiled egg? Sandy says they're good for the brain.'

'Oh, she does, does she?' Ellie says, looking as if the last thing she wants to do is make a boiled egg for the benefit of Alex's brain.

'I'll make you one,' I say. 'I quite fancy one myself.' Ellie looks grateful, but she has her standards.

'It's very kind of Billie to say she'll cook you an egg, but you can't have one unless—'

'Please!'

'All right. I'm going back to bed for a bit. I've got a terrible headache.' She's not said why Dad's taking Alex, and he's not asked – he's only interested in his own arrangements – but I can hazard a guess. There's no time for thinking when you're having breakfast with Alex, and it's not until I'm in the shower that I have time to consider it properly. Ellie never gets headaches; at least, she hasn't for years. Dad must have told her about the police visit after all. She was short with him when Alex went to bed, but she seemed fine for the rest of the evening, so she can't have known then. He must have told her late last night after we'd all gone to bed. Whether he was telling the truth about her knowing about Vanessa or not, it can't have been an easy conversation. Perhaps they were up late and she's tired. Or maybe she just needs some time on her own.

My muscles are aching from yesterday's climbing so I give myself a day off from running. A couple of messages came through on Facebook last night about rooms going spare in London and I send replies asking for more details. They're not from people I know so I'll wait before committing myself. While I'm busy on my phone I hear first Alex and Dad and then Sandy and Nora leave the house. Ellie must have encouraged them to stick to their usual Sunday outing and I suppose they accepted her story about having a headache. The house is quiet for the second morning in a row and I realise it's almost eleven o'clock and my brain's craving caffeine. There's no sign of Ellie, but the back door's open and I guess she's in the studio. I don't bother to go down there, knowing she usually has a drink at this time, and put the kettle on.

As if on cue, the doorbell rings. I don't believe it – are they going to turn up at this time of day for the rest of our lives? I put down the coffee jar, but Ellie's at the back door, pushing her hands through her hair to tidy it up and on her way to answer it herself.

'It's all right, Billie, I'll go. It's for me.' There's a grim expression on her face and she doesn't wait for a reply before striding out into the hallway. I stand there, spoon in hand, wondering what to do next. She knew. She knew they were coming. That's why she invented a headache and got rid of everyone. But if the police are here, when did they tell Ellie they needed to see her? Did she know last night? Or perhaps they left a message on her phone and she didn't see it until late? That must be it. Perhaps she'll loosen up on the no-phone policy now that she's fallen victim to it herself, but I don't suppose that question is uppermost in her mind right now.

The kettle's boiling and I wonder how many mugs we're going to need, but I don't have to wonder for long. Ellie's coming back into the kitchen, Twist and Carter in tow, saying, 'I hope you don't mind coming in here. We're just making coffee. Would you like some?' My mouth opens in surprise. Surely she doesn't want to have this conversation with me in the room? But maybe she does. It dawns on me that whist Ellie has managed to get the house almost to herself for this, she didn't suggest I tag along with Sandy. If she'd wanted to get rid of me too, I'm sure she'd have found a way. If I'm still here, it's because she wants me to be.

'Good morning, Billie.' DI Twist sounds almost friendly for once. She's still dressed smartly, but her hair's down today, flowing sleekly to her shoulders. She must have spent ages straightening it. Maybe she's going out for lunch or something. She notices my surprise, although she assumes it's their timing rather than Ellie's behaviour that's caused it.

'There's no such thing as a weekend in a murder investigation, I'm afraid,' she says, sitting at the table. 'And Ellie said it might be a good time to catch her without a houseful.' She turns to smile at Ellie, perhaps hoping to put her at her ease. If so, it's not working.

'It's okay for Billie to stay, isn't it?' she says. 'It's silly, I know, but I've not been interviewed by the police before – at least not before this week.'

'Of course,' says DI Twist. 'As I said in my message last night, you're more than welcome to have your husband with you, or anyone else you choose.' She pauses, looking around the room, as if Dad might be hiding in one of the cupboards. 'Was Mike not able to join you?'

'No, one of us had to take Alex to the minster.' Very neat. She's managed to avoid suggesting she doesn't want him here, and if the detectives think it's odd that one of the other adults in the house didn't volunteer, they aren't showing it. The coffee's almost ready and they wait in silence, Sergeant Carter turning on his tablet, while I pour it, wondering if they're going to mention yesterday's interview with Dad. Coffee distributed, I sit next to Ellie, opposite the two detectives, feeling uncomfortably like a solicitor in a formal interview.

'This is just an informal interview,' DI Twist says, as if reading my mind. 'We're looking into the events of Vanessa Forsyth's life in the days leading up to her death, and any information is helpful at this stage, no matter how unrelated you may think it might be.'

'Of course,' says Ellie. 'I understand. We weren't close friends, but we did know her. I'm hardly worried about being a suspect.' She laughs nervously.

'Quite.' DI Twist smiles politely but doesn't actually agree with her. And if Ellie's not worried about being a suspect, why am I here? Fortunately for her, no one asks that question.

'I expect your husband mentioned to you that we discussed his relationship with Miss Forsyth yesterday?' she continues.

'Yes. He did.' The answer comes quickly enough to sound true but Ellie's face has gone white all the same. She shoots me a quick look as if wishing she'd not asked me to be here after all, but it's too late now, and I get ready to look shocked when I hear what they were talking about.

'What, exactly, did your husband tell you about it?'

'I'm sure you know what Mike told me. Didn't you talk about that with him yesterday?' Ellie's voice is tight and hard. Maybe she does have a headache after all.

'We did, but we'd like to hear it from your perspective. If you don't mind.'

'All right, although I don't see how it can help.' Ellie takes a sip of her coffee as if giving herself time to prepare her answer, although I'm sure she's had it ready for long enough. 'About two months ago, Vanessa asked Mike for some financial advice. He used to be an accountant and she thought he could help.'

'Didn't she have her own accountant?'

'That's what I asked him, but he said no, she and Dean used the same firm and she didn't want him finding out she'd been asking for advice.'

'And the reason for that was...'

'She said she was planning on divorcing Dean. She told Mike that Dean had been unfaithful to her, bullying, and violent too. She wanted to make sure he didn't have the chance to run off with all her money when she told him she was leaving him.'

'And Mike said he'd help her.'

'Yes. He went over a few times when Dean was away. In the evenings, when the children were in bed and the housekeeper had gone home.'

'And you were happy for him to help her?'

'Of course. We'd been friends for a while by then and I felt sorry for her. It didn't surprise me about Dean having an affair. He was married when he met Vanessa and it seemed like history repeating itself, to be honest. I was surprised about the violence, though. I'd never particularly warmed to Dean, but he didn't seem the type. I suppose they never do.'

'No, I don't think they do,' DI Twist agrees. She's talking calmly, almost conversationally, no threat in her voice, her eyes fixed on the window, as if admiring the view of the garden. Ellie's finally starting to relax and I think that maybe Dad didn't tell her everything after all.

'I believe you were Vanessa's closest friend in Beverley?' DI Twist asks, still keeping it light.

'That's putting it a bit strongly,' says Ellie. 'I wouldn't say close. She hadn't been here long enough to get to that point. But she didn't have many friends locally, or the time to make any. She was busy filming most of the time; it was what she was here for, after all.'

'Of course. And as she got busier, you drifted apart, is that right?'

'Yes. We didn't have much in common other than the children.'

'It was a gradual process, was it? Not an abrupt ending?' DI Twist's voice has taken on a sharper edge, and she's focused on Ellie now rather than the trees.

'I'm not sure what you mean.'

'What I mean, Mrs Preston, is that your husband told us that you saw him kissing Vanessa at her son's birthday party, and that it was this, not a gradual "drifting apart", that caused your friendship with her to end.' There's a shocked silence, and I'm glad I'm sitting next to Ellie rather than opposite. She'd spot my 'surprised' face a mile off, but DI Twist doesn't know me so well, and she's looking at Ellie, anyway, not me.

'Is that what Mike told you?'

'Yes, it's what he told us. I'm surprised he didn't mention it to you himself.'

'We… we were busy yesterday evening. I didn't get back from Leeds until nearly five o'clock. The house was busy, we were having a party – a family party, not a big one. I went to bed before Mike. I was tired, and I was asleep before he came up. I didn't even check my phone.' She looks over at Sergeant Carter. 'That's why I didn't answer your message until this morning. We didn't have time to talk properly. Mike told me you'd been here yesterday but not what was said. There wasn't time.'

'So when you said earlier that Mike told you what he said about Vanessa yesterday, you were lying?'

'No. I… that is, I meant yes, he told me you'd talked to him. Just not in detail.'

'Hmm.' DI Twist sounds doubtful, but she seems to decide it's not worth pursuing. She pauses for a moment and looks towards her sergeant, perhaps deciding that it's time for a change of personnel. He puts his tablet down and smiles sympathetically at Ellie.

'So the friendship came to a sudden end. After you saw them together.'

'Yes, that's right.' I can feel Ellie sitting up straighter in her chair, perhaps preparing herself to tell an uncomfortable truth or two.

'Did your husband stop "helping" Vanessa at this point?'

'No, he didn't.'

'Why not?'

'We talked about it. I was… very angry with him. I'd seen her flirting with him dozens of times. She was all over him every time she saw him, little touches, you know, making private jokes with him. I'd told him I didn't like it before, but he said not to be silly, she was like that with everyone. And it's true, she was like that with everyone, I've even seen her flirt with the postman.'

'But you didn't stop him helping her with her finances?'

'I didn't like it, but I still felt sorry for her. She could be very sweet and charming. She was very kind to me at first, and lovely with Alex. Not everyone "gets" Alex, but Vanessa did; she asked him over to play with George and Heidi straight away. And after what she told Mike about Dean, I could hardly say no, could I?'

'But you had your suspicions?' Sergeant Carter's approach seems to be working and I can tell Ellie's loosening up now that she's decided to tell the truth.

'Yes. I did. I don't know much about finance, but it seemed to me that it was taking a very long time to sort hers out. I asked Mike and he said it was complicated. She had a lot of investments, apparently, some going a long way back, and it was hard to work out what had happened to some of them.'

'And then you saw them at the party?'

'Yes. Like I said, I was very angry. We had a big row about it. And that's when he told me…' Ellie hesitates, perhaps wondering if Dad told them this bit too.

'Please, Ellie, don't hold anything back. If you hide anything now it might not look good for you later,' DI Twist interjects quietly, but the message is clear. People who want to look innocent can't afford to keep secrets, and Ellie knows it.

'He told me Vanessa said she was in love with him and wanted to move in with him.' It all comes out in a rush, as if she can't wait to get it over with.

'And was he in love with her?' Sergeant Carter asks.

'No! He wasn't, I know he wasn't.' Ellie pauses, perhaps thinking it unwise to protest too much, but her pride wins the argument. 'She might have been a glamorous film star and I suppose I'm not much more than a dumpy, not-very-successful artist, but he loves me. He said so and I believed him. I still do. We've not lived together all this time, brought up Alex – and Billie – together, been through everything we have together, without it meaning something. He wasn't in love with her. I know it.' It's quite a speech, and even if they think it might not be true, it would be impossible to believe Ellie thinks otherwise.

'Okay,' he says. 'You believed him. But he didn't stop visiting Vanessa. Why was that?'

'He'd promised to keep seeing her. To get her off his back and to give us time to work something out. She only said all this the day before the party. He was going to talk it through with me once it was over. I think we'd have ridden it out, you know, waited until her filming was over and she moved back to London. I'm sure she'd have moved on to someone else; she'd never have handled a long-distance relationship.'

'But you couldn't do that, could you?'

'I suppose Mike told you, did he? No, we couldn't. She told him her contract had been extended. They were planning three more seasons of her TV series. She was going to be in Beverley for the foreseeable future.' Ellie sighs.

'So I understand.' Sergeant Carter nods encouragingly. 'That can't have been easy to hear.'

'No, it wasn't,' Ellie says wryly. 'Especially when she said she was hoping to buy the house and live on our doorstep. Even if Mike managed to stall her in the short term, we'd never be free of her.' This is sounding pretty grim to me. Doesn't Ellie realise she's providing the police with a great motive for either her or Dad to have killed Vanessa? I'm expecting DI Twist to say as much, but Ellie's still talking. 'I expect Mike told you about our plan?'

'Go on,' he says, neither confirming nor denying her assumption.

'We decided to move. Away from Beverley. Not a long way, but far enough to be out of Vanessa's range. Somewhere bigger, out of the town, where I could have a proper studio with heating and running water, and with space for Alex to work and play his piano, and Billie to have a room of her own.' I feel like I've been punched in the stomach again, but in a good way this time. It sounds amazing. It's a great idea. Ellie turns to me as if for confirmation, and I give her a big smile.

'I'm sorry,' she says. 'We'd not mentioned the idea to Billie before. I guess it's a shock for her to hear it.'

'Only you won't need to move now, will you?' DI Twist says, returning her sergeant to note-taking duties.

'No,' Ellie agrees. 'Although I think Mike would like to… well, to have more space, and so would I, to be honest. Who knows? Maybe we'll think about it anyway.' She turns to me again, but there's something in her expression that makes me wonder if she thinks it's a good idea. The detectives aren't interested in Ellie's potential moving plans, and they're already pushing their chairs away from the table.

'That'll be all for now, Mrs Preston,' says DI Twist. 'Thank you for your time, and for your honesty. As I said, it's essential for us to build up a full picture of Miss Forsyth's life and relationships. We're talking to lots of people – you're not the only ones who knew her.' She gives Ellie a little smile as if to reassure her, and perhaps it's true – who knows how many other people Vanessa upset since coming here? Ellie sees them out and comes straight back, sitting opposite me this time as if preparing for another inquisition.

'Go on. Ask,' she says.

'Ask what?'

'I don't know, but you must have at least one question after that lot.'

'I don't know where to start, to be honest. Is all that true about Dad and Vanessa?'

'Of course it's true. Why would I – we – make it up?'

'I suppose, but…'

'Why didn't we say anything about it? Why would we? We were sorting it out, and it wasn't anyone else's business, anyway.'

'But you've made it my business, making me sit there and listen to it all.' Even though I'd heard half of it from Dad yesterday, it's still far more information than I ever wanted to have about their relationship.

'I know. I'm sorry. I should have thought. But I needed someone there. For moral support. I could never have held it together without you Billie, honestly, I'm so grateful.' She reaches out her hand and I put mine on top. I can never stay cross with Ellie for long, and I guess I might have felt the same in her position.

'I was still angry with your father for being such an idiot, letting it get that far, and I don't suppose they'd have wanted him there anyway. And I couldn't do it to Mother, she's had enough to cope with already.'

'What about Sandy? Why didn't you ask her?' I'd have thought she'd be Ellie's first choice for support. She's more of a mother to her than a sister in many ways.

'Oh… I don't know. I suppose I feel stupid for letting it all happen in the first place. I'd have been embarrassed for her to hear about it. And anyway, I needed her to get Mother out of the house.'

'I suppose so.' I pause for a minute, thinking things through. 'Does Dad know about the police coming this morning?'

'No, there was a message on my phone last night. I didn't want to talk to him about it then; it was late and I didn't want another argument. It was easier to just get him out of the house and get on with it myself.'

'And what about yesterday? When they came to see him? Did he tell you about that?'

'Oh yes, but not in detail. As I said, it was a busy evening.' I have the feeling she's about to say more, but we're interrupted by a loud beeping from her phone. 'Oh my goodness – Alex,' she says. 'I knew I'd forget him if I wasn't careful. I'll have to go, Billie. I'll see you soon, and thanks again. You're a star.' She plants a kiss on the top of my head before rushing from the room. I hear her grab her keys and slam the front door, leaving silence in her wake.

I'm desperate for a smoke but my body seems to have lost every last ounce of energy and I find myself unable to move from the kitchen table. My limbs won't work until my mind's sorted itself out, and I try to untangle the thoughts which are disturbing me the most. Vanessa wanted to steal Dad from Ellie – it's a dreadful thought, but I've had twenty-four hours to get used to it. I can believe their story of how it started. Dad loves to put his accounting expertise to good use and Ellie's too kind for her own good. I bet Dean's never been violent towards anyone; Vanessa must have made that up to get Dad's sympathy. And I can easily believe she wouldn't take no for an answer when he said he didn't love her. But the rest of it? Did they really decide moving house was a sensible solution to the problem? It's a massive decision to make, and wouldn't they have needed to discuss it with Sandy? Or is the whole idea something they made up? They must have known the whole thing would come out in the end. And without a plan in place, Vanessa promising to make their lives hell for the foreseeable future sounds like an excellent motive for murder to me.

TWELVE

I go into the garden for a smoke, and it helps to get outside, but Ellie and Alex will be back any minute and I suddenly know I can't face them. How can I stay here, knowing what I do, making polite conversation, pretending everything is normal? Perhaps it is normal, perhaps Dad and Ellie are fine now Vanessa's gone, but I can't pretend I don't know about everything that's happened. I need to talk it through. With someone I can properly trust. I stub out the cigarette and pull my phone out of my pocket. I don't believe it. There's a text from Jay:

Hi babe

Babe?

Sorry for the silence. Been in the mountains, amazing times but no signal, no wifi, nothing! Just about to have my first shower in a week. Talk later? Xxx

It's the best thing and the worst thing. My head spinning, I type an automatic 'okay' and call Gaby.

'Billie! You okay?'

'Not really. Are you busy?' She doesn't even need to ask. She knows me too well.

'Meet you at the bandstand in… twenty minutes. Bring food.'

'Thanks, Gaby, you're a—'

'And Billie—'

'I know, I know. I won't be late – I promise.' I head back into the house to make a sandwich before Ellie and Alex get back. I'm not quick enough, though, and I've barely started when Alex crashes into the kitchen.

'You're going out?' His face falls. 'You said you'd help me with my model this afternoon.'

'I'm meeting Gaby. I'll be back later, we can do it then.'

Ellie picks up on my barely concealed impatience, no doubt knowing what's behind it. 'Billie's not home for very long,' she tells Alex. 'And Gaby works all week. It's probably the only time they have to get together, right, Billie?'

'Right.' I shove some crisps into a shopping bag.

'You can come in the studio with me and do some painting, if you like,' Ellie offers.

'The studio? Really?' Ellie hates other people being in her space and she only allows Alex to paint in there on the most special of occasions.

'Yes. As a start-of-the-holidays treat,' she improvises. 'Maybe you could paint something for Dad?'

'And for Sandy,' says Alex. 'It's her holiday too.'

'If you like.' Ellie's rummaging in the fridge. 'Now, do you want cheese or ham in your sandwich?'

* * *

It's not a bandstand, but that's what we call it. Sandy always tells me off, saying it's a market cross and a historical structure, but it looks like a bandstand to me. It's busy in town; sunny Sundays always are.

Gaby suggests we take our picnic to the memorial gardens, but there are too many people there and I make her walk to the Westwood and find a spot where we won't be overheard. We keep the conversation light, focusing on bouldering and whether there'll be another heatwave, until we're on the hill, overlooking the racecourse.

'Go on then. What's up?' Gaby says. 'No, let me guess. Jay called?'

'How on earth…'

'Just call me mystic Meg.' She grins. 'No, seriously, did he?'

'He texted. He said he's been in the mountains for a week with no signal.'

'Do you believe him?'

'I don't know. He wants to talk later. I said okay.' I bite into a sandwich, thinking that Jay's the least of my worries right now.

'That sounds good – or potentially good, yes?' She's not asking why the big drama over a text from Jay, but I can tell it's what she's thinking.

'I didn't call you because of Jay.'

'No?'

'You know what happened to Vanessa Forsyth?'

Gaby nods. 'Sure.'

'Well… I think Dad and Ellie might be suspects.'

Gaby nearly chokes on her crisp. 'You what?'

'The police have been round. A few times now. Because we knew her, you know. Like they talk to a lot of people when someone dies.'

'And specially when they've been murdered, I guess.'

'Yeah. Anyway, they've been twice this weekend. Yesterday for Dad and this morning for Ellie.'

'Yesterday? But you never said a thing about it when we were out.'

'I know. I… I wasn't ready, I needed to think about it more. And it was nice to switch off for a bit, to be honest.'

Gaby nods slowly, and I'm grateful for her understanding. 'That's unreal,' she says at last.

'I know.'

'So what was it about? Why do you think they're suspects? Just talking to them might not mean that. It's not as if they've been hauled off to the police station, is it?'

'No, that's true. They did say – at least they said to Ellie – that it was informal.'

'There you go,' Gaby says. 'Nothing to worry about. You do get worked up about things, Billie.'

'No, there's more.'

'Go on.'

'Look, Gaby, this is completely confidential, okay? You can't tell anyone, and I really mean anyone, not even Katie. Or your mum.'

'All right.' She looks serious enough, even though her mouth is full of sandwich, and I take a deep breath.

'My dad might have been having an affair with Vanessa.' There, it's out.

Gaby has stopped, mid-chew, but she doesn't splutter it out this time, just pauses, finishes her mouthful and takes a swig of water. 'That's ridiculous. Anyone can see your dad loves Ellie to bits. They're the perfect couple. Who says so?' She's so calm about it, it takes me by surprise, and I feel better already. She's right. It is ridiculous. Despite the obvious implications about Vanessa's death, my biggest fear has been that Dad and Ellie could split up over this, and Gaby's blunt assessment is immediately reassuring.

'Well, they do. Although that's not exactly what they said.'

'So what did they say?'

'They both told the police that Dad had been helping Vanessa with money stuff because she wanted to divorce Dean.'

'Okay, that makes sense. Film stars get divorced all the time, right?' That's a huge generalisation, but now's not the time to go into it.

'And apparently Vanessa fell for Dad and wanted him to leave Ellie and move in with her. And Ellie saw them kissing.'

'Wait a minute. Vanessa Forsyth fell in love with your dad? Are you sure?'

'I know. It does sound mad but it's what they said.'

'You actually heard them say it?'

'Yes. I was with Ellie when she told the police all about it.'

'Okay,' says Gaby slowly. 'But… sorry, Billie, I know she's your family now, but Ellie has had… I don't know, issues, in the past. Might she have imagined it? You know what actresses are like, they kiss everyone all the time. Might she have misinterpreted something?'

I'd love to think this is true, it would make life so much simpler, but I can't.

'No, Dad said it too.'

'He said that to the police with you in the room? That he'd had an affair with Vanessa?'

'No. He said the same as Ellie. About helping Vanessa and her falling for him. But I wasn't in the room.'

'So how d'you know what he said?'

'I was sitting on the stairs. I heard through the lounge door. They're not very thick, our doors.'

'Oh.' Gaby doesn't know what to say, and I'm not surprised. I take the opportunity to grab a sandwich before she eats the lot while she thinks. 'So are you saying they had a motive to murder her? To get her off your dad's back?'

'Well, yes. But no. Ellie said they'd planned to move house. To get away from her.'

'That sounds a bit drastic. Won't she be leaving soon anyway, once she's finished filming?'

'No, apparently they're doing three more seasons and she was planning to stay. Although I guess they won't be doing them now.'

'I see. So what you're saying is that they might have had a motive but they didn't because they were planning to move?'

'Yes. Does that make sense?'

'I suppose so. But you're still worried, aren't you? Or did you just need to talk it through?'

'Both, I guess.' A family walk up the hill, a little girl of about three toddling towards us, and we wait until they're out of earshot again. I roll a smoke and offer one to Gaby, who shakes her head.

'Do you think they made it up? The moving house plan?' Gaby asks once the coast is clear.

'I did wonder. They didn't mention it before, but Ellie said they'd only decided on it just before Vanessa died and they'd wanted to keep it secret for a bit.'

'So it could be a lie. To make the police think they didn't have a motive after all.'

'Yeah. But… I mean, is Vanessa wanting to cause trouble like that a good enough motive for murder anyway?' I say. 'I know people do it for love, jealousy, whatever, in books, but do they in real life?'

'Sure they do. Don't you ever watch true crime shows? People kill each other for those reasons all the time.'

'Yes, but Dad? Ellie? Really?'

'I know. They aren't like the people in those shows, but the police don't know that, do they?' She's right, they don't.

'You know what the best thing would be? To get the police off their case?'

'What?'

'If they could prove this moving plan was for real. Then there'd be much less reason for the police to think they might have done it.'

'That's true.' I have to admit she's got a point. 'Yes, they'd have to talk to Sandy if they wanted to do that. The house is half hers. At least it was when she and Ellie first moved in. Dad paid for the studio and the extension, so they might have given him a share too. I don't know – it's not something they'd discuss with me.'

'Never mind the details,' says Gaby, impatiently. 'The point is, maybe they talked to Sandy about it, and if they did, that's got to help, hasn't it?'

'Yes, it has.' I sit up a bit straighter. 'I'll ask Dad. I'm going to go mad soon if I don't find out what really went on between him and Vanessa, and I can ask him about the house as well.'

'Are you sure? I know you and your dad are really close, but won't it be the most embarrassing conversation on the planet?'

'Yes. It will be embarrassing. But I need to know whether to be really angry with him for having an affair or just annoyed because he's been naïve. He's a bit of an innocent, you know – I can just imagine him being completely clueless about Vanessa and her romantic ideas.'

'But you know what he'll say, Billie. Even if he was having an affair with her, he'll deny it straight off. Wouldn't you, if you were him?'

'I suppose so…' I bite my lip, trying to imagine how a conversation with Dad about Vanessa might actually play out.

'And you can hardly ask him if he murdered her, can you?'

'I guess not.' I sigh heavily. 'So what *should* I do?'

'Talk to Ellie. But just about the house and how it would help if she can prove Sandy – or someone else – knew about the plan before Vanessa died. There's no need to start telling your dad you've been lurking in the corridor while he talks to the police and suspecting him of murder. Think how upset he could be – it could take years to repair that sort of damage.'

'But what about him and Vanessa?'

'Leave it for now – at least until the police have stopped hassling him. Remember, you've only just found out all this stuff, but he and Ellie have been dealing with it for much longer. They're grown-ups, let them sort it out themselves – or at least give them a chance to. It shouldn't be a problem, should it? At least, not if they're telling the truth.' Gaby jumps up and hauls me to my feet, evidently deciding that the discussion is over. I don't reply, but we're both thinking the same thing: what if it's not the truth they're telling – what if it's a well-constructed, carefully thought-out, convincingly delivered pack of lies?

* * *

I deliberately delay my return to the house with a mooch around the shops, but they close at four, which is probably just as well as I don't have any money to spend. It's tempting to hide in the study when I get home, but I know Ellie will be struggling to work with Alex in her hair, so I get myself a cold drink and go down to the studio. Alex is washing brushes, so it looks as if I've arrived at a good moment.

'Billie!' The look of relief on her face is unmistakeable and I feel a twinge of guilt for having stayed out so long. Only a tiny one, though – if she hadn't involved me in her chat with the police, I wouldn't have needed to get away, would I?

'Hey there. Good afternoon?'

'You'd best ask Alex.' Ellie gives me a forgiving smile and gets back to her painting.

'It was great,' he says, wiping his hands on his apron. 'Look!' He pulls me across to the rack, where his efforts have been left to dry. Alex always paints the same thing. The minster. It started when he was small and didn't know what to paint. Ellie suggested he try copying one of her paintings and he's never tired of it, despite repeated suggestions and requests for different subjects. These are simple silhouettes, Andy Warhol-style, with swirly backgrounds which appear to owe more than a little to Van Gogh. Ellie's share of the home-schooling project has involved a good chunk of art history, and it shows.

'Nice,' I say. 'Which is which? Or will you let them choose?'

'The green one's for Dad. Because it's like the trees and he likes to look at them when he's cycling.'

'Okay, that works. And Sandy's is orange because…?'

'Because she likes orange.'

'Does she?'

'Yes, she told me so. Ages ago.'

'Great.' I'm fairly sure Sandy's favourite colour isn't orange, but who am I to say? 'If you've finished clearing up, we could do some work on your model if you like?'

'Yes! See you later, Mum.'

We're halfway out of the door by the time Ellie lifts her head to say goodbye, already immersed in her own work. I'm dragged upstairs to Alex's room and a lecture as to exactly which aeroplane is which and what I'm permitted to do to help, and I manage to pass a couple of hours without thinking about Vanessa or Dad or Ellie at all.

* * *

I watch Dad and Ellie carefully during the evening meal. They seem to be perfectly normal. I was up in Alex's room when Dad got back from cycling. Ellie might have told him about the police visiting, but Nora and Sandy were already home by then, so they can't have had much time on their own. My brain's had enough of worrying about them and I tell myself to stop. Thanks to Gaby, I've got a plan. I just need to get Ellie on her own tomorrow and ask her if she talked to Sandy about the house. If she did, that's one problem solved, and maybe if they can prove it to the police, the pressure will be off them both.

I do my share of the clearing up quickly and say I have stuff to do. Fortunately for me, Sandy has suggested watching a James Bond film, which everyone else jumps at with alacrity, Alex because he loves James Bond, Nora because she likes doing anything with the family, and Ellie and Dad, I'm sure, because it means they don't have to talk about other things. Like Vanessa.

Jay picks up straight away and spends nearly half an hour telling me about the mountains, camping, snakes, cacti and other stuff he thinks is adventurous. He's wise enough to apologise at length for not letting me know, saying he was sure he'd sent me a text before he left. It comes through while he's talking, with a send date that matches what he says, and we laugh about the useless signal he gets abroad and I forgive him completely. It feels good, very good. I'd made myself not think about him, and there's been plenty going on to distract me, but I was kidding myself. Jay's great. He's funny, talented and he gets me in a way that no one else does. And thanks to Gaby, I can tell him everything that's been happening without totally stressing out about it.

'Wow,' he says when I've finished. 'That's quite a story. And you've still not told them you were there that day?'

'No, what's the point? To be honest, there's been so much going on, I'd almost forgotten about that. Things have moved on a lot since then. I guess the police have got other stuff on their minds now. Like who wanted Vanessa dead.'

'Yeah, I guess. So you're going to ask Ellie if she told Sandy about the move, and if she did, that's proof she and your dad didn't need Vanessa dead?'

'Right. Fingers crossed she did tell her. I reckon she might have done. They're very close.'

'How d'you think she'll have taken it? Sandy, I mean?'

'The moving idea? I suppose she'd be all right with it. She's not one of those people who goes on and on about how much they love their house. Although she's lived here a long time. She and Ellie bought it together years ago, before Ellie met Dad.'

'So she'd move out, too?'

'What d'you mean?'

'Would she move too? Or would your dad and Ellie get their own place? There'd be no need for Sandy and your gran—'

'Nora's not my gran, she's my—'

'Sorry, Sandy and Nora wouldn't need to move too, would they? Unless they have a problem with Vanessa as well?'

'I don't know. I…' I'm stumped. It hadn't occurred to me that everyone wouldn't stay together. And Ellie was talking about space, wasn't she? I think back – she talked about a better studio, space for Alex to run around, a room for me… No, she didn't mention Sandy or Nora.

'I assumed she meant everyone, but maybe she didn't. And she did say that even with Vanessa gone it might be nice to have more space.'

'So perhaps Vanessa wasn't the only reason they were thinking about moving. Look, Billie, I don't know your family well – I've never met them – but maybe your dad and Ellie want a place of their own. With you and Alex, of course, but just not with… extended family.'

'Not with Sandy and Nora,' I say slowly, thinking it through. 'I hadn't thought of that. It'd be a big deal. Sandy's part of the family. She's... well, she's always been around. She helps out massively with Alex, and she and Ellie are super close. Ellie relies on her, you know. She had terrible post-natal depression when Alex was born. I can't imagine her coping without Sandy being around.'

'Hey, don't listen to me, what do I know? It's just an idea, and probably a stupid one. Don't spend time agonising over it. Ask Ellie tomorrow. And if she didn't talk to Sandy, maybe she talked so someone else – like Nora? It'll turn out fine, you'll see. And anyway, what about the husband?'

'Husband?'

'Vanessa's husband. The husband's usually the first person the police suspect, right? They must have been hassling him too.'

'Oh. Yes, of course. It's so long ago now, I forgot to tell you. He came over last week. And yes, he was worried about them thinking he did it.'

'There. Don't worry about it. They'll only be talking to your lot to prove they've done their job properly. Trust me, Billie, there's nothing to worry about.'

He's right, of course, about most of it at least. I put my misgivings to one side and change the subject, asking how many beautiful French girls he's had to fight off this week.

THIRTEEN

Life in our house doesn't change as much during school holidays as you might expect. Dad and Sandy are around a lot more, of course, but Alex keeps to the same routines, and so does Ellie. There's no chance of catching Ellie for a talk before they head out to the supermarket and for their Monday-morning swim, so I'm planning a morning learning lines in the garden. Nora has taken it into her head to go with them, rather to everyone's surprise. She says she needs to remind herself what a supermarket looks like and that she won't slow Ellie down if they leave her to her own devices. And apparently there's a senior swimming session she wants to try out.

'She reckons it will be good for her hip or something,' Dad says vaguely, wiping the counter while I put bread in the toaster.

'Good for her,' I say. 'What are you up to this morning?'

'I thought I might go for a bike ride,' he says. 'D'you fancy joining me?'

'Not unless you want to go at half your normal speed. But Dad…'

He straightens up, hearing the uncertainty in my voice.

'Dad, can we talk about something?' Despite Gaby's warnings, I can't hold back any longer. Talking to Ellie will answer some of my questions, but not all of them. Not the most important ones. The ones I've been trying to avoid asking. And with the two of us on our own in the kitchen, I've been given a chance that might not easily come up again.

'Sure.' He sits at the table and I do the same, abandoning my toast in the knowledge that I could easily avoid the question if I don't ask it straight away.

'Were you having an affair with Vanessa?'

'No!' It's completely instinctive, and I have to believe him. A huge weight I didn't know was there lifts from my shoulders.

'I know why you're asking,' he says. 'Ellie told me. About the police coming yesterday. You were there, you heard it all. She was telling the truth, Billie, I promise. I can't believe I was stupid enough to let it happen, but it's all true.'

'But the police...'

'The police are asking questions of everyone who knew Vanessa. Everyone, not just us.'

'I know.'

'They'll probably come up with a reason to talk to you in the end.'

'I hope not.' I try to match his light tone, but my stomach's churning at the thought of it. 'Dad?'

'Yes?'

'Ellie said you were thinking of moving? To get away from Vanessa. Is that true?'

'Or did she make it up to make sure the police didn't think we had a motive for murder?' His tone is anything but light now, and I can't let him know that's exactly what I've been wondering.

'I... no... look, if you move house, it affects me. I know I don't come home often, but I'd like to know which door to knock on when I do.'

'I'm sorry, Billie. Of course it does. And we'd have discussed it with you sooner if all this hadn't happened.'

'You'd have told me what was going on with Vanessa?'

'Not that, no. But about moving, of course.'

'So I guess you won't have to. Now that she's gone.'

'No…'

'But?'

'To be honest, Billie, I quite like the idea of a change of scene. It would be good to have more space, and we could get much more for our money if we moved out of the middle of town.'

'I guess. And it would be nice not to have to sleep in the study every time I come home.' I give him a smile to show I'm not complaining.

'I know, and I'm sorry about that too. Although Nora shouldn't be with us for ever. Once she's had her hip replacement she should be able to move into her own place.'

'Really?' I'm surprised to hear this. I'd thought Nora's immobility was permanent. 'Is that what Ellie and Sandy want? Neither of them have mentioned it to me.'

'No, I'm sure they haven't, but that's a conversation for another day.' Dad stifles a sigh and gets up. 'Don't you need some breakfast? Let me make you some for a treat. What do you put on your toast these days?' He puts my bread back in the toaster and fills the kettle.

'Dad?'

'Hmmm?'

'If you do move, would it be everyone? Sandy and Nora as well?'

He doesn't answer immediately, stalling for time while he gets out mugs for coffee.

'We've not discussed it with them yet,' he says. 'It's early days, we're not sure what we'll do, so there didn't seem much point in talking to anyone else about it.'

'Okay.' It clearly hasn't occurred to him that it might have helped to be able to tell the police that anyone else knew about the moving plan, and my heart sinks as the hope that they might have done fades away.

'So Billie…'

'Yes?'

'Please don't mention it to anyone else. Not just yet.'

'No worries. You're secret's safe with me.'

'It's not exactly…' The toast pops and he turns away to find the butter. But it is a secret. And I still don't know for sure that it's true.

* * *

It's nice to have breakfast made for me, but the conversation with Dad has made me uneasy, and I take my toast and coffee outside, saying it's nice to make the most of sunny mornings while we can. Dad goes for his bike ride and the house settles into its customary Monday-morning peace. I learn some more lines, have lunch with the rest of them and try to ignore the nagging feeling that Dad's lied to me about something. I know him well enough to be able to spot his evasions but I'm not psychic, and I can't work out what he wasn't telling me. He's back in time for his afternoon shift with Alex, and Sandy joins me in the garden with her book, although I don't suppose she can concentrate very well with Nora testing me on what I've learnt in the morning.

'It's sounding good to me,' Nora says as we finish. 'I'd love to see you do it for real.'

'I'd love you to see it too,' I say, taking the script off her. 'But it's just for schools, they wouldn't allow "the public" in. You'll just have to wait for me to get a part in a "proper" show.'

'I'm sure it won't be long,' she says. 'Of course, it's not me who should be helping you with your lines. I'm sure Ellie or Sandy would do a much better job than me. They were both a dab hand at acting when they were younger, you know.'

'Really?' It's the first I've heard of it, and I've been living with them both for more than half my life.

'Of course. Alex is always saying Sandy's the best at reading stories, isn't he?'

'Well, yes, but that's hardly the same thing.'

'No, it's not,' Sandy interrupts. Her nose might be in her book but her ears haven't stopped working. 'You're exaggerating, Mother.

Ellie might have liked drama at school, but she soon worked out that art was what she wanted to do. And I know you've always gone on about my star turn as the innkeeper when I was five, but that's about it as far as I can remember.'

'I'm sure there was more to it than that, dear,' says Nora. 'I know it was a long time ago, but still...'

'Yes, a long time ago is certainly what it was,' Sandy agrees. 'And didn't you tell me a story about Auntie Margaret doing a lot of amateur dramatics in her youth? I expect it's her you're remembering, not us.'

'Maybe it is,' Nora agrees. 'You look like her, you know. You have something of her about you. You're both pretty, of course...'

'Now you're flattering me!' Sandy says. 'Enough! Who's for a cup of tea?'

* * *

It's a bit hot for tea, but Nora has her routines, and afternoon tea is one of them. She likes to take a nap in the afternoon so Sandy takes her to her room, leaving me at a loose end in the garden. Dad's taken Alex to see a friend he used to go to school with. It's one of the few things Alex is happy to change his schedule for, and they won't be back for a while. It's too hot for a run, Ellie's in the studio and Sandy hasn't come back from helping Nora. Gaby will be at work, so I think it might be a good time to see if Jay's in Wi-Fi range. My phone's in the study, and there's a fan in there too, which appeals. I've just sat down on the desk chair when the doorbell rings. Sandy and I both go to answer it, almost colliding in the hallway, and I stand back to let her open the door.

'Good afternoon, Miss Henderson. I hope we've not come at an inconvenient time. Would you have a few minutes for a couple of questions?'

'Oh. Hello.' Sandy's blocking the doorway from my view but I recognise the voice. It's DI Twist. I fight the urge to run, and wait as Sandy asks them in, telling them that Dad's out but Ellie's in the studio and can be fetched if required.

'No, I'm sure you can help us, there's no need to disturb Mrs Preston if she's busy.' We lead them into the lounge and I offer them a drink, but Sergeant Carter refuses on behalf of them both, saying they hope they won't be taking up too much of our time. They've not told me I'm not needed, and I don't want to ask in case it looks like I'm trying to avoid them. We all sit down, Sandy and me on the sofa and the detectives on the same chairs as before.

'How can we help?' Sandy asks, as if they've come for a social chat rather than a murder investigation.

'It's a simple matter, really,' Sergeant Carter says, although I doubt that's true. 'We're trying to establish who had access to Miss Forsyth's gun in the weeks leading up to her death. Billie, we'd like to confirm again the date on which Vanessa showed you her firearm. As I'm sure you appreciate, it's important that we know exactly when this occurred.'

'Of course,' I say, glad that Sandy already knows about it. 'It was a week before George's barbecue. A Saturday, the last Saturday in June it must have been.'

'The twenty-fifth?'

'Yes, that's it. I remember Alex telling everyone we were halfway to Christmas.'

Sergeant Carter nods and taps briefly on his tablet. 'And you were at the party for George Westerby's birthday the following weekend, the second of July?' he asks.

'Yes, we both were. The whole family went.' I look across at Sandy for support and she murmurs her agreement.

'Did either of you go into the house during the afternoon?' We both shake our heads.

'It was a barbecue,' Sandy reminds him. 'We were outdoors the whole time.'

'Of course,' DI Twist says. 'But perhaps you went inside for the bathroom? Or to bring out drinks? People often pitch in at barbecues, don't they?'

'I suppose they do,' says Sandy. 'But I didn't go inside. We weren't there long enough to need "the bathroom". And it wasn't the sort of party where you "pitch in".' She might as well be miming the speech marks, and I find myself hiding a smile. Sandy's always been a fan of plain speaking.

'That's true,' I agree. 'Vanessa hired a catering firm. I think we'd have got into trouble if we'd tried to help out.'

'If you *had* needed to go inside, say, for…'

'For the toilet, you mean?' says Sandy – I don't think she can bear to hear her say 'the bathroom' again.

'Yes. If you had needed to go inside, there weren't any barriers to your doing so?'

'You mean guards on the door, that sort of thing?' Sandy smiles disbelievingly.

'It's not uncommon, when the host is, shall we say, a…'

'A celebrity?' I want to nudge Sandy and tell her to stop. Finishing her sentences is hardly likely to endear her to Ronnie Twist.

'Yes, if you like. It's not uncommon in such situations for people to restrict access to their homes. To protect their privacy.'

'You mean someone might have wanted to snoop around inside?' I say before Sandy has time to interrupt again. 'To be honest, I don't think she'd have minded much. She liked publicity, and the house was immaculate. She was always posting pictures of it on social media – she might have quite liked seeing other people posting it too.'

'Although I doubt anyone would have bothered,' says Sandy. 'Apart from us it was mostly people from the film company, and I daresay they've seen it all before.'

'I daresay,' says DI Twist, and she gives Sandy a look that suggests they might have similar opinions of film stars and their ways.

'Do you need to ask the others about whether they went inside?' I ask. 'Dad won't be back for a while, but Ellie wouldn't mind coming out, I'm sure.'

'No, we won't disturb her. We wanted to confirm that access to the property was freely available throughout the afternoon, and your answers are sufficient for now. But please do ask the others if they did go inside, and if so, if they saw anyone else in the house at the time, particularly in the area of the study.' They obviously think someone might have stolen Vanessa's gun that afternoon. But won't Dean have been able to tell them that? Why are they asking us?

'Of course. We'll be sure to ask them, won't we, Billie?' Sandy's taking charge now, clearly deciding the interview's over, and she starts to get up.

'There is one more thing we need to ask.' DI Twist stays firmly in her own seat, watching Sandy as she sinks back into her own. 'Mr Westerby has told us that you have a set of keys to his property. Is that correct?'

'Oh. Let me think,' says Sandy. 'We've lived here a long time, at least Ellie and I have. We used to have a set, I'm sure, back when Felicity Halford lived next door, but that was a long time ago. She died and the house went to her children. I seem to remember it lying empty for some time before it was bought. It went to a developer, and we worried that it would be turned into flats, but he did a wonderful job on it and it's rented now. Although you know that, of course.' Sandy's demeanour has changed completely from edgy to ever-so-slightly incompetent. She almost sounds like Nora, and I wonder if the strain of having a murder in the street is finally starting to show, even if she didn't know Vanessa as well as Ellie did.

'The history of the property isn't relevant right now,' says DI Twist, a barely concealed impatience creeping into her voice. 'Do you still have the keys given to you by Mrs Halford?'

'I suppose we must do. Forgive me, Inspector. I know you don't need all the detail, but going over it is helping me to remember each stage of the process, and I'm almost sure that… no, I'm quite sure that no one ever asked for the keys back. Mrs Halford's family had too much to deal with and we didn't like to bother them. And we've not had anything to do with the developer or the letting agent. So we must still have the keys.'

DI Twist's eyes have begun to glaze over, but on hearing Sandy's final sentence, she jerks slightly and clears her throat. 'Good. That's very helpful. Would you be able to find them for us? Mr Westerby feels that under the circumstances it might…'

'Be best if we returned them?' She's at it again, Sandy's never been able to let a sentence go unfinished if she thinks she knows how it should end, and this time it's done with a smile rather than a snap. 'Of course. I know where they'll be – if no one has moved them in the last ten years, that is.' She goes to get them, leaving me to sit on my own, wondering if I need to engage in polite conversation with the detectives.

'I hope you don't mind confirming one more thing for me Billie.' Sergeant Carter leans towards me while DI Twist appears to have developed a keen interest in one of Alex's drawings of the minster which is pinned up on his noticeboard.

'Yes?' He's looking back down at his tablet, swiping the screen as if looking for something.

'It's about your movements on the day of Miss Forsyth's death. Between two and five o'clock, to be precise. You told us you were shopping, is that right?'

'Yes. I was looking round town. I was hoping to get something new before going back to London. The prices are much lower up here.'

'And did you?'

'Did I what?'

'Get anything? In the shops?'

'Um… no, I didn't. I tried a few things on but there wasn't anything I liked.' A bit of extra detail won't hurt.

'Can you remember any of the shops you visited?'

'Um… they were all charity shops. I don't have a lot of money for clothes and I like older styles when I can find them. I definitely went to Scope and YMCA. I'm not sure which the others were. I go most weeks while I'm up so it's hard to remember which ones I went to on that particular day.' I've got DI Twist's attention again now, although

I hardly think we share a taste in fashion. She looks more of a Jigsaw girl to me.

'But you didn't buy anything?'

'No. I'm trying to save and there wasn't anything that was worth it.'

'I know how that feels,' she says with a smile. Is she trying to be nice? I know what that means in these circumstances, and remind myself to be on my guard. 'Did you see anyone you know?' she asks. 'I know what Beverley's like – you can't go out without bumping into someone you know.'

'I know, Ellie's always saying that.'

'Ellie's always saying what?' says Sandy, returning triumphantly with a bunch of keys. 'Look! Found! Just where I thought they'd be.'

'You can't go into Beverley without meeting someone you know. And thank you.' DI Twist passes the keys to her sergeant.

'Yes, that's true enough.' Sandy sits down and looks enquiringly at DI Twist. 'Are we done?'

'Almost,' she replies. 'We were just asking Billie if she met anyone she knew when she was out shopping in Beverley on the day of Miss Forsyth's death.'

'Oh.' Sandy's face falls. 'Does this mean you're… checking alibis? Surely Billie's not on your list of suspects?'

'We don't have a list as such. But yes, we do want to confirm exactly where everyone who was at George's party was that afternoon.'

'Because anyone who was there could have taken the gun?' Sandy asks.

'I really can't comment on our reasons for asking questions. I'm sure you appreciate that.' DI Twist's words sound like a cross headteacher, but there's a gleam in her eye that suggests she rather likes Sandy's cleverness.

'Of course you can't,' says Sandy with a grin. 'Go on, Billie, answer the question. Which of your many friends did you bump into that day? Gaby? Charlie? Rosie?'

'No one.' I can't lie about this. Making up visits to shops is one thing, but meeting someone I didn't is another. 'I didn't see anyone that day.' There's a pause which no one seems able to fill until Sandy offers her own contribution.

'She didn't even meet me, which isn't entirely surprising. I don't think we frequent the same outlets, do we?'

I smile weakly, grateful for her attempt to help.

'And which are those?' asks DI Twist. 'And did you make any purchases that afternoon?'

'Oh yes, I made quite a few. Now let me see, I don't want to leave any out…' Sandy closes her eyes to think and I can see the inspector rolling her eyes at Sergeant Carter. 'I started at Guest and Philips to get a new battery for my watch. And I needed a birthday present for a friend so I went into The Lemon Tree – they have lovely things in there. I went into Boots for some hand cream, and then to the library. I changed my books and ordered one too. It's a new one about Churchill. It won't be out in paperback for a long time and I didn't want to wait. Then I went to the Refill Jar, you know, that nice recycling shop, for some herbs and spices. We were low on a few so I took in half a dozen jars to fill.'

'You had a busy afternoon.' DI Twist looks drained at the thought of it, but I reckon it's listening to Sandy drone on that's done it.

'Yes, I like to make good use of my time. Perhaps because I have so little of it, especially since Mother came to stay with us.'

'Quite.' The two detectives exchange glances, and when neither has anything more to say, it seems the interview is over at last. 'Thank you, both of you,' DI Twist says, getting up. 'You've been very helpful.'

'Will you be coming back? To ask Ellie and Mike about their alibis?' Sandy asks as we file out into the hallway.

'Yes, in due course. Will they be in tomorrow morning, do you know?'

'Yes, it's my turn with Alex on Tuesday mornings so they should both be free,' says Sandy helpfully.

'Perhaps you could let them know we'll be coming around ten?'

'Of course.' They're finally out of the door, and although Sandy doesn't wave them a cheerful goodbye, it feels like a close thing.

'Since when were you best friends with the law?' I ask her as she closes the door.

'Believe me, Billie, that's the last thing I am, but antagonism gains you precisely nothing with that lot, I can tell you.'

'I suppose not.'

'You know not. They're just doing their jobs; they have to talk to everyone so that when they finally work out Vanessa killed herself after all they can prove they've done everything by the book.'

'Is that what you think? That she wasn't murdered after all?'

'Of course. This murder story's just something cooked up by Dean so he can get his hands on Vanessa's life insurance. They don't pay out for suicides, you know.'

'Oh. I suppose that's true.'

'Of course it's true. That's why they're taking their time. They weren't bothered about seeing Ellie today, were they? Or your father? Trust me, if they really had suspicions about anyone in this house they'd be sitting here now waiting for Mike to get back.'

'Of course they would.' Suddenly, I feel massively better. Sandy always talks sense and I wish I'd asked her what she thought about it sooner. Even if Dad did get himself into a mess with Vanessa, what can it matter now? There was clearly something going on that made her unhappy that no one else knew about. Probably Dean. I reckon he either pulled the trigger on that gun or made her so miserable she did it herself. Either way, it was his fault, not ours, or anyone else's.

FOURTEEN

It's Monday, so Sandy takes Alex off to the library as usual and I go for a run. Now Sandy's convinced me that Vanessa killed herself, I've forgotten to worry about anything. Jay agreed with her, saying he was glad I'd come to my senses at last and stopped trying to be a detective. That last bit wasn't true, I'd make a rubbish detective, but I let it go. If he really thought I was wrong thinking it was murder, it was nice of him to listen while I rabbited on about it. It was good to talk about other stuff, and I'm counting the days now till he comes back. He's got a friend in London with a spare room, and I might be able to move in next week, which would be amazing. It's nice to be home, but a month is more than enough, especially when you're living in a broom cupboard. My head's full of moving plans and which pictures I'm going to post this morning, and I get a shock when I see Ellie and Dad sitting at the table like schoolchildren waiting for the headmaster to arrive to tell them off.

'Are you two waiting for someone?' I joke, heading for the kettle. I pick it up to fill it but it's already warm. 'Were you about to make a drink?'

'Yes and yes,' says Dad. 'We're waiting for the police. They're coming at ten o'clock, remember?'

'And we thought they might want a drink so we boiled the kettle,' Ellie adds.

'Of course! Oh, sorry, I'll be quick and get out of your way.'

'Don't worry, we can take them in the lounge.' Ellie gets up and pulls some mugs from the shelf. 'And I don't care what they want or don't want – I need coffee. Mike?' Dad nods and I leave her to make it for all of us while I sort my breakfast.

'I'm sure there's no need to be nervous,' I say. 'Like Sandy said, they're just doing their job.'

'I know that,' Ellie snaps. 'But Sandy doesn't know everything, even though she likes to think she does.'

'What d'you mean?' It's not like Ellie to talk like that, even if she is stressed.

'Oh, nothing. But she doesn't know everything, does she? We didn't tell her about your dad and Vanessa. You're the only person who knows, and we'd like it to stay that way.'

'Sure,' I say. It's a horrible situation for them, I get that, but it gives me a little glow nonetheless knowing they've shared their secret with me.

'Sandy may well be right,' says Dad. 'And it's true, they weren't in a rush to talk to us yesterday, and that's good. But until it's sorted out, it's hard not to feel worried. It's different for you and Sandy. You didn't have any reason to dislike Vanessa. We did.'

'I know.' I spread peanut butter on my toast and sit at the table. Ellie pours coffee for us all and we sit in silence for a minute.

'All the same,' I say. 'If you know you didn't do it, surely all you have to do is keep telling the truth and wait until they work out what really happened, right?'

'Right,' says Dad. 'Simples, eh?' He's trying to make it a joke, but I catch a look pass between the two of them that makes me wonder if I'm missing something. If I am, I'd really rather not know, and I find myself saying anything that comes to mind in order to hide the awkwardness of the moment.

'I think it is simple. Either Dean did it for the insurance or he made Vanessa so miserable she killed herself. How do we know what was really going on between them? You're always saying no one knows what other people's relationships are like. Even with everything you've told me, I don't know what's going on between you two, do I?'

'Um, no, I guess not.' Dad's looking surprised that I've remembered his words of wisdom.

'So what is going on between you two? And why isn't anyone offering me a coffee?' We all jump as Nora comes into the room.

'Mother! I'm sorry.' Ellie gets up to help Nora into the room, but she shakes her off.

'Sit down, sit down, I'm all right. I got this far, didn't I?' Ellie backs off quickly and pours a coffee for her mother.

'So what's so distracting that you forgot to offer your poor parent a morning coffee?' Nora asks, a twinkle in her eye. 'Or did you think you'd starve me out? If so, it worked. These new painkillers seem to be working well. Or maybe yesterday's swim loosened me up.'

'No, we—' Ellie begins.

'The police said they needed to talk to us again.' Dad looks at his watch. 'But they're late. They said they'd be here half an hour ago.'

'Where are your phones?' I ask. 'Maybe they've been trying to get hold of you.'

'Mine's charging upstairs. I'll get it,' Dad says.

'Mine's in the studio,' says Ellie, looking out of the window as if her phone might make its way into the kitchen of its own accord if she stares hard enough.

'Wait and see if there's a message on Mike's first,' says Nora. 'There's no need to rush about for no reason.'

'No…' Ellie looks as if she's a million miles away. Maybe she's staring at the studio because that's where she'd rather be, and I can hardly blame her.

'There's a missed call,' Dad says, fiddling with his phone as he comes back into the kitchen. 'And a message.' He presses the loudspeaker button and we all listen to Sergeant Carter apologising, saying they've been delayed and can they come this evening instead.

He says they need to talk to Sandy and me again as well as Ellie and Dad, and they'll be here at six o'clock. No need to reply unless there's a problem. We sit in silence, taking it in, then Ellie pushes her chair back, the scrape of it on the floor giving us all a shock.

'No need to be nervous, Billie?' she says, a wobble in her voice. 'Is that still how you feel? Well, I don't know about anyone else, but I can't afford to waste any more of the morning. I need to paint.' She's out of the room before any of us can answer and it's only a few seconds before we hear the sound of the studio door slamming behind her.

* * *

Ellie doesn't come out for lunch. Dad pops his head round the studio door and comes back to say she wants a sandwich while she works. She's got an order to fill for next Monday and she can't afford to waste any more time. It's her afternoon with Alex, but when Dad suggests a trip to the beach instead, he's easily persuaded. Alex may be a genius at maths and a total geek, but when it comes to the seaside he's just like any other ten-year-old. The prospect of an afternoon at home trying not to talk about murder with Nora and Sandy is hardly appealing, and I jump at the chance to join them.

It's ages since I went to the beach, and we have the best time ever. It's busy, of course, but we walk a little way from the car park and find ourselves a quieter bit of sand. It's warm enough to swim, and we join forces to make an amazing sandcastle, complete with turrets, moat and the little flags Alex always brings for these occasions. I mooch up and down the tide line while Dad helps him add the finishing touches, collecting shells for Ellie. She likes to mix them in with the stones on the path in the garden, and I hope they'll perk her up a bit. I can't help worrying about her. The slam of the studio door this morning reminded me of those awful months after Alex was born. She's been okay for years now but I can't ever shake the fear that it might happen again, and I know Sandy thinks the same. She's always saying how it's not good for Ellie to get stressed.

My thoughts are interrupted by Alex, running up behind me and grabbing my shoulders.

'Hey! Careful – I'll drop all these lovely shells.'

'We've finished! Come and see!'

'All right, all right, I'm coming.' And we race back to Dad and the castle and a world where our only problem is whether to get an ice cream now or after another swim.

* * *

I love the itch of sea salt on my skin, but I don't suppose post-swim manky hair is a good look for a police interview, so I make sure Dad gets us home in time for a shower before they arrive. Dad and Ellie have remembered to keep their phones handy in case there's another postponement, but there are no calls or messages. Ellie's afternoon in the studio has done her good, and she gives each of us a hug when we get back.

'I'm sorry I was grumpy this morning. It's this big order, that's all. Waiting around for no reason annoyed me more than it should have done. We'll answer their questions and have a nice evening together. Sandy's made a lasagne for tea so it'll be ready for us when we've finished.'

'Finished what?' Alex asks.

'The police have a couple of questions to ask us about Vanessa,' says Dad. 'Because we were her friends.'

'Oh, okay,' says Alex, reassured by Dad's matter-of-fact tone. 'Can I play some online chess before dinner?'

'Good idea,' says Ellie. 'But shower first!' she calls after him as he rushes upstairs.

After this morning's fiasco, none of us feel inclined to wait together for them to arrive, and I'm in the garden with a can of Coke when Sandy comes to the back door to call me in. They're in the lounge again, only this time Dad has the chair instead of the piano stool.

'I'm sorry about this morning,' DI Twist says. 'Something came up at the last minute which we needed to attend to.'

'No problem,' says Dad. It was a problem, actually, but what else can he say? 'We're all here as you can see, but is this what you want? All of us together?'

'It really doesn't matter to us,' she says. 'There's no reason for anyone to absent themselves, but we've reached a stage in the investigation where we need to record what you say as formal statements. If you'd rather we spoke to you individually, that's fine.'

We look at each other uneasily. We hadn't thought or talked about it, but we all know it might look suspicious if we ask to speak to her separately.

'We're all here now, so we may as well stay where we are,' says Dad, and we all nod our agreement. 'We're all family, after all,' he adds, smiling round the room. I want to tell him not to, it's totally cringeworthy, but the detectives don't seem to care – perhaps they're used to people talking that way. Sergeant Carter seems to be in charge of alibis, as it's him who kicks off again.

'Mr Preston. We're asking everyone who was at the Westerbys' party on the second of July to confirm their whereabouts on the day of Miss Forsyth's death.'

'Yes, Billie and Sandy told us you'd been asking them what they were doing that afternoon.'

'You told us that you were out for a bike ride.'

'Yes. I'm out most Saturday afternoons. Sometimes Sundays as well.'

'Where did you go, exactly?'

'Oh. Let me think.' Dad looks taken aback, although he must have known they'd want details of this sort. 'I don't follow the same route every time, so I need to think back. I met Dean when I got home and I remember seeing him as I turned into the road, and he was on my left as I approached him, so I must have come across the Westwood…' Dad shuts his eyes, trying to visualise his route that day, and Sergeant Carter flashes a look at DI Twist as if to say 'we've got another one here'. I don't blame him, Dad's nearly as bad as Sandy. I guess they're both getting old.

'Oh yes, I remember now.' Dad opens his eyes at last. 'I did the Skidby circuit. I went down to Anlaby and Hessle, via Skidby, of course, then across to Market Weighton and back to Beverley through the villages. It's a good ride, and a lovely view of the minster, of course, as you come over the Westwood at the end.'

'What time did you leave?'

'After lunch, so about two. I got home a little before five. We were planning a barbecue and I'd promised to be home in good time for Alex. He wanted to help me set it up.' I'm sure Sergeant Carter isn't interested in these details, but he smiles nonetheless.

'And you met Mr Westerby as you returned home, I think you said?'

'Yes, he was pulling his golf clubs out of his car as I turned into the road. He said hello, we got chatting, and I asked him to join us for dinner. Well, supper, I suppose, you can't really call—'

'Who instigated the invitation?' DI Twist interrupts Dad's ramble and he does a double-take.

'Sorry? Who…?'

'Was it your idea to invite Mr Westerby to join you or his?'

'Mine, of course, he could hardly invite him… oh, I see what you mean. Did he invite himself? Well, I suppose… he did say right from the start that he was on his own. And how he loved a barbecue. And he said about what a good time everyone had at George's party. I suppose I did feel obliged to return the favour.'

'Of course you did,' Ellie says. 'It was typical Dean, he can't stand being on his own and he must have known you wouldn't invite him over otherwise. We were neighbours, not friends, as I've already explained to you, Inspector.'

'You have indeed,' DI Twist agrees, and she leans back in her seat, letting her sergeant take up the questioning once more.

'Were you out on your own, Mr Preston? Or do you cycle with friends? Or a club, perhaps?'

'I go out with the cycling club on Thursdays, but I prefer my own company at the weekends so that I can go at my own pace. It can be hard to keep up with the younger ones, you know.' Dad smiles.

'What about you, Mrs Preston?' Sergeant Carter turns towards Ellie. 'You told us you were at home that afternoon?'

'Yes, that's right. I didn't go out at all.'

'I suppose your mother was with you? She mentioned as much before.'

'She was in the house, but not exactly with me. I took her a cup of tea at about three o'clock, but she was in her room and I was in the studio.'

'You're very precise about the time,' comments DI Twist.

'Yes, Mother likes her tea at three. We tease her about it sometimes. I have an alarm clock in the studio so I don't forget.' I smile encouragingly at Ellie. She's doing well despite her nerves; perhaps an afternoon with her paints helped her after all.

'Did anyone call at the house during that time?' asks the sergeant.

'No.' Ellie shakes her head. 'I wouldn't hear the door from the studio anyway.'

'What about your son? Was Alex in the house?'

'No, he was at the minster. He sings in the choir and they've got a big performance coming up. They had a rehearsal with other choirs that afternoon. I took him down there after lunch and picked him up at four thirty.'

'Is there a back gate to your garden?' DI Twist asks. It seems a random question, but I think I can guess why she's asking.

'Of course,' Dad answers, perhaps not realising the question is directed at Ellie. 'It's a terraced house, as I'm sure you've noticed. There's an alley along the back and gates to all the gardens in the row. We use it to bring the bins out through the arch a few doors along.'

'Of course. Thank you, Mr Preston.' DI Twist suddenly beams at him as if he's a schoolboy who's answered a particularly challenging question. She's been taking notes while Sergeant Carter talks, and she gives her tablet a few final taps before putting it to one side. The sergeant picks his up and swipes it as she does so, and they remind me of those weather clocks where the little man goes inside when the lady comes out.

'We're also interested in the afternoon of George Westerby's birthday party. Did either of you go in the house during the afternoon? Or notice anyone else doing so?'

Dad and Ellie shake their heads, having been primed on this question by Sandy and me. The tension in the room subsides as we wait to be told that the interview is over, but DI Twist isn't going anywhere.

'The reason for our delay in coming to see you today is that we've received some information which has led to a new line of enquiry.'

We all sit up a little straighter, and there's a frisson of something in the room as I remember their request for me and Sandy to be present as well. How could I have forgotten? It's not a question, so we all wait for her to continue.

'We have reason to believe that Miss Forsyth had a visitor during the week before her death. A visitor with whom she had a strong disagreement. Do any of you know anything about that? Perhaps she mentioned it to someone in the days before she died?'

'I'm sorry,' says Sandy. 'But what has this got to do with us? We've already told you about the last time we saw Vanessa. We've given you information about George's party, details of our whereabouts on the day she died – and don't worry, we know full well that you've been asking for alibis even if you've not said it outright – surely we've answered enough questions now? We were only neighbours, for goodness' sake – what can this... disagreement... possibly have to do with us?'

DI Twist turns to look at Sandy as if she's suddenly become interesting, and the rest of us hold our breaths, sure she's about to say something about Dad and Vanessa.

'Come on, Sandy, they're only doing their job,' says Dad before she has time to open her mouth. 'Let's see what it is they need to know, eh? We want to help, don't we?'

145

'Thank you, Mr Preston.' DI Twist is still looking thoughtfully at Sandy. 'I do understand your concerns, Miss Henderson, but your brother-in-law is right. It's our job to piece together every piece of the puzzle that made up Vanessa Forsyth's life, and you, along with all her neighbours, can help us to find those pieces.'

'I'm sorry,' says Sandy. 'It's been a strain for us all, and I daresay I'm still tired from the end of term.' She gives the inspector a tentative smile, which DI Twist – somewhat surprisingly, I think – returns.

'As I was saying. We have compelling evidence to suggest that a woman visited Miss Forsyth on the Tuesday evening before she died. That would be the…'

'The fifth,' supplies Sergeant Carter, helpfully.

'The fifth of July. Were any of you in a position to see any visitors to the Westerbys' house that evening, at around eight thirty?' We all shake our heads.

'Although I suppose we should ask Mother,' says Ellie. 'Her window looks that way.'

'Thank you, we'll be sure to do that,' says DI Twist. 'And I must ask, of course, if any of you visited Miss Forsyth that evening?' She looks in turn at Ellie, Sandy and me, as we all shake our heads again.

'I hope you'll forgive the additional questions.' She looks briefly at Sandy as she says this. 'But we do need to ask what each of you were doing that evening. For elimination purposes, of course.'

'Of course,' Sandy murmurs, not quite under her breath. She gives herself a shake as if reminding herself of the benefits of being polite to the police. 'Shall I go first?'

'That would be very helpful, Miss Henderson.'

'Remind me of the day you mentioned?' Sandy says, and I have a feeling we're going to be treated to another of her 'let's see what I can remember' sessions.

'The fifth of July. It was a Tuesday. The week after George's birthday party.'

'Let me see. I'm with Alex on Tuesday mornings and in school for the afternoon. I run an after-school Latin club. That finishes at four thirty. I can remember the fourth because we had an event after school. It was a farewell do for the staff who were leaving, and one of them is going to the States so there was a Fourth of July theme. Some of them were a little jaded the next day.' She smiles with a definite air of superiority at the memory. 'Ah, yes, I remember. I was supposed to have a meeting with the head of sixth form but he said he needed an early night and postponed, so I did some marking.'

'It's the evening we're interested in,' DI Twist interrupts, with more than a hint of desperation. 'Were you still at school at half past eight?'

'Oh no, of course not. I was home by six. We had dinner at seven. We always have dinner at seven – Alex benefits from routines, you know.' Sandy pauses for long enough to look pointedly at her watch, which must be showing at least six forty-five already. 'I helped Billie clear up and spent the rest of the evening in my room planning for the next day.' It's a very efficient account in contrast to the initial ramblings, and DI Twist blinks at her for a second before turning to Ellie.

'Mrs Preston? Does this tally with your recollection of that evening?'

'Yes, it does.' Ellie's looking more confident than I might have expected. Perhaps because Dad has unobtrusively taken her hand, or maybe listening to Sandy has loosened her up. 'Mike and Alex were out. They went to the cinema to see the latest Marvel film. It was a big treat for Alex, he's not normally allowed to stay up so late, but there's a special deal on Tuesdays and Mike persuaded me to let him go.'

'What were you doing after the evening meal?'

'Working. As usual.' Ellie smiles ruefully. 'I've got a big order to fill before the end of this month and I've been working whenever I can. It's one of the reasons I let Mike take Alex out. To steal a couple more hours in the studio.'

'And you, Billie? What were you doing?'

'I was in the lounge all evening. It's more comfortable than the study. That's where I'm sleeping at the moment.'

'Watching television?'

'No, I was doing stuff on my phone. I called my boyfriend, Jay, posted some pictures on social media, checked messages, that sort of thing.'

'So each of you were on your own from, what... seven forty-five? Eight o'clock?' We look at each other and shrug.

'I guess so,' I say. 'No, wait, Sandy came down and made tea. When was that? About nine?' Sandy nods.

'Yes, that's about right. I took one out to Ellie. She never remembers to drink enough when she's working.' She smiles at her sister, and Ellie gives her a little grin in return. DI Twist looks at her sergeant and gives him the smallest of shrugs. He nods, taps a few final times on his tablet and puts it away.

'Sergeant Carter will type up everything you've said and print it out for you at the station,' she continues. 'We'll need each of you to come in tomorrow afternoon to confirm that his records are accurate and sign the statements.' She doesn't ask us to say that we'll be there, but we murmur agreement and nod our heads.

'In that case, I think we're done,' she says. 'Thank you all for your help. We appreciate the stress a situation such as this causes, and we're grateful for your cooperation.' She's laying it on a bit thick, but after everything Sandy said, I can see why.

'If we could have a quick word with your mother before we go?' She looks at Ellie as we all stand up.

'Of course. I'll take you to her room.' Ellie's all smiles and helpfulness now there are no more questions heading in her personal direction. Sandy says she'll see to the lasagne and Dad offers to help her. I follow them to the kitchen but then head out into the garden for a smoke before dinner. I sit at the wooden table to roll a cigarette, letting my thoughts unwind. It's not good to be asked for alibis again, but we are neighbours, after all, they're bound to ask if we saw anyone going into Vanessa's house on the night she had an argument. And we were all in the house, weren't we? If I'm sticking with the theory that it was Dean who did it, I reckon it was his girlfriend who came to see Vanessa. They had an argument, she and Dean had a bust-up and either he killed her or she did it herself. Roll-up complete, I strike a match, inhale and sigh with satisfaction. Simples.

FIFTEEN

It's amazing how quickly the stress caused by a police interview just trickles away when they leave you alone for a few days. All seems to have gone quiet on the Vanessa front. Dean's away again, in London, I guess. He's not been over, thank goodness. Perhaps he's realised that we're not his best friends after all. I'm back on social media properly again, posting every day and getting some good responses. I'll be back in London with Jay in a week, my lines are all learnt and I can't wait for rehearsals to start. I have a feeling it's going to be a good few months.

I'll have the house to myself for once today. Ellie's completed her order at last and says it's about time she had a proper day off. She and Mike want a family outing and they've taken Alex to York for the day. Sandy never passes up a chance to visit the Viking museum, and even Nora has said she'll join them now her hip's feeling better. She's been swimming every day, and she says it's making a huge difference. Sandy keeps telling her it's only temporary, but she doesn't pay any attention.

'I don't care,' she says at breakfast, sounding more like a child than a grandmother. 'It feels good now, and I'm going to make hay while the sun shines.'

'Make hay? Why?' I could have told her Alex would say that.

'It's a saying, Alex,' Ellie tells him. 'It means your gran's going to make the most of feeling a bit better while she can.'

'Oh. But why did she say—'

'Do you want to bring your iPad in the car?' Ellie interrupts.

'Yes! Wicked!' He sprints upstairs and normal conversation resumes.

'What will you do with yourself, Billie?' asks Nora. 'Are you sure you don't want to come? I expect they have lots of lovely second-hand shops in York.'

'No, I'm trying to save. I'd only be tempted to spend money I want for other stuff. I'll go for a run now it's not so hot, and I thought I might start packing.'

'Packing what?' Ellie asks. 'You only came home with one suitcase.'

'I know, but I want to take other things back with me. You know, warmer stuff for the winter. I thought I'd look through all my clothes while I'm at it and have a sort-out.'

'Then don't let me discourage you,' Ellie says. 'You know where everything is, don't you?'

'I think so. Clothes in the suitcases in Sandy's room and other stuff in boxes in yours, right?'

'Right. I knew we'd regret converting the loft at some point. At least the other rooms are big enough to put a few things in.'

'And maybe we'll have a bit more space one day,' I say, forgetting that Nora doesn't know about the moving idea. Fortunately, she has her own interpretation of my careless remark.

'You certainly will, as soon as this hip is properly fixed,' she says. 'The girls keep telling me I should stay here permanently, but I miss having my own home, and I'll be looking for one as soon as I'm able.'

'Mother, that's not true. You know perfectly well—'

'I'm ready!' Alex bursts into the kitchen, iPad and sunhat in hand. 'Are you *still* talking? You said we'd be leaving at nine thirty and it's nine twenty-nine. Sandy and Dad are ready – why aren't you?'

'I'm coming, I'm coming,' says Ellie. 'What about you, Mother? Are you ready to go?'

'I've been ready for at least twenty minutes,' says Nora. 'I've been waiting for everybody else to sort themselves out.'

'Well, what are we waiting for?' Ellie hands Nora her frame. 'Come on, Mother, your carriage awaits.'

'It's a car, not a…' I can hear Alex explaining their travel arrangements as the door closes behind them, and lean back in my chair in relief at the thought of a whole day of peace and quiet.

* * *

Ellie put all my clothes into two enormous suitcases when Nora moved in and left them in Sandy's room. It's a big room which used to be Ellie and Dad's, but when Alex was born he got Sandy's smaller room and they moved into the loft. I love Sandy's room. Most of the house is boring magnolia walls and IKEA furniture, although Ellie's pictures brighten it up. Sandy's room is different – it's like another century in there. She decorated it herself, but she let me help, and I remember the two of us covered in wallpaper paste, battling the textured paper on an old picnic table and debating the best shade of paint to use on the chimney breast. There's a huge old-fashioned bookcase, full of history books, classic literature and anything she can find to do with the Second World War. She has lamps everywhere, cosy blankets draped on the chairs and an old leather-topped desk to work at, overlooking the garden. She and Alex must share a tidiness gene because there's never any clutter on it, just a neat pile of papers and a pot full of posh pens and beautifully sharpened pencils.

The room's hardly changed in ten years, and I feel a wave of nostalgia wash over me when I step inside. It's years since I've been in here, but it feels like yesterday. I used to come up here a lot, especially when Alex was small. First to let Ellie rest, and then to avoid Alex and his noise. He's great now, and I love him to bits, but it was different when he was younger, barging into my room without warning and messing up my stuff. Sandy would get out a fold-up chair and we'd work at either end of the desk. Or we'd sit in her two armchairs, one either side of the fireplace, reading or chatting about stuff I was too embarrassed to talk to Dad about. I feel a sudden pang of guilt. Sandy was almost like a mother to me once, and I've not been up here to talk to her for ages. Maybe I should do something to show her I've not forgotten.

A good way to start would be to get some of my belongings out of her room. Sandy has a big Victorian screen in one corner that she uses to hide her empty suitcases and other 'unsightly items', as she calls them, and I can see it's been moved forward. A quick peep around the corner confirms my suspicions and I pull out the first of the two cases. There's no point in lugging it downstairs, and there's more room in here than anywhere else in the house, so I push the chairs to one side and open the case.

* * *

My phone's blaring out my favourite playlist, and I get a shock when it ends after two hours. It's taking forever, but that's only because I keep stopping to take photos. Sandy's old-fashioned full-length mirror is perfect for taking selfies, and I've got at least twenty pictures in the bag to post online. It'll save me loads of time when we're on the road. Putting outfits on and off takes time and energy, and I'm more than ready for a lunch break before starting on the next suitcase. I've got a pile ready to sell, and I lug it onto the landing to make room for the next lot.

I make a sandwich and take it into the garden. Poppy's messaged, saying she's looking forward to seeing me when I get back to London and can she ask a favour? She's putting on a production of *Twelfth Night* in Edinburgh and she's desperate for costumes. Have I got any of those blouses with big flouncy sleeves? I haven't but I know Sandy has. She lent me one for a school production once. She said it was from her flower power days, although I'm sure she's too young for that. Perhaps she used to have my taste in clothes and just doesn't want to admit it. Sandy doesn't buy a lot of clothes, but what she does have is made to last, and she never throws anything away.

I message Poppy saying I might be able to help and go straight back up to find the blouse before I forget. I've never seen Sandy wear it and I'm sure if I do the looking, she won't mind lending it. Sandy's wardrobe, in contrast to her bookshelf, is modern and extremely efficient – floor-to-ceiling and L-shaped, with a pull-out section in the middle. The clothes she wears most hang at eye level, and I know the blouse won't be there. Shelves hold jumpers and shoes, and boots are on the floor, together with a big White Stuff bag with a cotton jumper showing through the neatly tied ribbon they use to hold the bag closed. It must be a recent purchase she's not hung up yet. Everything's open, it's all within easy reach and I can see no sign of the blouse or anything else she might not wear nowadays. Her old clothes must be somewhere else, and the big chest of drawers is the obvious place to start.

A quick peek confirms that the top drawer is full of underwear. There's no way Sandy would want me looking through that, so I move on quickly. The next one contains more jumpers and a tracksuit. Two more to go, and I hit lucky. They're both full of what I recognise as Sandy's old clothes. I find a bright orange T-shirt that she once showed me in disbelief, saying she couldn't understand why she'd bought it in the first place, and a scarf given to her by a pupil that she couldn't stand. And there's a short black skirt she lent me when I had to dress up as a waitress for a murder mystery evening at Gaby's. It's all stuff she doesn't need or doesn't want, and I can't understand why she hasn't given it away. It's a much quicker job than sorting out my own clothes and it takes less than an hour to establish that the blouse is missing. I check again as I put everything back, one garment at a time, but it's definitely not there. I stand up, stretching the cramp out of my knees, wondering where else it could be. There's nowhere else to look. She's hardly likely to keep it in a desk drawer or the bookshelf. She must have lent it to someone else. I'll ask her about it when they get back from York. I pull the second suitcase out from behind the screen, start a new playlist and settle in for another session.

* * *

I'm in the garden when they get back, Alex rushing out to tell me all about his day. The others must be in need of a break from his chatter, so I let him fill me in on every detail of the Viking museum, the Railway museum, the pizza he had for lunch, and the seating arrangements on the park and ride bus. After half an hour, Ellie takes pity on me and brings out drinks – a glass of wine for each of us and a lemonade for Alex.

'Mike's making a salad,' she says. 'We had an enormous lunch, so we've not got room for much else. Is that okay for you?'

'Sure. I'll fill up on crisps if I get hungry.'

'How was your day? How did the great clear-out go?'

'It went well, thank you. I've got a bin bag full of clothes and one empty suitcase.'

'Impressive.' Ellie takes a sip of her drink, and Alex, uninterested in anything to do with clothes, wanders off inside, and none of us are surprised to hear the sound of Bach drifting out of the back door shortly after.

'It's amazing how the sound carries when it's quiet, isn't it?' Ellie says. 'I give thanks every day that he didn't choose the drum kit like your father.'

'I know. I can't imagine what that would be like. D'you think Dad would get a new kit if he could? If you moved somewhere with more space? He's not mentioned "the band" for ages, but maybe he'd like to get back to it one day.'

'I hope not! That definitely falls into the category of misspent youth, so please don't put any ideas into his head. And we probably won't do it. Move, that is.'

'No? I thought Dad sounded keen on the idea. Or was that just when he wanted to get away from Vanessa?' I look surreptitiously towards the house, making sure neither Nora nor Sandy are within earshot.

'Oh, he'd like the space, for sure, but...'

'You like it here?'

'Yes. I do. But perhaps he's right. Perhaps we do need to...' Ellie's voice trails away. She's looking into the middle distance, and I wonder for a moment if she's forgotten I'm here.

'You do need to what, Ellie?'

'Oh, I don't know. I'm talking rubbish as usual. Forget it. I'm not thinking straight at the moment. Once all this fuss about Vanessa is over we'll talk about it properly. We've too much on our minds to make big decisions right now.'

'All right,' I say. 'Just keep me informed, okay?'

'Okay. No more moving around of Billie's property without prior warning, I promise.'

'I'll drink to that,' I say.

'Drink to what?' asks Sandy, approaching with the wine bottle. 'I thought you two might like a top-up.'

'Mmm, thanks,' I say, thinking quickly as I hold up my glass for a refill. 'Ellie was just congratulating me on my success in sorting out my clothes today. I think you'll find you've got a bit more space in your room now.'

'That's certainly worth a toast.' Sandy smiles. 'Where are you taking your cast-offs?'

'Oh, the nearest charity shop I can stagger to, I guess. I was thinking of selling some online but I'm not sure I can be bothered posting it all.'

'Well, good for you, whatever you decide. I might follow your good example and sort through my own old clothes while I've got time.'

'No!' Ellie pulls a horrified expression. 'Sandy Henderson getting rid of her old clothes? Whatever next? Quick, Billie, look for the flying pigs!'

'Talking of old clothes,' I say. 'I hope you don't mind, Sandy… I had a bit of a rummage in your room today. D'you remember that blouse you lent me when I was playing a pirate that time at school?'

'Mmm, yes, I think so.' Sandy's not sounding very sure.

'It was white, with a few buttons at the top and big flouncy sleeves.'

'Yes. I remember that one.'

'My friend Poppy was asking today if we anything like that which she could borrow, and I thought you wouldn't mind lending it again, so I had a look while I was in your room.'

'Let me guess… you couldn't find it?'

'No. Did you get rid of it?'

'No, what do you take me for?' Sandy smiles at me, squinting against the sun. 'I took it into school last term. The drama department were doing *Pirates of Penzance* and flouncy blouses were in great demand, so I lent them that one.'

'Oh well, not to worry.'

'I'd ask for it back, but it's hard getting hold of people in the holidays.'

'No problem, I'm sure she'll get one somewhere else. She'll have asked loads of people.'

'And I hope you put everything back where you found it, young lady.' Sandy puts on her stern face.

'Of course. I value my life too much not to.'

'Quite right.' Sandy picks up the bottle. 'Now, who's going to help me finish this off?'

* * *

Everyone's tired after their day out and Alex manages to persuade Dad and Ellie to finish the evening in front of *Star Wars*. Nora and Sandy say they have other plans, which I suspect involve nothing more exciting than tea and books, retiring to their respective rooms straight after supper. Neither option appeals to me, and I'm glad I've arranged to see Gaby. It is Friday night, after all, and my last one in Beverley until Christmas, so we need to make the most of it. I know it's going to be a late night so I take a key and tell them not to wait up for me.

It's not quite the night I'd hoped for, although I earn Gaby's extravagant praise for not being late for once. Gaby's had a row with Katie and she wants to talk, not party. We sit outside in the Spoons garden while she tells me all about it, but it starts to get crowded and we know everywhere else will be just as bad, so we buy a couple of bottles of cheap supermarket wine and some snacks to mop them up and come back to my place. It's not eleven o'clock yet, but the house is quiet and I reckon they've all gone to bed early. We tiptoe through the house and into the garden, picking up a couple of glasses on our way through the kitchen. We're still tiptoeing for some reason as we make our way to the table, when we run smack bang into Sandy.

'Oh my…' Gaby shrieks, before I put my free hand on her arm to stop her dropping the wine.

'Sorry, Sandy,' I say, as Gaby sits down, fanning herself in mock dismay. 'We came back early. Gaby's a bit upset. We wanted a quiet drink so we came here.'

'Is she okay?' Sandy asks, peering round my shoulder at Gaby, who seems to be having some difficulty opening a bag of crisps.

'She'll be fine. Her dad'll pick her up soon. I'll tell him not to ring the bell and wake you all up.'

'All right.' Sandy heads towards the door.

'What are you doing out here anyway?' I ask her.

'What?' The question seems to take her by surprise. 'Oh, I forgot to water the plants. I suddenly remembered about it while I was cleaning my teeth. Ellie would never forgive me if they died.'

'I don't suppose one night off would hurt,' I say.

'No, I'm too conscientious for my own good.' She smiles. 'Night, Billie.'

'Night.' Gaby's won her battle with the crisps and has wisely left the wine to me. I pour us each a glass and lean back in my chair.

'Look up, Gaby.'

'Why?'

'The stars look nice. It'll make you feel better. Go on, try.' We both look up, and I'm trying to remember how you're supposed to find the pole star when the studio door opens and we both nearly shriek again.

'Who's there?' Ellie's voice sounds shaky and fierce all at once.

'Ellie, are you all right?' Dad's outline emerges behind Ellie's and I realise there's been a dim light glowing in the studio all along. I've been too busy coping with Gaby to notice. Why didn't Sandy warn me they were in there? Or was she too busy watering to notice?

'It's all right, Dad, it's only me, Billie.' I turn my phone on and tilt the torch towards my face. 'And Gaby. We wanted a quiet drink, not a noisy one, so we came back here. We didn't mean to give you a fright.'

'Sorry, Billie's dad, sorry, Ellie,' says Gaby. 'Didn't mean to frighten you… would you like a crisp?'

'It's a kind offer, but I think we'll pass, thank you,' Dad says, taking Ellie's hand as they walk down the path towards the house. 'You have a good night, now. Don't stay up too late.'

'We won't. Night, Dad. Night, Ellie.' We wait for the door to close and burst into fits of giggles.

'What were they doing in there?' Gaby splutters. 'With no light on?'

'There was a light on,' I say. 'But it was just a little one.'

'A very, very, little one.' Gaby's slurring a bit, but she's still with it enough to make up her mind about what was going on in there. 'A very little, *romantic* one, if you ask me.'

'No!' I can't help laughing, despite myself.

'There's a lot of people in your house, right? You, your dad, Ellie, Sandy, Alex…' Gaby counts them off on her fingers, and looks at me questioningly, knowing there's one more.

'And Nora, Ellie's mum.'

'That's right. Nora. Nora the explorer, right?'

'No, Dora's the explorer, not Nora.'

'Dora… right. Anyway, lots of people in the house. Not much privacy, right? So they go to the studio to… you know.' Gaby grins wickedly and sloshes more wine into her glass. 'Well, good for them, that's what I say. You're never too old for romance!'

'Gaby, shush, they'll hear you!'

'Sorry, Billie, sorry.'

'It's okay. Just don't talk about it, please? Or shall we talk about what your mum and dad get up to as well?'

'No! No! Spare me!' And we collapse into fits of giggles. It's a good night in the end: Gaby says I'm the best friend in the whole world and makes heartfelt, drunken promises to visit me in London. I know she won't come, but it's nice that she wants to. She calls her dad and he picks her up without ringing the bell. It's late, but I lie on the sofa bed for hours with my eyes wide open. I'm glad Gaby had a good time, but she got it wrong about Dad and Ellie. They weren't 'up to something' in the studio. There's only one thing they'd go there to do late at night when they don't want anyone to hear them. They'd been arguing. Vanessa's gone, you'd think they'd be happy now, so what was it about this time?

SIXTEEN

I sleep in the end, but it's nearly ten when I wake up and the house is quiet. Everyone except Nora's gone out, and by the time I've made breakfast it's late enough for her to join me in the garden with her morning coffee.

'This is the life, eh?' she says, taking her first sip. 'William and I had a much bigger garden than this, but I like this one. It's cosy.'

'You can say that again.'

'I suppose it was bigger before the studio was built, but there's still room for everything you need, and without any of the hard work you get with a larger garden. It makes me wonder what the point is in having acres of space that just takes time and effort to maintain.'

I look at her in surprise. 'I thought you loved the garden in your old house.'

'It was William who loved it, not me, and he never let me help or choose any of the plants. Oh no, it needed specialist knowledge, he said. That was a favourite phrase of his – specialist knowledge. He had a lot of specialist knowledge, and he didn't hold back in letting you know about it. It didn't do him much good when he became ill, though. It wasn't the right sort of specialist knowledge for that.'

It sounds a harsh assessment to me, but I remember what Dad said about relationships. Maybe Nora and William's marriage wasn't as straightforward as it might have seemed.

'I suppose not. Who managed the garden when he became ill? Did you take over?'

'Oh no, it would have been far too much for my knees. And William needed looking after, there wasn't much time for gardening. Ellie and Sandy helped, of course, but I got someone in to take care of it.'

'What was William's... I don't know... well, specialist subject?' I ask. 'I know he was a historian, but not much more.'

'Oh, history wasn't his subject. He was a classicist. He specialised in Ancient Greece, although he could read and write in half a dozen different languages. It was only in English that he struggled to communicate.'

'Nora!'

'Well, it's true, dear. I suppose Ellie and Sandy are too polite to have told you the whole truth about their father. Too loyal, perhaps.'

'Loyal to William?' From what little I've heard about him, this doesn't seem likely.

'Loyal to me. They wouldn't want to suggest that I'd been... I don't know, perhaps downtrodden's the word. Yes, downtrodden. Although I was. I daresay intelligent young women don't allow that to happen so easily these days, but when I was young, wives of promising young professors were supposed to look after their families, not have careers of their own. It was different for the girls, times had changed by then, and William was proud of their achievements, even if he didn't show it very often.'

'Is that what happened to you? You had to give up a career? What did you do?' I'm intrigued. Ellie and Sandy have always been tight-lipped about their parents, and only visited them infrequently before William's death.

'I was a historian. The Victorians were my period. I still read a lot, of course, and it's always made me happy to see Cassie pursuing a historical path herself.'

'Who's Cassie?'

'Oh, I mean Sandy. I don't forget very often these days.'

'What do you mean, Nora? Forget what?' My toast is finished, our mugs are empty and I turn my chair to look at her face on.

'Didn't they tell you? The girls changed their names. Both of them, a long time ago. First Sandy – or Cassie, as she used to be – and then Ellie.'

'What was Ellie's other name?'

'Helena. She never shortened it when she was young, but she always liked to copy her big sister, so I suppose it was inevitable.'

'Sandy's a lot older, isn't she? Like me and Alex?'

'Yes, although the gap's wider for you. Sandy was eight when Ellie was born. We weren't expecting another child after so long.' Nora smiles, perhaps remembering a time when she and William still shared such things as the joy of a new baby.

'So what was Sandy – Cassie's – proper name?'

'Cassandra. After the Trojan princess. And Ellie was named after her twin brother, Helenus. I was rather grateful she wasn't a boy. Helenus would have been a real trial to him at school.'

'So Sandy was Cassie, short for Cassandra. I suppose Sandy's another way to shorten it. I've always thought of it as a musical theatre name rather than an ancient Greek one.'

'I know. William was furious. He was very attached to the name and he always used the full version, even when she was tiny. Cassie was bad enough, but I think Sandy was the last straw.' Nora smiles mischievously, and I wonder if she didn't rather enjoy her husband's annoyance when the name he'd chosen so carefully was hijacked without his permission.

'So when did she change it? Was it when she went to uni?'

'Yes, but not straight away. Sandy went to university in London, as I'm sure you know already. We saw very little of her in that time – she was always off travelling or staying with friends. Ellie missed her terribly, of course.'

'I suppose she studied history?'

'Yes. I was pleased to see her following in my footsteps, but I was surprised she stuck with it. She always seemed to do better in English literature, and she loved Shakespeare, poetry, that sort of thing.'

'I think she still does,' I say, thinking of Sandy's bookshelves, crammed with as much fiction as history.

'Yes, and despite what she said the other day, she was a lovely little actress when she was young. They both were.'

'But not when they were older?'

'No, William discouraged it. He wouldn't let them take part in drama clubs or anything like that.'

'That's a shame.'

'Oh, I don't know. I'm sure they'd have moved on to other things in time. And it wasn't just William who wanted them to do well in their studies, I did too. I wanted them to have the chance I never did – to pursue their own careers, you know. They couldn't afford distractions.'

'But Ellie's an artist. How did that happen?'

'We weren't keen on it, I can tell you. I know you've chosen a creative path for yourself, Billie, and I respect that, of course, but it's a difficult world to make a living in, as I'm sure you'll agree, and art's no different.'

'I know. Dad made me think about it super-carefully. And I'm glad he did: it makes me less likely to give up when times are hard, knowing I thought it all through first.'

'I guessed as much. He's a good man, your father, and I'm sure being married to a singer helped him to understand that performing can be a career, not just a hobby.'

'Like him and his drums.' I smile.

'Exactly. But William and I weren't enlightened in that way. We didn't want Ellie to take art GCSE, but she went ahead and did it anyway. I could see she was talented, but William wouldn't have it. When the time came for her to choose her A-level subjects he said she'd to give it up or leave the house. So she did.'

'She left home?' I'm amazed. The Ellie I know wouldn't run away from home, but maybe I don't know her as well as I thought I did.

'She did.' Nora can't help a hint of pride creeping into her voice. 'She got herself onto a course in Hull and came to live here. Sandy had become tired of London and of studying, and she went to Hull to do a one-year teaching course. William was devastated; he wanted her to follow him into academia. He'd encouraged her to do a PhD, and she'd been accepted at UCL. He was all set to be the proud father of an academic genius, but she changed her mind at the last minute. She'd been living in Beverley and calling herself Sandy for a couple of years by the time Ellie moved in with her.'

'And that's when Ellie changed her name. Like her sister.'

'Like her sister.'

'So why did Sandy change her name in the first place? Did she just want to be someone different, not the person William wanted her to be?'

'It seems likely, doesn't it? I can't blame her, really. After all, I'd been pushed down a path I didn't want. Why should she let the same thing happen to her? I was very angry at the time, though. I'd have given anything to be offered the opportunity to do a doctorate, and I couldn't understand why she was throwing it away. It wasn't just William who was furious with her. I was too.' Nora turns her face away from my gaze, perhaps feeling she's said too much.

'I understand, Nora. I do. It must have been very hard. But you're here now, aren't you? You must have made it up with Sandy at some point?'

'Yes, I did,' she sighs. 'Although it took Ellie leaving to do it. I couldn't bear to lose both of them. We'd not seen Sandy for years when Ellie took herself off, and I wrote to her. To thank her for looking after Ellie, and to apologise. For both of us. We started writing, and eventually William agreed to let them visit. He kept out of their way, it still made him furious to see them, and he wouldn't call them by their new names, but he let them come.'

'Well, that's good,' I say. 'You must have worked hard to persuade him.'

'Oh, I said I'd leave too if he didn't.'

'Nora! Really?'

'Yes, really. We Henderson women are tougher than we look.'

'So it would seem.' I give her a big grin. 'That's quite a story, Nora. I can't believe I've not heard it before.'

'I don't suppose there's been a reason for anyone to tell it. It was all in the past by the time your father met Ellie. We were seeing them quite regularly by then, although William hid in his study most of the time in protest. He came out more often after Alex was born. Even William couldn't resist getting to know his own grandson.'

'I suppose that's why I don't remember him hiding away. I only came to see you the one time, didn't I? And it was a long time ago.'

'That's right. Your father took an instant dislike to William and refused to come again.' She looks embarrassed at the memory, and I wonder if William said something to upset Dad. I can imagine what someone like William might have said to the widower of a Caribbean jazz and blues singer, and think it best not to upset Nora by asking for details.

'Well, all I can say is I'm glad you're here now,' I say.

'Even if I have stolen your room.'

'I'm coping,' I tell her, remembering just in time not to say anything about potential house moves. 'And I'll be off soon, back to London to start rehearsals.'

'Of course you will,' says Nora. 'And I'll miss you. Perhaps you'll find time to FaceTime me now and then? I'm a dab hand at online meetings, believe it or not.'

'I'm ready to believe anything about you after everything you've told me this morning.' I put the mugs on the tray and get up. 'And I don't know about you, but I need another coffee. How about taking me through my lines while we've got the place to ourselves?'

* * *

I think I might get roped in to entertain Alex in the afternoon, but I'm let off the hook when Sandy and Dad agree to play *Risk*. Nora decides she's had enough sun for one day, and retires to her room with a book, and Ellie says she needs to get back to work, heading into the studio as soon as the kitchen's tidy. I have another go at the online yoga class and then decide to make myself useful by making tea. I deliver drinks and biscuits to Nora and the *Risk* players, and then – before I can change my mind – take two mugs to the studio.

'Mind if I join you?' I ask, opening the door with my elbow.

'Billie! Oh dear, I forgot to set the alarm. I was supposed to be making that.'

'No worries, I wasn't exactly busy.'

'Well, thank you. And yes, sure, come in.' Ellie gestures to the sofa, which is supposed to be where she has creative thoughts, and I sit down, forgetting how squishy it is and splashing tea on the floor.

'Oops, sorry.'

'Don't worry, this floor's got plenty of spills on it already, one more won't hurt.' Ellie considers the sofa with a critical eye. 'I suppose I should think about replacing that with something with springs in it, but I sit on it so seldom it never seems worth it.'

'Don't worry on my account, I've sat on worse.'

She smiles and returns to her easel. She's immersed in a matter of seconds, and watching her quiet concentration is surprisingly soothing. She seems to have forgotten I'm here, and I take the opportunity to study her with an objective eye. Sandy's always been the more striking of the two sisters. Slim, elegantly dressed, even though she's in her mid-forties, you can see that she was attractive – maybe even beautiful – when she was young. Ellie's the arty one but you'd never guess it to look at her. Not much taller than me, she's more dumpy than svelte, and most of her clothes are about ten years old. She puts makeup on for special occasions and jewellery when she remembers, and it's always surprised me that it's Sandy who has the talent for interior décor, not Ellie. Maybe all Ellie's creativity goes into her work and there's none left over for anything else.

When she got together with Dad my thirteen-year-old brain couldn't comprehend why he'd picked her and not Sandy. The ten years between them seemed an insurmountable gap, not to mention Sandy being the intellectual, level-headed one, much more like Dad than her sister. I'd forgotten about Dad liking the creative type. Married to a singer first time round, what could make more sense than an artist for a second wife? Maybe he'd have led a creative life too, given the chance.

Ellie's rinsing her brush, and notices my glazed look. 'You look miles away. Is everything all right? No more problems with Jay?'

'No, he's good. This time next week I'll be only a couple of hours away from seeing him.'

'So? What were you thinking about?'

'About you,' I say, truthfully.

'Me?' Ellie returns to her palette. I can't see what she's painting but there seems to be a lot of green in it. Maybe it's the Westwood. 'And what conclusions did you reach? Or shouldn't I ask?' She shoots me a quick grin.

'I'll miss you when I go back to London. I'd forgotten how nice it is to be home.'

'Even without a room to call your own?'

'That's what Nora said this morning.'

'Did she?' Ellie dabs her canvas a few times and stands back to look at her efforts. 'It's been good to see the two of you getting to know each other. She'll miss you when you go.'

'Mmm. I said I might FaceTime her.'

'She'd love that.' Ellie reaches for her tea and takes a sip, her eyes never leaving her painting. 'So what were you talking about?' She's made it easy now, and it just slips out.

'The past. You, Sandy, how you came to Beverley, how you used to have different names.'

'Goodness me, you have got to know each other well if she's told you all that.' Ellie stops in her tracks and looks at me.

'I know.' It's true: it's a huge amount of family history for Nora to have shared with me, but none of it sounded particularly scandalous, so why shouldn't she?

'Was it a secret? Your changing your names? You've never mentioned it before and neither has Sandy.'

'Not exactly.' Ellie returns to her paints, adding purple and grey to the mix. 'It happened more than ten years before I met you and your dad so it was old news by then. It only became a big deal when our parents got in a tizz over it. Father because he'd picked the names specially, and Mother because she never liked it when he got cross.'

'I see.'

'I suppose she built it up into a big saga?'

'Something like that,' I agree. 'And she said that Sandy made William cross by becoming a teacher and you ran away from home to become an artist.'

'Well, you could put it like that.' Ellie laughs. 'I only ran as far as Sandy's spare room. It wasn't as if I was absconding to Paris to live in a garret.'

'So you were what… fourteen when she came back up north?'

'Yes, I was just about to start my GCSEs. We'd not seen her since Christmas. She'd seemed all right then, happy with her course and her life in London. She didn't talk about anything other than her work, and I remember thinking she was hiding something. I thought it was a boyfriend, but she wouldn't say. And then she called out of the blue at the end of August to say she'd changed her plans. Our parents were furious but they couldn't make her change her mind. She wouldn't even tell us where she was living for the first six months in case they drove over and pulled her out.'

'Wow. That is dramatic.'

'I suppose it was. It's just a long time ago now. I'd almost forgotten about it.' Ellie pauses to rinse her brush again. 'She inspired me, you know.'

'Who? Nora?'

'No, Sandy. My parents had said I had to take academic subjects at GCSE. There was no way they'd let me do art and drama, which was what I wanted. But after Sandy changed her plans and did her own thing, I decided I could too.' Ellie pauses, adding a deep blue to her palette.

'What happened?'

'I marched into the deputy head's office on the first day of term and said I wanted to change my options. I dropped history and Spanish and took drama and art instead. My parents didn't find out until Christmas, by which time it was too late.'

'Ellie! You rebel!'

'I know,' she says, grinning widely at the memory. 'And then I wrote to Sandy just before my mocks saying I wanted to do art and I knew they wouldn't let me. I'd got a place at Hull College and I asked if I could come and live with her.'

'And she said yes?'

'Of course she did. She said she wished she'd had my guts years ago, her life might have turned out differently, and I could come as soon as my exams were over.'

'What did she mean about her life turning out differently?'

'I'm not sure. She might have done English rather than history, or maybe an education degree, she's always loved her teaching.'

'So you left home at sixteen.'

'Yup. Mother and Father wouldn't give me an allowance or anything. I think they hoped I'd go home if I was skint, but I waited tables, stacked shelves, that sort of thing, to pay my share of the rent. I didn't want Sandy supporting me, that wouldn't have been fair.'

'She helped you a lot, didn't she?'

'We helped each other.' Ellie's added white to her palette and she's touching the canvas with the very tip of a tiny brush.

'Can I see?'

'Sure.' She carries on dabbing while I struggle my way out of the sofa's embrace and come up behind her to see. It is the Westwood, but at night. It's only a small canvas, but every detail is perfect. The greens are almost invisible, blended in with a mass of purples, greys and blues, the solid black outline of the mill only just visible on the horizon. A faint wisp of cloud is barely there, in a sky dotted with stars.

'It's beautiful, Ellie.' I find myself whispering, as if the sound of my voice might break a spell.

'Thank you.' She takes a step back.

'What's it for?' Some of her paintings are for sale, others for shows and a few are commissions, and I can never keep track of what she's doing.

'It's for you. To remind you of home.'

I can't speak. There are so many things I want to say to her but I don't have the words for any of them.

SEVENTEEN

Sunday starts in its normal way, everyone carrying out their normal routines of cycling, singing, running and coffee-drinking. I brave the loft room and sort out two boxes of my belongings, deciding that perhaps the time has finally come to get rid of my *Jackie* magazines, and finding a couple of hidden gems in a box full of nail varnishes. Dad's gone for a long cycle ride, saying he reckons he's earned it after being annihilated at *Risk* yesterday, and Alex has a new model to start, so we know we won't see much of him this afternoon. The rest of us linger over our lunch in the garden, enjoying the sunshine and talking about not very much in particular.

'Will you be busy in your studio this afternoon?' Nora asks Ellie.

'Yes, I suppose so,' she sighs. 'Although it seems a shame to be inside on such a sunny day.'

'Why don't you give yourself an afternoon off and help me in the garden?' Sandy suggests. 'I've been meaning to sort it out for ages, but I never have time during the term.'

'It could certainly do with some attention,' says Nora, casting her eye around. 'Particularly in the weeding and pruning department.'

'Not to mention the deadheading,' Ellie and Sandy say in unison, leaving me to assume this is a well-worn family phrase.

'All right, why not?' Ellie says, loading the lunch dishes onto a tray. 'I'll put on my scruffy clothes and rendezvous by the shed in ten minutes.'

'Great.' Sandy gets up to help her. 'It'll take half the time with two of us.'

'Scruffy clothes?' I turn to Nora for enlightenment.

'Of course. You can't garden in anything that matters, it's bound to get stained or ripped.'

'I didn't realise gardening was such a dangerous activity,' I say. 'I'd better leave quickly before they drag me in too.'

'You can walk me to my room,' says Nora. 'That should keep you out of range for at least five minutes.'

'And after that I shall make myself deeply popular with Ellie by sorting through the final boxes in her room,' I call loudly in Ellie's direction.

'You do that!' she replies over her shoulder. I smile to myself, thinking that the least I can do after she painted that picture for me is to clear out my junk before I leave.

* * *

It's not such a sacrifice after all. It was more fun than I expected this morning, going through all my childhood possessions, and I tell myself it's part of the growing-up process, leaving all my teenage bits and pieces behind. I'm halfway through the first box when Ellie's voice drifts up the stairs.

'Billie?'

'Yes?'

'Can you come down here a minute?'

'What for?'

'I can't explain when you're all the way up there. Can you just come down, please?'

'All right.' I haul myself up from the floor and step carefully over the pile of hair accessories I've decided I don't need. Ellie's gone by the time I reach the landing and there's no one downstairs, so I go into the garden, where the two of them are looking at something on the table.

'What's up?' I say, squinting in the sun and wondering if I should have stayed outside after all.

'We just found this in the shed,' Ellie says. It's a plastic bag, one of those bags for life you get at Tesco's and then forget to ask them to replace when it breaks.

'Found what? And why do you need my expert opinion?'

'Just come over here and look, Billie.' There's more than a trace of impatience in Sandy's voice, so I shut up and do what she says. Ellie's holding one of the handles to the side so that I can see what's inside. A checked cotton shirt, like the ones Dad wears, nothing else. With blood on.

'What the…' I sit down heavily on the nearest chair.

'I know.' Ellie lets go of the handle and does the same.

'Where did you find that?'

'On a shelf in the shed. Next to the slug pellets.'

'Let me look again,' I say. I only took a quick glance the first time, and I need to be sure how much blood there is. Sandy pushes the bag towards me and sits down too. Her face is pale, and when I look in the bag, I can see why. There's more blood than I thought, not less. There's no way this is just someone's 'scruffy' clothes, stained from the scratches of a rose bush. Blood spatters are all over the shirt and it doesn't take much imagination to work out what the last person to wear it was doing. Despite myself, I reach into the bag, wanting to see if there's blood on the back of the shirt too, not just the front, but Sandy leans forward, putting a hand on my arm.

'Don't touch it, Billie. It might be evidence.' I drop the bag as if it's red hot and sit back down, looking up at them in turn. 'So what do we do? Call the police?'

'Maybe.' Sandy's still as white as a sheet, and so is Ellie, the shock drawing their faces in and giving them a sisterly resemblance that I've not seen before. She turns towards me. 'Billie, I think we need the brandy. Will you get it? It's in the—'

'I know where it is,' I say, interrupting her for once rather than the other way round. 'But do you think it's a good idea to talk about this outside?' I say, looking meaningfully at the fences bordering the sides of the garden.

'Oh. Maybe not.' Sandy picks up the bag and we all retreat indoors. Sandy puts the bag on the counter while I find the brandy and Ellie gets out the glasses. I shut the door to the hall before we settle ourselves around the kitchen table, but we talk quietly anyway, knowing how thin the doors are in this house. Sandy sloshes a generous slug into each glass and we sip in silence, none of us wanting to be the first to speak.

'Okay, let's think about this logically,' Sandy begins.

'Logically? How?' Ellie asks. I think she has a point, but it's probably safer not to interfere.

'We look at the facts. We have a bag. With a shirt inside.'

'And the shirt's covered in blood!' Ellie hisses. 'For God's sake, Sandy, it's obvious, isn't it? Someone wore it to murder Vanessa and hid it in our shed. What's there to be logical about?'

'Ellie, stop.' Sandy puts her hand on top of Ellie's, but she won't be stopped.

'No, I won't stop! Did you see that shirt? Did you? It's Mike's. He's worn shirts just like that one for years. I should know, I've been ironing them for long enough.'

'You can't know that,' Sandy says quickly. 'They're hardly custom-made, are they? Hundreds of people could have the same one.'

'Yes, but hundreds of people don't live in this house, do they? You know what it means, don't you?' Ellie looks at us in turn, as if challenging us to disagree with her. 'I'll tell you.' She looks Sandy hard in the face. 'I'll tell you what it means *logically*. It means one of two things. Option one: Mike killed Vanessa, which is clearly not true. Or option two: someone's trying to set him up.' She takes a deep breath and a swig of brandy, her face clearing as she does so. 'And I reckon I know who it is.'

'Who?' I need her to tell me. I don't care who she thinks it might be, as long as it's not Dad.

'Dean, of course.'

'Dean?' Sandy looks flabbergasted. 'How d'you work that one out? I mean, of course Mike couldn't have done it, but how could it be Dean? How would he have got hold of Mike's shirt?'

'He snuck in here, pinched it from the wardrobe and then snuck back to hide it in the shed.'

'But how could he sneak in? The back gate's always locked, never mind the front door. And this house is never empty.'

'It was on the day of George's barbecue. It's not only us that has spare keys,' Ellie says triumphantly. 'I always worry about getting locked out, so when Vanessa moved in I gave her one to the front door. He used that.' We sit, stunned for a minute, trying to work out what's wrong with the idea.

'I suppose…' Sandy says slowly.

'That does, actually, make sense.' I look at Ellie, searching her face for any sign that she's hiding something. There's nothing there, other than satisfaction at having figured it out.

'But will the police agree with you?' Sandy asks.

'Why not? Oh, they'll have to jump through their hoops, of course they will, but they have to "explore every avenue", don't they? They can't ignore the fact that Dean had access to this house any more than we had access to his. Can they?' I can't help but think it's going to be a lot more complicated than that, but it's hard to disagree with her in theory.

'I suppose not,' I say, uncertainly. 'What do you think, Sandy?'

'I don't know.' There's a sort of frozen look on her face, as if she's thinking at a million miles an hour. 'You're right, of course. It could easily have been as you describe. But I'm not sure the police will reach that conclusion without an awful lot of unpleasantness first. Who knows how long it will take them to work through the rest of us as suspects first? Because that's what they'll do. Why look at Dean first when any of us could have done it?'

'You don't think they'd arrest anyone, do you?' Ellie looks horrified.

'I think it's very likely they would. Starting with Mike. It's his shirt, after all, or at least you think it is.'

'I didn't say—'

'Well, you did, actually,' Sandy points out. 'And we're on his side. Can you imagine what DI Twist will think when you say it looks just like his?'

'Well, I don't have to say so, do I?'

'Are you really prepared to lie to the police, Ellie? And are you asking us to lie too?'

'I...' Ellie's face falls, and she buries her head in her hands. It's all too easy to see how quickly she'd tie herself up in knots if she tried to hide the truth from DI Twist.

'There is another option,' Sandy says.

'What's that?' I ask.

'We don't tell them.'

'We don't tell the police we've found crucial evidence in a murder investigation?' I can't believe what she's saying.

'We don't have to. We could put it in the bin and never tell anyone about it.' Sandy looks at me steadily, as if daring me to argue with her. 'It's the logical thing to do, really. If you don't want to run the risk of the police arresting Mike.'

Ellie and I look at her in astonishment, our mouths open.

'But that would mean Dean getting away with it,' says Ellie. 'And those poor children being brought up by a murderer.'

'It might be better than having their father in prison for murdering their mother.'

'Sandy, I know it makes sense. In a weird way. But it's also totally wrong.' Ellie looks at her doubtfully and turns to me for confirmation.

'Of course it is,' Sandy says, her face grim. 'But I needed to say it anyway. To make you think about it properly. When we do call them, and call them we must, you need to remember why we're doing it. For those children. No matter how hard it gets, and it will be impossibly hard, I can promise you that, we need to know we've done the right thing.'

'Will they arrest Mike?' Ellie's voice wobbles as she reaches out her hand to me.

'I don't know, Ellie. I hope not, but we have to be prepared, don't you think?' Sandy covers both our hands with her own. 'But he's not alone, and neither are you.'

* * *

Sandy does it. We sit around the table like the three witches in *Macbeth* and listen while she calls the number on Ronnie Twist's card and says yes, she knows it's Sunday, and no, it can't wait until tomorrow, and yes, she'll wait for the inspector to call her back. Ellie wanted to wait for Dad to come back from his cycle ride but Sandy said no, she couldn't face talking it all through again; it was now or never. I think I'd have preferred never on the whole, but I knew she was right. I can't imagine how Dad's going to feel when he gets home, finding the police there, but Sandy said that if we warn him it will look suspicious, and I knew she was right about that too.

We're waiting for the call back when Nora comes in, looking for her afternoon tea. None of us have noticed the time, and we realise that we're going to have to tell her something. It's Sandy who takes charge as usual, saying there's been a call from the police, they need to pop round to see the three of us again and can she keep Alex out of the way for a while? Nora takes one look at our faces and leaves the room, calling up to Alex to ask if he'd like to join her for a game of chess. He's down the stairs and into her room in record time, and when I take in Nora's tea she's already got him busy explaining some fancy move I've never heard of. Sandy's on the phone when I get back to the kitchen.

'Yes, a bag of clothes. Well, a shirt to be exact.' She pauses and the phone chatters briefly. 'Yes, it's definitely blood.' She listens again. 'No, we've not removed anything from the bag.' Another pause. 'It's in the kitchen. I'm standing next to it.' There's silence at the other end and then more chatter. 'All right. Thank you.' Sandy turns the phone off and puts it gently on the table.

'They're coming right away,' she says. 'She said not to move it again and not to touch it and we're all to stay here while we wait for them to arrive.'

'Well done. That can't have been easy,' I say, joining them again at the table.

'No, it wasn't.' Sandy looks exhausted. It must have felt like signing someone's death warrant, making that phone call, and I can see her hands shaking as she picks up her tea. Ellie's got hers wrapped around her mug, probably to hide the fact that hers are shaking too. It's hitting me too, now Sandy's made the call. Knowing they're coming, that something awful is about to happen, has put us all into what I can only think is a state of shock. The brandy's worn off in double-quick time, and all I can feel is a sick, sinking feeling inside. We sit in silence, not sure whether it's worse to speak or keep quiet. Just as I'm thinking I can't stand it another minute and I need more tea, the doorbell rings. It's them.

* * *

It's their efficiency that's the most frightening thing of all, although I'm relieved at first when Sandy brings them into the kitchen. I thought there might be a crowd, but there's only four – DI Twist, Sergeant Carter and two men in high-vis jackets who say they're scene of crime officers. The detectives take a look in the bag and then the officers put it in a big plastic bag, seal it up and ask where it was found.

'In the garden shed. Would you like me to take you down there?' Sandy asks.

'Was it you who found the bag?' DI Twist asks.

'It was me.' Ellie's not moved from her chair. She looks completely drained, and I wonder for a moment if she's going to faint, but she stands up and leads them out of the back door without being asked.

'They'll need to know exactly where it was before they examine the scene,' DI Twist explains.

'Of course. Won't you sit down?' I don't know how Sandy manages to stay so calm; she sounds as if they're here for nothing more than a cosy chat and a cup of tea. Although I notice she doesn't offer them a drink this time. We sit in a kind of stupor, watching Sergeant Carter getting out his tablet yet again, and Ellie comes back, saying they're looking over the shed.

'Thank you, Mrs Preston,' says DI Twist. She turns to Sandy. 'And thank you for making the call this afternoon, Miss Henderson. It can't have been easy, and we appreciate both your clarity and your patience.'

'You're welcome.' Sandy's looking a bit bemused, but I suppose the inspector wants to show us she's human after all before hitting us with the hard stuff.

'When exactly did you find the bag?' she asks Ellie.

'This afternoon.' It's Ellie's turn to look bemused now, but she quickly realises more detail is required. 'Oh, I suppose… about an hour ago?' She looks at Sandy and me for confirmation and we nod our heads.

'And whereabouts in the shed was it?'

'It was on the shelves at the back of the shed. We've got an old bookcase in there and it was sitting on the bottom shelf next to the slug pellets.'

'You were doing some gardening, I assume?'

'Yes. Sandy and I were working out there together. She saw that something had been eating one of the plants. She thought it might have been slugs, so I went to get the pellets. We don't keep plastic bags in there – we used to but the mice shredded them. I thought someone had forgotten so I pulled it out, thinking I'd put whatever was in it in a box instead.'

'I see.' DI Twist doesn't sound as if she sees at all, but she lets it go. 'So you took it out and looked inside and saw…'

'I saw a shirt. Nothing else. With blood on it.' Ellie must have rehearsed what she was going to say, because it comes out calmly and clearly, nothing like the way she told me about it.

'What did you do next?'

'I showed it to Sandy and we brought it inside. We showed Billie what we'd found and then we called you.' She's left more than a bit out of her account, but I suppose it's true enough.

'All right. Tell me more about the shed. What's in it?'

'Just gardening things. And the barbecue. There's not room for much else, it's not a very big shed. Do you want to take a look?'

'That won't be necessary right now, we'll take a look at it before we leave. You say you were gardening with your sister?'

'That's right,' Sandy says. 'It always gets a bit neglected during term time, and we decided it was time to sort it out.'

'You must have gone into the shed to get equipment out before discovering the slug damage?' DI Twist seems happy to let Sandy answer her questions, and Ellie relaxes visibly now that her moment in the spotlight seems to be over.

'Yes, of course. But we didn't need to go to the back, we keep everything we need most often close to the door. It saves climbing over the clutter in the middle.'

'I see. When were you last in the shed? Any of you?'

'It's only Ellie and me that use it as a rule,' says Sandy. 'I suppose Mike would have gone in there to get the charcoal last time we had a barbecue, but that was some time ago. When did we last have a barbecue, Billie? Can you remember?'

'It was the day... the day Vanessa...' How can she possibly have forgotten? I can't make myself say it, and fortunately DI Twist spots my discomfort and is kind enough to rescue me.

'The day of Miss Forsyth's death?'

'Yes. That day.'

'So you're saying no one's been in the shed since that time until today? Not even to mow the lawn?'

'It's not needed mowing recently,' Ellie says, looking out of the window. 'It's not rained in weeks.'

'Of course.' DI Twist can't be much of a gardener if she's not noticed that herself. Whereas Sergeant Carter appears to be better informed.

'Do you have a lot of problems with slugs?' he asks Ellie sympathetically. 'I'm no expert, but my granddad's a keen gardener, and he swears by coffee grounds and eggshells. He's not a fan of chemicals. In fact, he says every garden needs a few slugs to break down the mulch. Or something like that. He reckons it's only young plants they go for, and if you have plenty of sturdy bushes they shouldn't be too much of a problem.' He cranes his neck to look out of the window. 'You've got a well-established garden out there, I wouldn't have thought you'd have too much of a problem.'

'Well, I wish our slugs listened to you.' Sandy smiles. 'We'll have to try the eggshells, won't we, Ellie?'

'Yes, I suppose so,' Ellie says. DI Twist gives her sergeant a sharp look, as if to tell him they've more important matters to worry about, and he returns to tapping at his screen, a chastened expression on his face.

'Tell us about the contents of the bag,' says DI Twist to Ellie. 'You all had a look inside, is that correct?'

'Yes. We did.' Ellie's twisting her hands in her lap, and she looks at the table, seemingly unable to say anything more.

'And as we've already seen, there was a checked shirt inside.'

'Yes.'

'Had you seen it before, Mrs Preston? The shirt? Or the bag, come to that?'

'We've got lots of bags like that,' Ellie says. 'And so have half the people in Beverley, I daresay.'

'And the shirt? Did it look familiar in any way?'

'Yes… at least I thought it did. I'm not so sure now… I'd have to look again to be certain…'

'What do you mean? You thought you recognised it but perhaps you were mistaken?'

'Yes. At least, I didn't look at it for long, so I might have been wrong.'

'But your first thought was that you recognised it. Is that correct?'

'Yes.'

'And?'

'And… it looked like one of Mike's shirts. Only lots of people have shirts like that. Mike's aren't anything special. Just from Marks and Spencer's.'

'Just from Marks and Spencer's,' DI Twist repeats. She looks out of the window, eyeing up the shed. 'Who has access to your shed? Apart from the family?'

'No one,' says Sandy. 'As long as the back gate's locked. Mike doesn't always remember to lock it when he comes back from a bike ride.' I'm not sure that's strictly true, but it won't hurt to plant a seed of doubt in their minds.

'Does he keep his bike in the shed?'

'No, there's a lean-to at the side of the studio, we all keep our bikes there.'

'I see.'

'How often do you check the back gate? To make sure it's locked?' We exchange glances.

'I never check it,' I offer. 'But I'm hardly ever here anyway.' The other two look at each other.

'Mike takes the bins out every week, so he must lock it then,' Ellie says. 'He doesn't have an evening ritual of checking all the doors, if that's what you mean.'

'I see.' DI Twist looks out of the window again. 'I think we'll take a look at the shed now. Will you all wait here, please?' She leads her sergeant outside without waiting for an answer. I walk over to the window to watch. I'm desperate for a smoke, but there's no way I'm going outside while that lot are in the garden.

'Sit down, Billie,' hisses Ellie. 'They'll see you.'

'So what? Why shouldn't I look out of the window? They're not looking this way, anyway.'

'What are they doing?'

'They're talking to those other guys… they're going in the shed now.'

'What, all of them? That must be cosy,' says Sandy.

'No, just her and Sergeant Carter.'

'That'd still be cosy if you ask me.'

'Sandy!' Ellie can't help herself, and we all dissolve into nervous giggles. 'D'you think it would be all right if we made another cup of tea?' Ellie asks. 'I'm desperate for one.'

'Of course it's all right. It's our kitchen, isn't it?' There's a definite bolshie tone in Sandy's voice, and she gets up and fills the kettle, turning the tap to full blast as if daring it to disagree with her.

'Wait a minute,' I say, still glued to the window. 'They're coming out.'

'Quick, Sandy, put the kettle down,' Ellie hisses again.

'No, why should I? Maybe they'd like a cup too.'

'Oh, carry on, Sandy, for goodness' sake, what does it matter?' They're really starting to annoy me now. 'They're not coming in, anyway. They're talking now. The yellow jackets are going. They're leaving through the back gate... no, wait, they're just looking at it, all of them, from both sides...'

'Great commentary, Billie, you should be on *Match of the Day*,' says Sandy, putting tea bags into mugs. 'Do you want sugar in yours?'

'Mmm, two, please. Oh, they are leaving now. Through the back gate.'

'What, all of them?' Ellie asks, hope and disbelief mingling in equal measure in her voice.

'No, just the yellow jackets.'

'What are the others doing?'

'Why don't you just come here and look for yourself?'

'I don't want them to think I'm spying on them.'

'I don't think that would make a difference. If they want to arrest us, they'll do it whether we've spied on them or not.'

'So what *are* they doing?'

'Talking. The Twist woman's on her phone now.' Ellie finally joins me at the window, standing to the side of it and leaning in so that they won't see her if they turn round. Instantly, DI Twist puts her phone away and they head back towards the house.

'I knew that would happen!' I can't help laughing as we rush back to the table like a couple of naughty schoolchildren. I can't believe we're behaving this way – it must be the shock. Sandy joins us, but only after making the tea and handing it round. She's taking her own seat just as they come back in.

'Sorry to keep you waiting so long,' says DI Twist. 'We're just about done now.'

'So what happens next?' asks Sandy, rather bravely, I think.

'We need to ask you all to come to the station with us.'

Ellie gasps, looking as if she's been handed an instant death sentence. 'Are you arresting us? All of us?'

'No, not at all. But we would like to take copies of your fingerprints. For elimination purposes. We'd need more evidence than this to arrest you, Mrs Preston, but we can't ignore the fact that what appears to be vital evidence has been found on your property. It's purely voluntary, of course, but—'

'Of course we will. Anything to help,' says Sandy briskly, interrupting the inspector before she can outline the potentially dire consequences of our refusing to do what she wants.

'What about Mike?' Ellie asks.

'A uniformed officer will wait at the house and escort him to the station on his return. He'll need to take a look at the contents of the bag, and we'll take his fingerprints too, of course.'

'Will you be arresting him?' Ellie seems to be obsessed with the issue of arrest, but I suppose it's understandable.

'That's not something we can confirm at this time,' says DI Twist. 'We'll need to ask him the same questions as we've asked you, and it makes sense to do that at the station at the same time as everything else.'

'I see.' It's clear Ellie wants to ask more questions, but she doesn't. Perhaps she's afraid of what the answers might be.

'I'll tell Mother we're going out for a bit,' says Sandy, pushing back her chair.

'Will you tell her why?' asks Ellie.

'I'll tell her enough, don't worry.' Sandy gives Ellie a reassuring pat on the hand, and Ellie and I clear our mugs in silence before following the detectives outside.

* * *

I thought I'd watched enough TV dramas to know what it's like inside a police station, but I was wrong. Beverley only has a small station, and it's not as if the entrance is crowded with what Nora would call 'unsavoury characters', but it still feels like everyone in there is looking at us accusingly. I suppose they've got good reason to, but it doesn't help. We each press our fingerprints onto a funny screen, a bit like a scanner. At least we don't have to go home with ink all over our fingers, and Sandy asks what will happen to them after the investigation is over.

'We'll remove them from the system,' says Sergeant Carter. DI Twist has disappeared, no doubt with more important things to do than taking fingerprints. 'We're only allowed to keep the prints of people who are convicted of a crime.'

'I thought as much,' Sandy says. If she thought so, why is she asking? Is this really the time for polite conversation? Or maybe she's been fingerprinted before and wants to be sure she's not connected to a previous crime. I tell myself not to let my imagination run away with ridiculous ideas, and ask if we can go now.

'I'll just ask the inspector,' he says, and goes out, leaving the three of us standing awkwardly around the machine, not sure what to do with ourselves.

'Let's just go,' says Sandy. 'We're here voluntarily, we can leave whenever we like. We don't need anyone's permission.'

'But what if they still need us for something?' Ellie looks around the room nervously, as if checking for hidden cameras.

'Then they can ask us to come back another day. And learn how important it is to be more organised,' Sandy replies tartly. She hates wasting time, I've seen her drying dishes for ten seconds at a time rather than sit around waiting for the kettle to boil. Sergeant Carter's return saves them having to continue their argument and we all turn to look at him expectantly, Sandy picking up her bag in a rather obvious fashion as she does so.

'DI Twist would like you to stay just a little longer. She wants the SOCOs to undertake a complete search of your garden shed before you return home.'

'Just to clarify things,' Sandy says, a hint of tension in her voice, 'is she requesting permission to search our shed? Or does she have a warrant to do so?'

'DI Twist has instructed me to ask for your permission to search the shed,' says Sergeant Carter, as if reciting a carefully prepared response. 'This will enable us to permit you to return to the property as quickly as possible.'

'What do you mean, as quickly as possible?' Ellie asks.

'We can't allow you to return to the property until the search has been completed.'

'Of the whole house?' Sandy can't keep the outrage from her voice. 'I mean... we can't give permission for that, not with Nora and Alex in there and Mike not back yet.'

'No, we're only interested in the shed. If you prefer, we can cordon off the garden and place an officer there on duty until we obtain a search warrant tomorrow.' I can't help wondering if it's a bluff. It's how they do it on the telly. They say they'll get a search warrant if they need to, but it's better to be helpful and then it turns out they'd never have got one in the first place.

'What's the problem?' I say, before Sandy can antagonise him any further. 'Let them search the shed, then we can go home. You'll just need to warn Nora they're coming. We don't want to give her a heart attack, opening the door to find people in hazmat suits on the doorstep.'

'I'm sure that won't be necessary.' Sergeant Carter allows himself a grateful smile.

'All right.' Sandy shrugs. 'But let me call Mother first. Billie's right, she needs to know they're coming. Do we have to wait here? Or can we go into town for a cup of tea or something while they're there?'

'DI Twist would like to take formal statements from you all while you wait. If you're agreeable to doing so, that is.' I'm sure this last phrase is directed towards Sandy, although he's careful not to look at her.

'Formal statements?' Ellie must know what they are, having signed one already, but her nerves have got the better of her.

'About your whereabouts on the day of Miss Forsyth's death and on the day of her son's birthday party. And on the evening of her… disagreement with another woman.'

'But we've already told you where we were on those days,' Ellie says, her exasperation clear despite her effort to be polite.

'That was before we found a bloodstained shirt in our shed,' says Sandy. 'I think you'll find that's changed things rather. Am I right?' She turns from Ellie to the sergeant, resignation in her tone.

'That's correct, Miss Henderson. Under these new circumstances we are required to take an additional statement from each of you. We realise that you may feel you are being asked to repeat information you've already given us, and I'm sorry about that, but it is an essential part of the process.'

'So you're not asking us this time? You're telling us?' Sandy must know the answer already, but I guess she thinks Ellie needs to hear it.

'That's correct.'

'Come on, Ellie, let's just get it over with. Then we can get home to Mother and Alex.'

'But what about Mike?' Ellie asks in desperation. 'What's going to happen to him?'

'Mr Preston will be interviewed, just the same as you, Mrs Preston,' Sergeant Carter says reassuringly. 'I can't make you any promises, but I wouldn't be surprised if he's home in time for dinner.'

'Really?' She looks at him hopefully.

'Well, that all depends on when you eat your dinner, doesn't it?

And when he decides to come back from his bike ride.' He smiles at her. 'Now, come along. We've got interview rooms ready for you all, and the sooner we get these statements taken, the better.'

'Rooms?' Sandy asks. 'Are you taking our statements separately?'

'If you don't mind,' he says. 'We'll be able to let you all go home quicker that way.' There's an undeniable logic to his answer, but his reassuring manner only makes me think he's good at his job, at least when it involves getting people to make statements they'd rather not have to. He doesn't fool me for a minute. Separate interviews might speed things up, but they also give them the perfect opportunity to look for contradictions in our stories. I've no idea who Vanessa argued with that night, but there's no doubt in my mind. They think it was one of us.

EIGHTEEN

It's nearly six o'clock when we finally get home. We let Nora make us hot sweet tea and take turns filling her in on what's happened.

'I'm sorry, Mother,' Ellie says when the story is finished. 'Maybe we should have told you straight away. When we found the bag in the shed.'

'Don't be silly, dear, there wasn't time for that. I'm only glad I could help out with Alex. He seems fine, by the way. I couldn't keep him completely in the dark, not after those officers came to look at the shed. But he seems happy with the explanations I given him. And I've told him we'll be getting a takeaway this evening. I didn't think any of us would be up to cooking.'

'Thank you, Mother, that was very thoughtful.' Sandy pats her hand and pushes her chair back. 'Now, if you don't mind, I'm going outside. I don't know what state they'll have left our shed in, but I'd like to deal with it sooner rather than later.'

Ellie watches her leave and turns to Nora. 'How long do you think they'll keep him, Mother? Do you really think he'll be back for dinner like the sergeant said?' She sounds more like a little girl than a wife and mother, but they're not unreasonable questions.

'Oh, I think he will,' Nora says decidedly.

'You're very confident,' I say. 'How can you be so sure? I mean…
I want Dad back home as soon as possible, obviously, but what
makes you think they'll let him go so quickly? They can keep people
for twenty-four hours, you know.'

'Yes, I know, Billie. I may be old but I'm perfectly capable of
remembering what they tell you on those TV detective programmes.'

'Sorry, Nora.'

'It's all right, dear, we're all under strain. No, it's because of the
fingerprints.'

'But how can our fingerprints help Mike?'

'Not yours, his, dear. Although I must say, it was very good of
you all to provide them so readily. You weren't under any obligation
to do so.'

'I know,' Ellie says. 'It just seemed better at the time to be helpful.
We thought it might look suspicious if we objected.'

'That's as may be, but it's Mike's that matter. As I'm sure even
Alex could tell you, they'll have gone over Vanessa's dressing room
at the theatre with their dust and brushes, or perhaps one of those
ultra-violet devices they use nowadays. They'll have fingerprints from
"the scene", won't they?'

'I suppose.' Ellie's got her 'let's humour Mother' expression
on, but I can see where Nora's going, and even as she's talking, my
stomach is plummeting into my shoes.

'So,' Nora continues happily. 'Mike won't be there, will they?'

'Won't be where?'

'Mike's fingerprints won't be in the theatre. And when they find
that out, which I expect they are doing right now, they'll have to let
him go.'

'Oh. I see.' Ellie's face clears as her exhausted brain eventually
understands what Nora's saying.

'At least, they shouldn't be, unless he was the murderer after all,'
Nora continues. 'But you don't seriously think that's possible, do you?'

'Oh, Mother, I've not known what to think,' Ellie sighs. 'No, I
didn't think it for a minute, but there's been a lot going on – more

than you know – and he's not been himself. You must have noticed.'

'I don't know Mike well enough to notice, Ellie. And your marriage is your own affair. I'd never want to pry. But if you ever need to talk, you know where I am.' Nora smiles at her daughter and reaches for her frame. 'And for the next half an hour, that's going to be my room. I think I need a lie-down before dinner, if you don't mind. No, don't worry about me,' she says as Ellie starts to get out of her chair to help. 'A little bit of exercise is good for my legs.' She shuffles out of the kitchen, leaving the two of us staring at each other across the table.

'I'll just…' I have to get out but my brain's frozen and I can't think of an excuse. Fortunately Ellie's miles away, staring into the middle distance, and she just nods absently as I leave the room.

I just make it to the downstairs loo in time for my stomach to do its worst, and then go to the study, where I sit on the sofa, heart pounding, clutching my water bottle as if it's the only thing keeping me alive. How could I have been so stupid? I was so busy worrying about Dad and that awful shirt, I couldn't even realise it was a bad idea to give the police my fingerprints. What kind of idiot am I to forget they'll have found my prints all over Vanessa's dressing room? Where *did* I leave them, anyway? It's been almost impossible to block the memory from my mind, and now that I need to remember, I can't. Slow down, Billie, breathe. Count in and out. Slowly. I make myself relax, and it works. I take myself through what happened one step at a time. The doorknob – I grabbed it when I felt faint. The gun? No, I didn't touch it, I know that for certain. The window, on my way out. Anything else? I don't think so, but it's bad enough. How long will it be before they match their prints with mine and turn up here again, maybe to arrest me this time? I'll have to hand myself in. It's got to look better if I go in myself. They'll find out anyway, and every minute I delay is another minute for Dad in the police station.

Now that I've made up my mind, I want to get it over with as soon as I can. The police station is at least a mile away. I'd take one of the bikes, but Sandy's still in the garden and I don't want to have to make up an excuse. I pull on my running gear and put my head round the kitchen door to tell Ellie I'm going for a jog. She looks surprised but nods absently.

'I just need to clear my head. Save me some food if I'm not back for dinner.'

'Okay.' Ellie looks up at the kitchen clock. She's not moved an inch since I left her, and it's clear she's forgotten about eating altogether.

'Didn't Nora say something about a takeaway?' I remind her. 'Maybe you should ask her what she'd prefer?'

'Oh. Yes. I'll do that.' Ellie stirs herself at last. 'See you later.'

I remove myself with relief and head out in the direction of the police station before I have time to change my mind.

* * *

Weirdly, I'm calmer going in this time than before. Maybe because the worst has already happened. At least it feels that way, although I'm sure there's more to come. At any rate, the entrance is empty this time, no one's staring at me and even the constable on duty doesn't comment on my appearance, which is definitely on the hot and sweaty side. She takes my name, says she'll find out if DI Twist or Sergeant Carter are in the building and tells me to wait over there.

'You will tell them it's urgent, won't you?'

'I will.' She picks up the phone on the desk, repeating my words and listening for a few seconds before putting it back. 'Come with me.' She emerges from behind the desk and holds a door open beside it. I follow her down the corridor and past the fingerprint machine, finishing up in an interview room that's a lot like the one I was in only a few hours ago. There's a table with two chairs on either side of it, a recording machine and not much else.

'Wait here. The inspector will be with you soon.'

'Okay.' I sit down, shivering a little as the sweat dries on my skin in the cool of the room.

'Do you want a drink of water?'

'Yes, please.' My throat's dry with nerves now that I'm here, never mind the running. She's back in short time with a bottle of water, and leaves me to it. I drink the water and hope they won't take forever, as I don't know if the door's locked and I might need a pee soon. I'm just wondering whether to try to open it when they come in.

'Billie.' There's no apology for the wait this time and I can see shadows under DI Twist's eyes. I suppose it's been a long day for her as well as for me, and I wonder for a moment what Sunday plans we've ruined for her.

'Hello.' It's the first time I've been with them on my own, and I'm not sure what to say. It was a constable who took my statement this afternoon, and it feels much more serious this time when I say my name and address for the machine.

'So.' DI Twist suddenly seems anything but tired. 'What do you want to tell us?'

'I was there. That day.' I've been thinking and thinking of how to say it, and this is the best I've been able to come up with.

'There as in…?'

'The theatre. I was at the theatre on the day Vanessa died.'

'We know you were. We found your fingerprints there.' She looks at me as if waiting for a response, but I don't know what to say. 'You've saved us a journey, Billie,' she continues. 'We were on our way to arrest you.' And before I even have time to open my mouth, Sergeant Carter is standing up and saying I'm under arrest on suspicion of murdering Vanessa Forsyth and something about what I say and don't say, and I tell them I understand, even though my mind refuses to take in anything at all.

* * *

They tell me I'm allowed a phone call and a lawyer. I say no to the phone call. Something tells me I need to keep all this secret from the family, and I ask for a text instead. I tell Ellie that I've bumped into Gaby and I'm going over to hers to hang out for a while. They've not said how long they'll keep me, so I say I might stay the night and not to worry if I'm not back before the morning. I can't believe they've got a lawyer waiting around at the station, so I say no to that too in the hope that they might let me go once I tell them my story. Surely they can't hold me indefinitely, especially when I've got no motive? They've gone out of the room to get some more water, and when they come back, they tell me I'm being interviewed under caution and I have to say my name and date of birth, and sign a piece of paper to say who I am and what I'm there for. The recording machine's on but the sergeant has his tablet out anyway, his fingers poised above the keyboard like a pianist waiting to begin a concert.

'So. Billie. You were at the theatre on the afternoon of Vanessa Forsyth's murder.' DI Twist is sitting upright in her chair as if for a job interview, and I decide it might help me to stay calm if I pretend that's what it is. I sit up straight too and try to look sensible and grown-up.

'Yes.'

'Why were you there? Were you involved in the film too?'

'No. She'd invited me to visit her in her dressing room. To… to see what it was like.'

'Hadn't you ever seen a theatre dressing room before?' Her tone is understandably incredulous.

'Of course I have, but not when it's being used for a film. And it wasn't just for that…'

'What was it for?'

'She said we could have a talk about… about the business, about how she might be able to help me.'

'But why would she invite you to the theatre? Wouldn't it have been easier to talk to her at her home?'

'No, she wasn't often there, and when she was she was busy with her kids. There are long breaks when you're filming. She said it was boring waiting around in that tiny room and she'd enjoy a visitor.'

I hope this sounds reasonable. It's true, after all, even without her wanting me to bring her those pills.

'All right, she invited you to visit her that day. So why is there no record of you going into the building? The security logs don't include your name and no one's mentioned seeing you.'

'I went in round the back. Through the fire escape. Vanessa said it was always open, to let the cool air in.'

'Hmm.' DI Twist pauses, looking out of the window, which can't be very interesting as it's so high up it's only showing a bit of sky. 'What time was this? Your visit to Miss Forsyth?'

'She told me to arrive at three o'clock. I got there at about ten past. I'm not very good at being on time.'

'So she was alive shortly after three o'clock.' DI Twist's eyes swivel back to me and neither of them can keep the surprise from their faces.

'No. She was dead.'

'You arrived in Vanessa Forsyth's room at ten past three on the afternoon of her death and found her dead?'

'Yes.'

'If that's true – and I'm far from being convinced that it is – why didn't you tell us this before? And why didn't you call the police when you found Vanessa Forsyth dead?' It's the first time I've heard her sound angry, and I don't know what to say. I don't even know what to think. I've been a total idiot. I should have done what Jay said and told them sooner. Why on earth didn't I listen to him? We all sit in silence, the only sound in the room the soft tapping of Sergeant Carter's fingers on his tablet, and even that stops eventually.

'Billie? Why didn't you tell us?'

'I… I thought I'd get into trouble.'

'You're in more trouble now for not telling anyone in the first place, as I'm sure you realise.'

'I'm sorry. Really I am.'

'I'm sure you are, now that you've been found out. I'm equally sure you had no intention of telling us about it before we requested your fingerprints. Am I correct?'

'I suppose so.' I don't know where to look. The floor seems the best option.

DI Twist looks at me as if trying work out what sort of puzzle I might be, and it seems to help because the anger's been replaced by what sounds like resignation when she speaks again.

'Why did you think you'd be in trouble?'

'Well, I knew I wasn't supposed to be there. And I thought someone else might get into trouble too. For leaving the fire escape open.' I raise my head to meet her gaze again, hoping this might make me appear truthful.

'You didn't want to get some unknown film company employee into trouble. Really?'

'No. I didn't. It could have cost someone their job. I didn't want that on my conscience.'

'I'm sorry, Billie. I'm not buying it. What was the real reason?'

'I… I can't say. But it doesn't have anything to do with Vanessa dying. Honestly.'

'Billie. Please. If you can't give us a good reason for avoiding the police when you found a dead body, we'll have no option but to view you as a potential suspect. More than that – a prime suspect.'

'But I didn't kill her! Why would I do that?' I'm shivering now, although whether with cold or fear, I can't tell.

'I don't know yet, but you're not convincing me otherwise just now.' She's like a dog with a bone, and I know she won't give up. And I guess admitting to having a few pills on me is a lot better than being suspected of murder. There's no need to mention that Vanessa was going to buy them off me, is there?

'All right. I had some pills on me. I thought my bag might get searched if I called the police and I didn't want them found.'

'What kind of pills?'

'I don't know what they were called. They were to help you sleep.'

'You don't know what they were called, but you knew what they were for?'

'Yes.'

'Where did you get them?'

'A… a friend gave them to me.' I can see where this is going. Jay will never forgive me if I drag him into it. 'But I don't have them anymore. I flushed them down the toilet the same day.'

'Well, that's very convenient for you, isn't it,' DI Twist says drily. 'We may come back to those pills later on, but I think we can agree that they're not our prime concern right now.' She raises her eyebrows ever so slightly as she turns towards Sergeant Carter and he nods as if in agreement.

'I suppose we can let the machine take the strain for a while,' she says, and this appears to be a signal for him to take over the questions, as he puts his tablet to one side and leans across the table towards me.

'So, Vanessa was dead when you arrived at three ten?'

'Yes. I'm so sorry I didn't say anything before. I was in such a panic, and then afterwards I didn't realise how much it might help you if—'

'Never mind that now,' he says, and there's something in his low tones that tells me things aren't so bad after all. 'Just tell us what you saw. Please think carefully, Billie. If you can give us an accurate description, it may help to improve your position.'

'Okay.' I take a deep breath. 'Although there's really not much to tell. I came into the room and she was in the chair. I knew straight away she must be dead because of the…'

'You could see she'd been shot in the head? Is that right?'

'Yes. That's right. I could see the bullet hole straight away.' Somehow it's easier to say now that he's done it already.

'What did you do next?'

'I felt faint. I had to kneel down for a bit. It was the shock.'

'I understand. And then you stood up again?'

'Yes. I held onto the doorknob as I got up. I expect you found some of my fingerprints there.'

'Go on. What did you do next?'

'I thought I should tell someone. Dial 999 or call for someone in the theatre. And then I remembered the pills and I panicked and just wanted to get out.'

'Did you see the gun?'

'Yes. I was looking around the room. In case... I'm not sure really... in case there was something out of the ordinary that I might need to remember later on. I thought she'd been murdered at that point. And then I saw the gun and I knew it was hers so I knew it must be suicide.'

'Did you touch the gun?'

'No, I didn't touch anything except the doorknob. And the window. That's how I got out. I didn't want anyone seeing me in the corridor, so I opened the window and climbed out that way. There'll be fingerprints on the window too... sorry, I expect you know that already.' Sergeant Carter clearly isn't going to share what he does or doesn't know with me, but he doesn't contradict me.

'You say you looked around the room for anything out of the ordinary? Was there anything that looked wrong? Out of place? Unexpected, perhaps?'

'I'd not been in there before so it was hard to tell, but it looked just like any other dressing room.'

'What about when you arrived? Were there any sounds coming from the room? Was the corridor empty? Did you get the sense someone had been there just before your arrival?'

'I don't remember anything like that. I was running late, so I wasn't thinking about anything much. I was just hoping Vanessa wouldn't be cross that I'd kept her waiting.'

'Was the room hot, Billie?' DI Twist asks.

'Oh...' The question takes me by surprise. 'No, not really. There was a fan running, but I did think it funny that she'd not opened the window further.'

'Did you notice any particular smell?'

'A smoking gun, you mean?' I almost find myself smiling at the cliché, and then I remember. 'Wait. Yes, there *was* a funny smell. I remember thinking it should smell like bonfires or something if a gun had just been fired, but it was a musty sort of smell, more like eggs. And there was something else mixed in with it. A perfume. It felt a bit familiar, but I couldn't place it. I might know it if I smelt it again, but I'm not great with smells, I never notice if I burn the toast.'

DI Twist gives me a tight smile and nods at Sergeant Carter to take over the questions again.

'So, you climbed out of the window?' he continues.

'Yes. I walked out through the car park and round to the library. I needed to go to the ladies. I wasn't feeling too good.'

'And you had some pills to dispose of?'

'Yes, that too.'

'Did you see anyone you knew? On your way to the library, or perhaps in the library?'

'No. I was looking at my phone most of the time. I didn't want anyone to talk to me. I just needed to get to the toilet as quickly as possible.'

'I see. How long were you in there? In the library toilet?'

'I don't know. Ten minutes? Maybe fifteen? There was someone else in one of the cubicles when I arrived. They were in there for ages – it sounded like they were unwell – and I didn't want to bump into them. So I waited until they'd washed and dried their hands before I left.'

'I see. What about when you were shopping? Didn't your aunt say she was in town as well that afternoon? You didn't bump into her?'

'No. Like I said, we don't go to the same shops. And I went straight home. I couldn't face town after that.'

'I understand.' Sergeant Carter pauses, and I hope he's going to say I can go now, but after an exchange of glances with his boss, he carries on. He's still talking calmly, as if there's nothing to worry about, but I'm beginning to wonder if he's as friendly as he'd like me to think.

'We have CCTV footage of you entering and leaving the library at times which fit with your account,' he says. 'But nothing before that point. You've given us the names of one or two charity shops, but you say you didn't buy anything. Is that right?'

'No, I didn't. I'm trying to save money, so I need to really want something to buy it, even if it's second-hand.'

'It's unfortunate that the shops you mentioned don't have CCTV. Without any footage, or receipts, it's difficult to confirm your movements prior to your arrival at the theatre.'

'What are you saying? D'you think I'm lying? That I did it? That I murdered Vanessa?'

'We're not saying anything of the kind, Billie,' DI Twist says, leaning forward. 'But it doesn't help your position that we've not been able to corroborate your alibi. And your accounts of what you were doing at George's party and the evening of Vanessa's argument with another woman can only be described as vague.'

'I'm not the only one with a vague alibi! Sandy's the only one with proper proof for that afternoon. And anyone at the party could have pinched Vanessa's gun and gone over to argue with her any time they wanted.'

'That's true. But you're the only one Vanessa showed her gun to, Billie.'

'What about Dean? He knew where it was, didn't he? And would I really be stupid enough to wipe my fingerprints off the gun but leave them on the doorknob and the window?'

'I don't think we said anything about them being wiped off the gun, did we, Luke?' DI Twist asks her sergeant. 'What makes you think that they were?'

'Perhaps the fact that if they weren't wiped off, you'd have arrested someone by now and you'd be talking to them instead of me.'

'Perhaps we would.' She smiles at me. 'You're not daft, are you, Billie? Even if you are silly enough to wander around with dubious pills in your bag.' The abrupt change in her expression takes me by surprise, and I shut up, hoping I've not overstepped the mark.

'I'm sorry, I wasn't trying to—'

'Tell us how to do our jobs? Don't worry, even if you were, it wouldn't be the first time. You'd be amazed how many people think they know how it's done just from watching a few cop shows on the telly.' She grins at Sergeant Carter as if at a private joke, and I allow myself to hope that they're not going to bang me up in a cell after all. He turns off the machine and the two of them get up and say they'll be back shortly, leaving me to fidget and shiver on my own. I realise I must be in shock, and I make myself recite as many lines as I can remember from the play to stop myself thinking about what might happen next. They're gone for ages, and I'm halfway through act three when they come back, making me jump when the door opens suddenly and without warning. DI Twist's on her own this time, which has to be a good sign.

'All right, Billie, you can go home now.'

'Really?'

'Yes. I can't pretend you've been anything other than irresponsible in not reporting Vanessa's death as soon as you found her, but that's not a crime in itself. And we don't have sufficient evidence to charge you at present.' I don't know what that means but I don't dare ask. The pills are another matter, though – I don't want that hanging over me, even if they don't think I'm a murderer after all.

'What about the pills?'

'Since they are no longer in your possession, there's not much we can do about them,' she says, and my stomach finally stops churning in fear. 'But let this be a warning, Billie. I'd advise you to avoid carrying anything of that sort around with you in the future. I don't know if you had an illegal substance in your possession or not, but it's not worth the risk.'

'I know. I won't. Thank you, DI Twist.' I don't care if I sound like a small child coming off the naughty step, I'm just so relieved to be allowed out of there.

Sergeant Carter opens the door and takes me back out through the main entrance. As I emerge into the late evening light, I want nothing more than a smoke to calm my nerves, but I've not brought anything with me other than a door key. I don't even know what time it is, but as I work up gradually from a jog to a run, I know I've never been so pleased to be heading in the direction of home.

* * *

'You're back!' Alex dashes out of the living room as soon as I'm through the door.

'So I am,' I say, casting my eyes around for signs that Dad's home too. I've been so bound up in my own worries, I forgot to ask if they'd let him go. I don't want to ask Alex, and it's a relief to see his cycling helmet hanging up in the hall.

'I said we didn't need to keep you any dinner, but Ellie said we should,' Alex informs me. 'There's pizza keeping warm in the oven if you want it.' He sounds doubtful, although I expect this has more to do with him wanting extra pizza than concern for the quality of my meal.

'Yeah, Gaby's got an early start tomorrow so I thought it best to come home. I'll have a shower first and then pizza. If there's any left, I'll let you know.'

'Cool. We're watching *Return of the King*. You can watch too if you like.'

'I might just do that. Thanks, Alex.'

I stand in the shower, my brain in shock and my eyes suddenly streaming, although whether it's tears of relief or fear, I'm not sure. They stop in the end, and I let the water wash over me as my thoughts first race around and then finally calm down. I'm brought back to reality by Alex as usual, banging on the door and asking if I'm ever coming out. Glancing at my phone as I rub my hair dry, I realise I must have been in there for nearly half an hour. Resigning myself to Dad's inevitable comments about long showers, I go in search of reheated pizza. I'm surprised to find myself ravenous, but there's still enough for both Alex and me, and the idea of an hour or two of Middle Earth appeals. I'd planned to call Jay, but I can't face going through it all again. He'll only say I told you so and tell me off for nearly getting him into trouble. I text him to say it's been a difficult day and I'll call him tomorrow, thinking I might put it off until I see him in London at the end of the week. Alex says I'm the best sister ever for sharing the pizza and Nora makes his day by suggesting ice cream afterwards. There's no sign of the others, and Nora says they all wanted an early night. I saw a light on in the studio when I was in the kitchen so I know this isn't strictly true, but I don't question it; I'm just relieved not to have to answer any questions.

I almost fall asleep in front of the film, but as soon as I lie down to sleep in the study, my brain's wide awake again, fizzing with questions. Who put that bag in the shed? It must have been Dean, but if so, who was the woman arguing with Vanessa? Was that even connected? Maybe it was Dean's girlfriend and she was in it with him. Maybe she did it? Or perhaps another couple killed her together. I fight the thought, but I can't help it – what if it was Ellie arguing with Vanessa, and Dad who killed her? And if not that, why are they still weird with each other? Is it just the stress of the murder or is something else going on? And do the police really believe it was just stupidity that stopped me reporting Vanessa's death? I almost find myself wishing I'd kept those pills as proof of my reason not to. I know I've got no motive for wanting Vanessa dead, but my alibis are rubbish and my fingerprints are all over her dressing room – what if they think I did it?

NINETEEN

All I want to do is hide away. I don't want to tell anyone else about being in Vanessa's room, and I decide that I don't have to. It would be too much explaining it all to Dad and the others right now. Maybe one day, just not today. I know it'll come out in the end. I didn't dare ask DI Twist to keep it a secret, and I don't suppose she would anyway, but perhaps by the time they do find out I'll have thought of a way of explaining it myself.

I've got a thumping headache, which feels unfair when all I had to drink last night was water and a cup of Nora's inevitable tea. I guess it's dehydration, so I drink a pint of water and go back to sleep. My head's a lot clearer by eleven o'clock and I make myself go for a run, knowing I'll feel better if I do. A shower finishes the job, and it's a relief to find only Nora in the kitchen when I go to make some food.

'Where is everyone?' I ask her. It's only just dawning on me that the house is unusually quiet.

'They went out. I'm not sure where – the beach, perhaps? Although I think Sandy said something about York…' She sounds unusually vague, and I realise that yesterday's events must have been as traumatic for her as for the rest of us. I've succeeded in burying my thoughts for a morning, but none of us can escape from the cloud of suspicion surrounding us right now.

'Would you like something to eat, Nora? It's nearly lunchtime.'

'That would be lovely, dear. I was just bringing back my coffee mug. Ellie made it before they left. I was hoping to swim today, but I thought I might have a little walk around the garden instead.'

'Go for it. I'll get started in here. Don't overdo it, though. Sandy will never forgive either of us if she comes home to find you exhausted.'

'I'll be careful,' she promises, rolling her eyes at the thought of Sandy on the warpath. I set to in the kitchen, and we spend a few hours eating, clearing up and going over my lines in the garden. We avoid discussing anything to do with Vanessa, murder, bloodstained shirts or fingerprints, and I wonder if I should leave for London tomorrow instead of the end of the week, where I might be able to forget about it altogether.

Ellie and Dad return with Alex as I'm putting the kettle on for some tea. They look windblown and happy, sand scattering from their shoes as they come into the kitchen.

'Oh, is that tea I see?' Dad says. 'Is there any cake to go with it?'

'You've just eaten an enormous lunch, the last thing you need is cake,' Ellie tells him, but there's a smile in her voice and she picks up the cake tin just the same.

'You look like you've had a good day,' I say.

'We have.' Dad puts his arm round Ellie and gives her a kiss. 'A very lovely day, thank you. The beach has blown more than a few cobwebs away, hasn't it?'

'Yuk, don't *do* that!' Alex's arrival in the kitchen has been delayed as always by his careful closing of the front door and removal of shoes. 'And look at all this sand. You know you should take your shoes off as soon as you come inside.' It's impossible not to laugh at his reproving face, but I get the dustpan and brush out anyway, knowing he won't shut up about it until it's cleared away.

'Shoo!' I tell Dad and Ellie. 'Get out there and take off your shoes. No tea or cake for people with sandy shoes on their feet.'

'Can I have some cake?' Alex asks as his wayward parents remove themselves.

'If you've got room for it, you can. But haven't you eaten an enormous lunch too?'

'Not really. I only had—' Alex is interrupted by the doorbell ringing, and he scoots down the hall, pushing Dad and Ellie out of his way. It would be comical if only I wasn't dreading it being the police again. I find myself holding my breath, dreading the sound of DI Twist's voice again, but it's Dean's deeper tones that come down the hallway. The kitchen door swings shut behind Alex so I can't hear what they're saying, but it's not long before Alex is back, demanding cake for three children, not one, and telling me that George and Heidi have come over.

'They've been with their grandparents for two whole weeks, and they were desperate to see me,' he says, puffed up with pleasure. 'George and me are going to start my new Spitfire model. I've said he can do some gluing if he's very careful.'

'That sounds nice,' I say, putting cake and cold drinks onto a tray. 'What about Heidi? Is she allowed to glue too?'

'No. She's going to do a jigsaw. And watch us.'

'You've got it all planned out, haven't you? D'you want me to bring this upstairs for you?'

'Yes, please.' Alex holds the door open, and we find George and Heidi standing at the bottom of the stairs looking lost, while the grown-ups talk above their heads.

'Come on, you two,' I say. 'We're taking this upstairs. Can you go ahead and hold the door open?' They scurry upstairs, glancing back at Dean for reassurance, and I follow them into Alex's bedroom. The boys head to the desk and start to unpack the model. I sit on the bed next to Heidi, keeping her company while she eats her cake. She's clutching a canvas shopping bag, and only places it on the bed reluctantly in order to hold her plate. She's looking totally lost, poor thing, and I'm sure she's only here because Dean needs to do something else.

'What's in your bag, Heidi?' I ask.

'It's Mummy's things,' she says, looking at her plate. I look at the bag. It's not very full, so 'Mummy's things' can't include much more than sheets of paper.

'That's nice.' It's a rubbish thing to say, but I don't know much about talking to children. Apart from Alex, of course, but he's not like most children, and he's definitely not like Heidi.

'I expect they're very special,' I say in desperation.

'Yes, they are.' Heidi's picking up cake crumbs with her fingertips. 'My granny gave them to me.'

'That was kind of her.'

'After the police gave them back to her.' I don't know what to say. How awful must this poor kid feel, losing her mother, being sent away from her father and having the police invade her life so completely.

'She said I could have them when I'm grown up. But Daddy said I can have them now if I'm careful with them.'

'Oh, I see. I'm sure you'll be very careful, Heidi.'

Heidi's finished her cake. She puts the plate on the bedside table and picks up the bag again, clutching it to her chest as if fearful it's about to run away from her. All sounds of conversation have disappeared from the hall below. Dean's clearly left them here for goodness knows how long. The boys have got their backs to us, there's no sign of a jigsaw and I know I can't leave Heidi here. I don't know much about entertaining little girls, but I do know what it's like to lose your mum, even if I was only three when it happened to me.

'Do you want to come downstairs with me, Heidi? I was clearing out my room the other day and I found some cool hair bands and some magazines that you might like. Would you like to have a look at them?' It's hardly the most enticing of offers, but she jumps at it unquestioningly.

'Yes, please.' She slides off the bed before I have a chance to say anything more, and the boys don't even notice us leave the room.

We head for the understairs cupboard, where my cast offs-are waiting, and I'm glad I wasn't more efficient in taking them to the charity shop. I didn't expect Heidi to find much of interest, she must have everything an eight-year-old could wish for at home, but she's easily amused by the magazines and we have a lot of fun with the weird and wonderful hair accessories I used to think were cool. We dig out an old pink rucksack and pack it full of goodies for her to take home with her. The canvas bag has been relinquished and is sitting on Dad's swivel chair. I fetch us some more drinks and think I might suggest we snuggle up on the sofa bed and watch a movie on my laptop, but when I come back she's sitting there with the bag on her lap.

'I want to show you this.'

'Oh.' I put the drinks down on the desk. I suppose it's the natural thing for her to want to show me something of her own after spending the last hour delving through my forgotten treasures. 'Okay. But best keep the drinks away from it, we don't want to spill them.'

'Sit here, and I can show you properly.'

I take a seat beside her, and she reaches inside the bag as if it was her stocking on Christmas morning.

'This is Mummy when she was very little.' Heidi passes me a photograph of Vanessa when she was small, maybe two or three. I wouldn't know it was her without being told. She was cute rather than pretty, in the way that all tiny children are. Heidi's looking at me expectantly, waiting for a response.

'She was very cute, wasn't she? Is this your granny's garden?'

'Yes. But that bush is much bigger now.'

'I expect it is. What's next?'

Heidi peers inside the bag, apparently not satisfied with the random items approach.

'This one is when she was eight, like me.' Vanessa's in her school uniform, and I can see the resemblance to Heidi now.

'She looks a bit like you in this one, doesn't she?'

'It's a different uniform, though.'

'Well, yes, but her hair's a bit like yours, isn't it? Brown and a bit curly.'

'Yes, it is. She made hers straight and blonde, though. When she grew up. Do all mummies change their hair when they grow up?'

'No, some keep it the same. You can choose, it's your hair. I think yours looks nice as it is.'

'Yours looks nice too.' Heidi cuddles into me and I just want to cry for her and tell it will be all right, even though it's horrible right now.

'What's next?' I manage to keep the wobble out of my voice and brush the tears which have appeared in my eye aside while she looks in the bag again.

'This is a picture that Mummy drew for Granny for her birthday. And this one was for Granddad. They're not very good, but I like them anyway.'

'And so you should,' I say, bursting out laughing at Vanessa's hilarious attempts to draw an elephant and a lion. 'I expect she was only little when she drew these. And they're lovely, even if they aren't very…'

'Accurate?' Heidi says. 'Granny told me what that means. It means exactly right.'

'Yes, it does. No, they're not accurate, but they're a lot of fun.'

'This is Mummy when she was a grown-up,' Heidi says. 'Can you see her?' It's a group of about twenty people, and Heidi might think the subjects are grown-ups but I'd put them at only just my age, if not younger. They've got the look of students about them, some sitting on others' laps, a few crouching or sitting on the ground, one or two making silly gestures. They're in front of a building that looks vaguely familiar, although I don't think I've been there. And some of them are in costume. The girls are wearing fifties-style dresses, some of them very smart, but a few of the boys are dressed as cow hands, and others in jeans and T-shirts must be backstage crew. It looks like student production, and I wonder what the play was.

'See if you can find her,' says Heidi. 'I did, straight away, but it took George ages. He guessed wrong three times.'

'Oooh, let's see. I hope I can do better than George. Can I hold it? To see better?'

'All right. But be careful, it's very old.' Heidi passes it across, and I scan the faces one by one, looking for one that resembles the eight-year-old Vanessa. Would she still have brown curls, or would the sleek blonde look have taken over? At least half the group are boys, so that helps, and she's more likely to be in a costume than jeans. I'm reminded of a game Alex used to play, where you had to identify a face by asking questions – 'Who am I?', it was called. I expect Heidi would like it too.

'Come on, you have to guess!' Heidi's bouncing up and down with excitement. 'Can you see her?'

'Give me one more minute, I want to get it right if I can…' I move my finger along the rows of faces, looking for a girl who could be Vanessa. They're all similar in many ways, none are particularly tall or short, fat or thin. There's one on the back row who *could* be her, and another in the middle, or… My finger stops abruptly.

'No, that's not her – guess again, guess again!' Heidi's leaning up against me, looking over my shoulder.

'I… I don't know. Um… is it this one?' I point to the one on the top row. I can't take my eyes off the girl in the middle. The one who isn't Vanessa.

'Yes, it is! You guessed second time! Well done, Billie.' Heidi reaches over to take the photograph from my hand. 'Billie? You need to let go now.'

'Oh. Sorry. Here you are.' The words come out of my mouth as if of their own accord. 'Wait a minute, Heidi. Can I have another look, just a quick one?'

'All right.' She hands it back to me and I turn it over. As I'd hoped, someone – Vanessa, perhaps? – has written on the back of the photo. *Edinburgh, 1997.* I don't know for sure how old Vanessa was when she died, but it's fair to assume she could have been a student in the late nineties. And I'm sure I remember someone saying she'd got her lucky break in Edinburgh.

'Here you go, Heidi. Now what else is in that bag?' Somehow, I'll never know how, I hold it together, saying all the right things as she shows me her treasures and then finding something she'll enjoy on my laptop. But my mind is full of only one thing. That photo. And the girl in the middle of the second row.

TWENTY

I have to talk to Sandy, but it's impossible. Dean doesn't pick up Heidi and George until dinner time. Ellie asks them if they'd like to stay and eat with us, but Dean says no, we've done enough already, and I can see she's relieved at not having to make a meal for six feed an extra three people. Alex keeps us entertained with a detailed account of his afternoon with George, and Ellie's grateful to me for looking after Heidi.

'I came looking for you, and put my head round the door, but you seemed engrossed in playing hairdressers, so I didn't interrupt,' she says.

'Haha, very funny,' I say.

'No, seriously, it was sweet of you to take her under your wing. She looked like a frightened little mouse when she arrived, but she clearly had a lovely time.'

'She's very sweet, it's easy to spend time with her.' I push my chair back, even though not everyone's finished eating. 'But I'm tired now, and I need to tidy up the study. I might have an early night.'

'Are you all right, Billie?' Ellie asks. 'You're looking a bit washed out.'

'I'm fine. Just tired. I might call Jay, see if he's in Wi-Fi range.'

'I expect you're missing him,' says Sandy. 'You must be excited to be going back to London and seeing him again.'

'Yes, I am.' I suddenly need to get outside, and I leave abruptly, not caring if they think I'm rude. I grab my cigarette pouch from the study and sit on the front doorstep, rolling a smoke and wishing we had a proper front garden. I can't face going out through the kitchen and talking to anyone again. It's not their fault – at least, not most of their faults – but I'm prickling all over with anger and resentment and I need to work out what I'm going to say to her. When I get the chance. I lean against the porch wall to smoke my cigarette and some of the tension starts to seep away. I sit up with a start when the door opens and Sandy steps out, looking down at me with a wry smile on her face.

'Escaping the hordes?'

'Something like that.' I want to blow the smoke in her face, just to see what she'd say, but I resist the temptation and direct it at the ground instead.

'D'you fancy a walk? It's a lovely evening. If you're not too tired, that is?' Is she psychic or something? I need to talk to her more than anything, and here she is, offering me the perfect opportunity. I inhale and pretend to consider the offer.

'All right. Will you tell Dad? I don't want him thinking I've gone missing.'

'Sure.' She retreats inside and I put my cigarette pouch in my pocket, thinking I might be glad of it before we get back. I let Sandy lead the way, and it's no surprise when she heads for the Westwood. It's where she always likes to walk, even though the fields are closer. She starts out briskly, her pace discouraging conversation, and I'm grateful for the chance to think about what to say. Once we're through the stile, she heads in the direction of the mill, but she stops before we get there, sitting on a bench to admire the view.

'I can never get enough of this place,' she says as I sit beside her. 'Don't you miss it when you're away?'

'Yes… and no. I love London, and it's where I need to be for work, anyway.'

'I suppose so. It's a young person's city, and I'm past all that now.'

'But you liked it when you were there?' Maybe this is my way in. I pull out my pouch and start to roll another smoke.

'Yes. But I prefer it here. I've always been a northerner at heart.'

'Sandy?'

'Mmm?'

'Nora said you liked acting when you were young. Ellie too.'

'I suppose we did, but no more than a lot of girls our age did. Not like you.' She smiles at me before turning back to the view.

'What about when you were at uni? Did you do any then? Acting?'

'No. I was busy with my course. There's not much time for activities like that when you're aiming for a first.'

'So you didn't go to Edinburgh? When you were at uni? To act in a play?'

'Edinburgh?'

'Yes, for the fringe festival.'

'What makes you ask that?' She's looking at me now, a strange expression on her face. I take a deep breath. It's now or never.

'I saw a picture of you. In a group of people. You were dressed up in a costume, something from the fifties. The photo had *Edinburgh, 1997* written on the back.'

Sandy stares at me for a moment and then laughs. 'Where on earth did you find that?'

'So it's true? You were there?'

'Yes, I was.' She looks away and into the distance as if recalling a faraway time, which I suppose she is doing. 'Good lord, it's so long ago I'd forgotten it even happened.'

'What happened?'

'Oh, a friend persuaded me. We were flatmates, she was in some drama society, someone dropped out at the last minute and she persuaded me to fill in at the last minute. I'd stayed in London to work over the summer holidays, no one else was around, or I'm sure she'd have found someone better than me. It was only a tiny part, mostly dancing. I'd forgotten all about it until now.'

'Oh. All right.' I inhale while we both think, wondering who'll speak next.

'So where did you find this photo? Was it while you were clearing out your stuff?'

'No. Heidi showed it to me.'

'*Heidi?*'

'She had a bunch of photos and stuff that Vanessa's mother had given her. The photo was in there. She wanted me to see if I could spot Vanessa, and I saw you.'

'Let me get this straight. Heidi showed you a photo of a group of people. One of them was Vanessa and another was me. In Edinburgh in 1997?'

'Yes. Why didn't you say that you knew her before?'

'Sorry?'

'You knew Vanessa when you were young. From this play in Edinburgh.' I can't keep the impatience from my voice. Is she being deliberately obtuse? 'Why didn't you say that you knew her?'

'I didn't say I knew her because I didn't know her.' Now it's Sandy's turn to sound annoyed.

'So why is there a photo with the two of you in it?'

'Look, Billie, I've not seen this photograph, but I can tell you categorically that I was not in a play with Vanessa. I was in a play, and yes, it was set in the fifties. It was *Grease* if you're desperate to know, and I was just a dancer in the chorus. But Vanessa wasn't in it with me.'

'But…' My mind's doing overtime. *Was* it Sandy in the photo? Maybe it was just someone who looked like her. But no, Sandy admitted to being in a play with those costumes, how many like that could there be in the festival at once? Well, maybe a few.

'Look, Billie, it may well be the case that Vanessa was in an Edinburgh show in the same year as I was. But there are plenty of plays set in the fifties, as you well know.'

'Yes, I know.'

'And if it was me, wouldn't Vanessa have mentioned something herself? I know she was a successful film star, and I'm just a teacher, but if she cared enough to keep the picture, don't you think she'd have recognised the people in it?'

'Maybe. Although you have changed quite a lot, you know. Your hair was long in the photo, and you looked a lot younger, of course.'

'Cheeky!' Sandy pokes me in the arm. 'Anyway, it wasn't me, as I've already told you.'

'It really did look like you, Sandy. Perhaps you'd both grown up a lot. And you changed your name, didn't you? If she knew you as Cassie, she might not have connected you to the girl in the photo. And maybe she changed her name too. Vanessa might be her real name, but I bet Forsyth isn't. I think you should look at the photo, or at least we should find out what her real name is and whether you knew her after all.'

'But what difference would it make if I did know her? And anyway, it wasn't me. You only looked at the picture for a minute, you were looking for Vanessa and you saw someone who looked a bit like me.' She pauses, waiting for my agreement, but something's stopping me from giving it.

'How clear was this photo anyway?' she says. 'I'd guess the faces were no bigger than your thumbnail, right?' I nod silently. 'And you were distracted by Heidi, tired from everything that's been happening and saw someone who looked a bit like me. It's an easy mistake to have made.'

'I suppose so,' I sigh, and stub out the end of my smoke.

'Careful,' Sandy says. 'You don't want to start a wildfire, do you?' She picks it up and walks to a nearby bin to dispose of it responsibly. I watch her as she comes back to the bench, starting to feel like an idiot for jumping to conclusions.

'But Sandy?'

'Yes?'

'Why didn't you mention it the other day? That you'd been in

217

a play at uni? When Nora was going on about you and Ellie being good actresses?'

'Because it wasn't relevant. And it would only have encouraged her. Ellie was much better than me. She really loved drama, but Father wouldn't let her act in anything outside school time, so she never got the chance to find out how good she could have been. She's a great artist, of course, but I sometimes wonder if she could have been an even better actress. Neither of us like talking about it; it only reminds us of what our father was like.'

'I see.' It's the only thing I can say. I suppose it all sounds plausible, and arguing with her isn't getting me anywhere. 'Shall we be getting back now?'

'Sure.' We head down the hill towards the town, more slowly this time.

'Sandy?'

'Yes?'

'Who do you think did it?' I don't know why, but it's easier to ask when we're walking and I don't have to look her in the face.

'Killed Vanessa?'

'Yes.'

'Now there's a question.' She sighs heavily and walks a while before answering. 'If you ask me, the only person that makes sense, logically speaking, is Dean. He had motive, means and opportunity. Isn't that what you're supposed to look for?'

'Yes. I guess so.' We pause to cross the road for a minute and the interruption gives me time to think some more. 'Do you really think he came in and stole a shirt of Dad's? Why would he do that if he was going to set it up to look like a suicide?'

'That's another good question,' Sandy admits. 'And one which I think the police are better trained to consider than we are. If you ask too many questions, Billie, you'll end up finding a reason for anyone to have done it. Even your own father.' I can't answer her. It's too close to what I've been most fearful of all along. 'At this rate, you'll tell me Mike did it to protect his marriage from Vanessa's evil

218

designs and to save Ellie's sanity into the bargain.' There's a laugh in her voice, but my brain doesn't register it. I stop dead in my tracks, and Sandy's several steps ahead of me before she notices.

'Billie?' She turns round and comes back up the path towards me. 'Billie, you don't think I'm serious?' She puts her hands on my shoulders and pulls me into a hug. 'I'm sorry, I shouldn't have said that. I only meant it as a joke. And to remind you not to try and solve everything yourself. That's what the police are here to do, right?'

'Right.' It comes out as a whisper and I'm talking into her shoulder so she can't hear me anyway.

'Right?' She holds me at arms' length.

'Right.' It's only a croak, but it's just about audible this time.

'Come on.' Sandy takes me by the hand as if I were a child. 'Let's go home, have a stiff drink and watch something mindless on the telly.'

'Okay.'

'And don't worry. You'll be back in London before you know it and by the time you come home for Christmas it will all have blown over.'

'You make it sound very simple.'

'That's because it is simple. You've been working yourself up about it, and I'm not surprised. It's a horrible thing to happen to someone you know, even if only slightly. And it's even harder knowing that she was… involved with your father.'

'Only she wasn't involved with him. She wanted to be, but he wouldn't.'

'I know. But…'

'But what?'

'Oh, nothing. The point is, she was a very unpleasant person, and that doesn't make it any easier dealing with the aftermath. You'd think it would be worse if she'd been a nice person, but it's the other way around.'

'Nora said that too.'

'Did she? Well, that's probably where I got it from.' We're turning the corner into our road, and Sandy changes the subject, asking if she should open a bottle of wine or would I rather have a beer, and which film do I fancy watching?

* * *

I go along with Sandy's plans because it seems pointless asking more questions, but my mind is buzzing all through the film, getting itself into a tangle that I know I can't unravel on my own. It's nearly midnight by the time we finish, but I know Jay won't mind me calling now, and I go to the end of the garden with a beer and a smoke where I can be sure no one will hear me. It's a warm night, and I can almost imagine I'm in France too. Jay's in the hotel so the Wi-Fi's working properly and we can have a video call for a change. He finds a quiet place on his own where he won't be disturbed and it's wonderful to see his face, even if there is a bit of a time lag with the words. He listens carefully, not asking any questions and giving me time to explain everything properly. When I finish, it feels as if a huge weight's been lifted off my shoulders.

'Wow, Bills. It's… unreal.'

'I know. Only it isn't. It's very real. It's too real.' I pause to roll another smoke, my phone providing just enough light to see by. 'So, what d'you think?'

'About what?'

'Any of it? All of it, I guess.'

'Well, just let me say, Billie, how very grateful I am…' Jay puts on an actorly voice as if giving an Oscar acceptance speech, 'for everything you've done to prevent my arrest for possession of dubious substances.'

'Quite right.' I laugh. 'And I don't ever want to be anywhere near your nasty little pills or anything else again. I hope you've got that straight.' I use my sternest voice for his benefit, but I mean it, and I know he can tell.

'Okay, okay, I've got the message.'

'So what about the rest of it?'

'To be honest, Bills, it sounds dodgy to me.'

'What d'you mean, dodgy?'

'Well, first off, the police have seen those pictures Heidi showed you, right?'

'Yes, she said so.'

'So they'll have seen this photo. The one with Vanessa and Sandy in it together.'

'Yes, but why is that so... oh, I see what you mean. If it is Sandy in the picture, they'll recognise her too. Only they might not. She did look very different. Not only younger in the face, long hair too. If it was her. I'm in a total muddle about that now. And why would they be looking out for her anyway?'

'They'll be looking for anyone connected with Vanessa. Detectives always poke into murder victims' pasts – don't you know anything about this stuff, Billie?'

'Not really, no. So you think it *was* Sandy in the picture?'

'I don't know, I didn't see the picture, but it's a big coincidence if it wasn't. The police may not have spotted this person – whether it was Sandy or not – but I reckon they'll be asking for photos of her and Ellie when they were young before long. And why didn't Sandy mention it before? What she said to you sounds like a lame excuse to me.'

'I know.'

'There's something else that's odd.'

'What?'

'You told me before that your dad and Ellie didn't want Sandy or Nora to know about the thing between Vanessa and your dad, right?'

'There wasn't a "thing" between them.'

'All right, so there wasn't, although you've only got their word for it. Anyway, whatever it was, they didn't want Sandy to know about it.'

'No, they didn't want Nora upset, and I suppose they thought she might find it hard to keep it from her. I guess it wasn't her business anyway.'

'So how come she mentioned it to you? When she was telling you not to ask too many questions?' He's right. I was too busy worrying that DI Twist might think Dad was a murderer to question how Sandy knew about his 'thing' with Vanessa.

'One of them must have told her. It was ages ago when they said that to me. A lot's happened since then; they might have decided she needed to know.'

'Or maybe she's been eavesdropping like you were.'

'Jay!' But he's right. It's all too easy to overhear other people's conversations in this house, as I know only too well. It's why I'm sitting outside in the garden, never mind wanting to smoke. I inhale deeply, thinking, and imagining Jay doing the same.

'Billie...' he says.

'Yes?'

'I think you should be careful.'

'Careful of what?'

'Look, I don't want to scare you, but you seem to know quite a lot of stuff that maybe the police don't.'

'What stuff?'

'About what was going on with your dad and Vanessa – she talked to you about it, remember? Maybe there *was* more going on between them than your dad has admitted.'

'But—'

'Wait, Billie. Let me say it. It's not just your dad who would have a motive if that was the case. It would hardly have made Dean happy, would it?'

'I guess not.'

'And there's Sandy. You might have made a mistake with the photo, but you might not have done.'

'What are you saying?' The night's still warm, but I'm starting to feel chilly, and I reach behind me for my jacket, forgetting I've not brought it out with me.

'I'm saying… I'm sorry, Billie, but I'd never forgive myself if I didn't say this and something happened to you… Look, Vanessa didn't kill herself. Someone else did it. And it sounds like it could be someone you know. What do you suppose they'll do if they think you know something the police don't?'

I grip the phone tightly, feeling that if I let it go my whole world will fall apart. There's a silence at Jay's end while he waits for a response, but my mind has frozen as completely as my body, trapped in a battle between fear and denial.

'Billie? Are you there?'

'Yes.' I can't keep the tension from my voice, and it feels as if another person is talking.

'Are you okay?'

'Not really.'

'I'm sorry, I didn't mean to frighten you.'

'Well, you did. A lot. You're basically saying I know stuff about a murderer and I'll be next on their list. Have you any idea how crazy that sounds? And what d'you want me to do? Run round to the police station and spill the beans on my whole family? They're not murderers, Jay. These are people I've known my whole life, not random strangers.'

'Dean isn't.'

'Okay, Dean isn't, but the others are.'

'I know.'

'So you think I should do what?'

'I think you should go to the police first thing tomorrow morning and tell them everything you know. Everything. What Vanessa said about your dad, and about the photograph. What you say might make things better for your dad. And if it isn't Sandy in the picture, it'll be easy to prove.'

'But Jay… if I go telling that Twist woman every little personal detail about everyone, they'll never trust me again. Never mind the fact they'll think I suspected them of murder.'

'Perhaps. I know it's difficult—'

'Difficult? Impossible, more like. My life will never be the same again if I do that. It's hard enough living in a family that's only half mine already. They're already trying to get rid of me, sticking me in that tiny study, telling me to get rid of my stuff. There's no way I could come back here if I went snitching to the police, don't you see that?'

'I'm sorry, Billie, I didn't realise—'

'No, you didn't. You know nothing about me, Jay, nothing.'

'Look, Billie, I'm sorry, I—'

'Oh, never mind. It's late. I need to go to bed. Bye, Jay.'

'Bill...'

My fingers are trembling with anger, but I manage to press the little red symbol in time to stop him saying any more. I steady my hand enough to roll another cigarette and smoke it slowly, my face turned up to the stars. I remember sitting here the first night I came home, and I can't believe it was only six weeks ago. I try to remember how it felt to be inside my head that night. What was I thinking of then? They seem such easy, innocent thoughts now – missing Jay, wondering how I was going to get through six weeks without him. Annoyance at myself for not saving enough money to go with him. Looking forward to seeing Gaby again. Excited about my new part and to get started on learning my lines. And anger at Nora for taking my room. It all seems so trivial now. I want the old me back, the me who didn't have to worry about murder. I've less than a week to go. Dad's promised to drive me to London on Friday, or Saturday at the latest, but why wait that long? I've packed most of my stuff already; I can easily finish it off tomorrow. I'll ask him to take me on Wednesday. The sooner I'm out of here, the better.

TWENTY-ONE

I wake up late and muzzy-headed and it all feels like a bad dream. The photo, the walk with Sandy, the fight with Jay. I can't believe it all happened yesterday, and in the space of only a few hours. But I can't believe a lot about my life at the moment, at least not where the last few weeks are concerned. I pull on my running clothes as if on autopilot, not wanting to face anyone else just yet. As I pound the streets, I focus on practical matters. I need to talk to Dad as soon as possible and persuade him to drive me down south tomorrow. I'm sure he won't have anything important planned, not with it being the school holidays. Then Jay's friend Alice. She said her housemate was due to move out today, so it shouldn't matter to her if I turn up a couple of days early.

I'll need to message Gaby too. I'd promised to see her again before I leave, so it'll have to be tonight. I'll have to think about what to talk about – the last thing I want is another argument like last night with Jay. Jay… I feel bad, shouting at him and cutting him off like that. There was a string of messages from him last night, ranging from how sorry he is for upsetting me to I'm an idiot for not listening to him, to please call him right away. It'll look mean if I block him, even if only for a day. I'll just have to ignore them. It'll be better when we're both back in London; FaceTiming's nowhere near as great as people make out.

The house is quiet when I get back. It's Tuesday, which is usually Alex's day with Sandy at the library. His routines have been a bit haphazard recently, but maybe they've decided it's better to stick to them again. I guess Ellie's in the studio and Dad's probably working. I half expect to find him in the study, but he's not there, or at the big table in the lounge. Thinking he must be out on his bike, I resign myself to waiting for his return to ask about travelling tomorrow. All my other plans depend on his agreement, but I can still do some packing after a late breakfast. I'm wondering what other belongings I might have scattered around the house as I come into the kitchen, and I get a shock when I find Sandy there, standing at the sink. She starts when I open the door, splashing water onto the floor as she does so.

'Oh! You gave me a fright. I didn't realise you were back.'

'You gave me a fright too. I thought you'd be out with Alex. Didn't you hear me in the shower? I've been back for ages.'

'I was in the garden. I've only just come in. Ellie's taken Alex swimming, Mother too, to make up for missing it yesterday.'

'Oh, right. She thinks it helps her hip, doesn't she?'

'Yes.' Sandy shakes her hands before drying them with a towel. 'I'm sure it's all in her mind, though. There's a lot more wrong with her hip than she wants to admit. I don't know how she'd manage if she was on her own.'

'She will be one day, though, won't she?' I ask as I fill the kettle. 'D'you want a drink?'

'Yes, please, coffee would be great. And no, I doubt it. She'll need to live with us permanently now. Only don't say so to her, there's no need to upset her.'

'Sure.' I put bread in the toaster, glad we're talking about something that doesn't involve Vanessa.

'On the subject of not saying so...' Sandy's looking sheepish, which isn't like her.

'Yes?'

'I'd appreciate it if you didn't mention that photograph to anyone else. As I said, I don't want to bring up the subject of my acting in that play. It will only get Mother going again, and I don't want Ellie upset.'

'Why would Ellie be upset? Surely she knows about it already?'

'No, she doesn't. It happened at a time when she was desperate to take part in a school play and Father wouldn't let her. It would have added insult to injury if she'd known I was in a production, especially when I wasn't even interested in acting myself. I didn't say anything about it at the time, and there was no need to afterwards. They thought I was in London for the whole summer and I didn't see any reason to tell them otherwise.'

'I see. Okay.' It's funny, I'd never heard anything about Ellie wanting to act before, but Nora seemed sure of it, so I suppose it must be true. Maybe she is still sensitive about it – who knows? The toaster pops and the kettle boils at the same time. Sandy makes the coffee while I butter my toast, hoping she won't bring up something else that I don't want to talk about. Perhaps she wants to avoid the same subjects, because she picks up her coffee, saying she has some work to do and she'll take it upstairs. I manage to hide the relief in my voice as I say I'll take my breakfast outside and I'll see her later.

* * *

In the interests of ignoring unpleasant matters and burying my head in the sand, I spend longer than is strictly necessary in the garden, checking my social media accounts and posting some pictures. I've fallen behind recently, and it helps me feel as if my life is getting back to normal. I tell myself that with any luck, I'll be on my way to London by this time tomorrow, and decide if that's going to happen I need to start gathering up my belongings from around the house. I'm sure some of my socks have made their way into Alex's room, and I should make the most of his being out of the house to reclaim them now. I dump my dishes in the kitchen and make my way into the hall, but the sound of voices brings me up short. Someone's in the living room. The door's closed but I can hear Sandy's voice quite clearly. And I know the others only too well. It's DI Twist and her sergeant. My head pulls itself out the sand with no prompting, and I tiptoe forwards in my bare feet just far enough to hear what they're saying.

'Yes, I brought the receipts in as you asked,' Sandy's saying. 'I left them at the front desk. I assume you received them?'

'Yes, we did,' says DI Twist. 'They confirm, as you say, that you purchased items from a number of shops during the afternoon of Miss Forsyth's death.'

'In that case, what else is there to say?' Sandy's got her imperious tone on her, the one I've always imagined she uses for telling off troublesome teenagers.

'We've been looking at CCTV footage from a number of locations around the town on that day. It's been helpful to us in tracking the movements of several people connected to Miss Forsyth.'

'Like Billie, perhaps?' There's a sneer in her voice that I've not heard before, and I can't work out what it means. Is she trying to suggest that I've got something to hide?

'I really can't comment on that.'

'Or maybe Mike? I'd say he needs all the help he can get in the alibi department, especially now his shirt's been found with blood all over it. I was surprised you didn't arrest him. I'd have thought he was a prime suspect after that.' My mouth drops open with shock. Not only at the words, but the venom behind them. Sandy sounds like a vicious gossip of the very worst kind, almost a caricature. Is she *trying* to get them to arrest Dad?

'We're here to talk about your movements, Miss Henderson, not anyone else's,' DI Twist says firmly. 'We'd like you to take a look at some CCTV footage and confirm that it's you on the screen.'

'Certainly, if it will help to verify my movements I'll be more than happy to help.' Sandy's tone is all sweetness and light again, and there's a pause while I imagine Sergeant Carter gets out his tablet to show her the film.

'This first one's at the library,' says Sergeant Carter. There's a longer pause, and I use it to decide what to do if the door opens before I have time to move. I can't get to the study without passing the door, but I can easily go back into the kitchen and pretend I've just come in from the garden.

'Yes, that's me,' Sandy says.

'Thank you. There's another section, also at the library, but around half an hour later.' Another pause.

'Yes, that's me too. I spent some time browsing and I had a word with the librarian about a book I wanted to order. As I told you before.' It was Sandy who told us to be polite to the police, but she can't keep a shade of superiority out of her tone, and it's clear she thinks this is a waste of their time.

'And there's this one,' Sergeant Carter carries on, ignoring Sandy's remark.

'Certainly, now where was I this time?' Her tone's indulgent now, as if humouring a small child. 'Oh yes, Boots. That's me, Sergeant, on my way to buy some hand cream.'

'And this one?'

'Goodness me, you have been thorough, haven't you? Is there anywhere you haven't got me on camera?' There's no response from the detectives, and I can't help wondering where this is going.

'Yes, that's me again,' Sandy says. 'The Refill Jar was my last stop.' I'm surprised she isn't telling them what a wonderful shop it is, but maybe she's starting to wonder what's going on too.

'Thank you, Miss Henderson, that's very helpful,' DI Twist says.

'You're welcome.' I can hear the creak of the sofa and I'm guessing Sandy's getting out of her seat. I turn round silently on my tiptoes, ready to scoot if they come out, but they're not done yet.

'Before we go, we'd like to go through the places you visited that afternoon again.'

'Is that really necessary? I've already been through this twice, you know.'

'Yes, we're aware of that. But please do think carefully, Miss Henderson. We want to be absolutely sure you haven't missed any out.'

'Very well.' Sandy's sigh is heavy enough to hear through the door, and I can easily imagine the look of resignation on her face. 'The jewellers for the watch battery, The Lemon Tree for a birthday present, Boots, the library and the Refill Jar.'

'You're absolutely sure that's all?' There's something about DI Twist's voice that reminds me of Mrs Williams, my year five teacher, giving me a last chance to come clean about cheating in a spelling test. Sandy of all people should be aware of it, but she's been too busy showing off her wonderful memory to notice.

'Yes. I'm sure.'

'You didn't make any purchases in a clothes shop?' DI Twist asks.

'No.' Sandy doesn't sound so sure of herself now.

'Please take a look at these photographs. You should recognise them as they're taken from the videos you've just seen.' DI Twist pauses briefly, no doubt so that Sergeant Carter can produce the photos.

'This one shows you at the jewellers. They have several cameras, and your arm is shown quite clearly as you pick up your watch from the counter.'

'Yes, I see.'

'And this one,' there's a rustle as the photos are moved around, 'is from the Refill Jar. It shows you opening the door.'

'Yes, I see.'

'So you'll also see that your shirt sleeve is different in this picture. In the first photograph it's loose-fitting with a ruffle at the wrist, but the second one has a tighter fit with a plain cuff.'

'Oh, I *see*.' Sandy laughs with genuine merriment. '*This* is what all these videos and photos are about. I'm sorry, I shouldn't laugh, it's a serious matter.'

'Yes, it is serious,' DI Twist agrees. 'So perhaps you'd like to explain why it's so funny.'

'I'm sorry, I really am, it's just... Oh dear, I'll start again, shall I?' Sandy says graciously as if offering a queen's audience to a commoner.

'Please do.'

'All right. And I'm so sorry to have caused this confusion. I went out shopping, as you know.' Sandy's voice shows every sign of embarking on another lengthy story, and there's nothing they can do to stop her now. 'I was wearing the blouse you saw in the first photograph – in both photographs, actually, but we'll come to that in a minute. I was starting to get rather hot, especially with those ruffles hanging around my hands. They're very pretty, and I love that old-fashioned style, but I began to wish I'd put something different on. So when I was in the library I went to the toilet and rearranged them. I turned the ruffles inside, you see, so the cuffs would have looked plain on the photograph. The ruffles fitted inside the sleeves easily enough, but it gave them the look of a tighter-fitting sleeve. Those photographs are rather grainy, of course, so it's difficult to see that level of detail, but I suppose that's the way of it with CCTV footage, even in this modern age.' There's a pause while the detectives take in Sandy's story. Not being able to see the photos myself, I have no way of knowing how plausible this explanation is, but the lack of a speedy response suggests it's not easily challenged.

'You're saying this is the same shirt? With the cuffs tucked inside the sleeves?' DI Twist sounds only a little incredulous, which I think is a great achievement.

'Yes, that's right,' Sandy says. 'Look, Inspector, I'm an intelligent woman and I know what you're thinking. I'm sure you came here today with a nice little theory about how I murdered Vanessa and then changed out of my blood-soaked shirt in the library. You'll have had me carrying a change of clothes in my bag, disposing of the first shirt and hiding Mike's in the shed. A feasible proposition, I'm sure, but with just one or two holes in it, I fear.'

'Oh yes?' There's a note of challenge in DI Twist's voice, but she lets Sandy continue nonetheless.

'Yes. If I *had* killed Vanessa, I'd have been clever enough to visit a clothes shop as well to cover my change of clothing. And I'd also have been clever enough to dispose of Mike's shirt just a little further away from my own home.'

'Would you really,' says DI Twist calmly.

'Yes, I would.' Sandy's sounding rather pleased with herself, and I'm starting to feel sorry for DI Twist, despite everything. 'One thing intrigues me, though, and that's my motive. The one you had for me. I assume you did have one? There wouldn't be much point in your coming round here to accuse me without one, would there?'

'Miss Henderson.' I have to hold on to the nearest stair newel to stop myself jumping with shock. DI Twist must be on her feet; no one could speak that loudly without taking a proper big breath first. 'Miss Henderson, you have been helpful this morning, and I'm sorry if you feel your time has been wasted, but please be assured that we have very clear protocols for the investigation of deaths of this kind, and they do not include making unfounded accusations. You have been accused of nothing this morning; however, your explanation of our observations is barely convincing. The images we've shown you aren't perfect, I'll agree, but our investigations are far from over, and I strongly advise you to keep your views of such matters to yourself.' There's a silence so thick I'm sure I could hear a pin if it was dropped on the other side of the door, but it's Sandy's sigh that I hear instead.

'I'm sorry, Inspector. I really am, please accept my sincere apologies. We've all been under a lot of strain recently. I'm sure you understand.'

'Of course I understand. We both do,' says DI Twist.

'I'm just so worried about…' There's a hint of tears in Sandy's voice.

'Worried about what?'

'What will happen to us. If it's someone… someone in this

house...' Sandy's voice becomes muffled, as if she's talking through a hanky.

'Miss Henderson, do you have reason to believe someone you know killed Vanessa Forsyth? Because if you do, you must tell us now.'

'No, no, I don't. I mean, I know Ellie had fallen out with her, and Mike... well, Mike...'

'Mr Preston has informed us fully of his dealings with Miss Forsyth, as has Mrs Preston,' DI Twist says, somewhat crushingly.

'Oh, yes, I'm sure he has. But I can't help wondering if... well, if there was more going on between them than he's admitted to...'

'Do you have any evidence to confirm this? Or is it...'

'It's just a feeling, that's all. At least, it *was* just a feeling until we found the shirt. I know this will sound terrible, Inspector, but I've not always been absolutely sure about Mike. He's a lot older than Ellie, and I wondered at the time if she'd... well, if she'd be enough for him.'

'Enough? In what way?'

'Oh, I don't know. Ellie's lovely, of course she is, it's just that she's... well, fragile. She's suffered with stress, anxiety, that sort of thing. She's always lived with me; she'd never have managed otherwise. I wonder if Mike started to feel the need for someone more confident, more assertive, more exciting, perhaps? I saw him with Vanessa, and I could tell. There was definitely something between them. And from where I was standing it looked like it was on both sides. And I doubt very much if your CCTV footage has helped him with *his* alibi.'

I can't listen to any more of this. She's trying to pin it on Dad. All she cares about is her own skin. If it wasn't her, why can't she tell them it must have been Dean? Why all this talk about Dad? I want to run as fast as I can, but I make myself tiptoe as far as the kitchen door and rush back to the garden. I sit at the table and roll a smoke with shaking fingers. I can't avoid it now. It was her. It was Sandy. It has to be her. That blouse. I know which one they meant; it's the one that's missing from her room, the one she said she'd lent to someone at school. She doesn't 'love' those sorts of clothes; she'd never wear anything like that out in public. She must have worn it to kill Vanessa, thinking she could get rid of it afterwards. I bet Dad's shirt wouldn't have covered up everything. She's always so well prepared, she'll have had a spare top with her. But where's that blouse now? In a dustbin somewhere?

My mind's racing at a hundred miles an hour, but it comes to a screeching halt as I realise I can't think of a motive. Would Sandy kill Vanessa for Ellie's sake? To stop her breaking up the marriage? She's always been protective of Ellie, saying she needs to look after her. It's why we're all living here together, because she helped out so much when Ellie was ill after Alex's birth. But after what she just said about Dad, I can't believe she'd kill Vanessa to help him out. She sounded more likely to want him gone than keen to protect his marriage for him.

My cigarette's almost finished, and I cast around for the saucer Ellie gave me to stub it out in. I need to talk it through with someone, but I'm not ready for Jay. My phone must have buzzed a hundred times in the last hour, and I'm sure it's messages from him. Gaby would be better, but I'd have to explain too much to her. I'll look at Jay's messages and see if he's still mad at me. I pull my phone out of my pocket, but before I get a chance to look at it, Sandy comes out.

'Here you are!' she says brightly. The sun's behind her so I have to squint when I turn around to look at her, and I can't quite see her expression. 'Have you been out here all this time?'

'Yes. I've been catching up with messages on social media and stuff.'

'Where are your breakfast dishes?'

She misses nothing, does she? My stomach's suddenly churning with fear, and the knowledge that I'm alone with someone who is more than likely a killer.

'Oh, I took them in ages ago, just after you went up.' I can't let her suspect for a minute I've heard what's been going on. 'What have you been up to? Don't tell me you've been doing schoolwork on a lovely day like today?'

'What else?' she says. 'I'm just off to the shops for a bit now, do you need anything?'

'No, I'm good, thanks.'

'All right, see you later.' She seems very keen to get away, which is fine with me. My thoughts are still too scrambled to work out what to say to her.

I wait until she's gone inside before I heave a sigh of relief and roll yet another smoke to steady my nerves before turning to my phone. There are about a million messages waiting for me from Jay and a voicemail from Gaby. I think I'd prefer to hear her voice first before dealing with the Sandy situation, so I press the little phone picture first.

'Billie, listen. I know you're mad at Jay, he called me and he sounded pretty desperate. I don't know what's gone on between you, but he's sent you an email. He says you can ignore all his messages, but please look at the email, okay? And when you're done, maybe give me a call?'

I hang up and look at the email. My hands are still shaking, even while I'm wondering how long it took Jay to find Gaby in my massive list of followers. It's a long email, and there are several attachments. I tap my fingers impatiently on the table while I wait for them to download, unable to focus on Jay's words beyond the first few sentences:

Billie, I'm sorry. I got it wrong last night. I hate not being with you, FaceTime's rubbish and I can't say things properly to you online. Please read this, and if you hate me forever, at least you'll know that I loved you enough to risk losing you.

He's never said he loved me before. I didn't expect him to, not at all. It's probably just to get me to read the email, but if he's desperate enough to do that... A picture pops up on the screen. It's the one

Heidi showed me. Where on earth did Jay get it? I look at it again, enlarging it on the screen so that I can see the faces more clearly. It's not a great photo, and enlarging makes it grainier, but I'm sure it's Sandy. I go back to the email again. Jay's been busy, he must have been on the internet half the night, and the rambling sentences reflect what must have been a totally exhausted brain. He could have set it out in a quarter of the space; he didn't really need to write anything at all, the attachments tell the story, but perhaps he needed to explain it for himself as much as for me.

The second attachment is a page from a book of some sort. The picture is there again, only smaller this time, with three others of groups of what look like production casts and crews. I enlarge it enough to read the caption below it: '*Hairspray', Edinburgh, 1997.* According to Jay, it's from an album he was given a few years ago to mark the sixtieth anniversary of the London Youth Theatre. I never managed to get in, but he was a member for a few years, and they were all given a copy of this book. I can't imagine what his mum said when he called her at seven in the morning asking her to dig it out and take pictures from it. I can't believe he remembered that Vanessa was an LYT member too, but he's always been a bit of a geek about stuff like that – knowing where famous actors trained is his favourite party trick.

The next picture is of a cast list. Jay says the book included these as well – someone in the LYT archives must be as big a nerd as he is – and it doesn't take long to spot them. Cassie Henderson's top of the list as Penny Pingleton, the role I remember seeing Ariana Grande play in an online version ages ago. And there, almost at the bottom, is Vanessa Gamble as Jackie. I don't remember her in the film so it has to be a minor character. There are no other Vanessas, and it's easy to believe that the Vanessa I knew wasn't keen to keep her original surname. Vanessa never liked to talk much about how she started out in acting, but she did say she'd been spotted by an agent in a play at the Edinburgh fringe. But from this information, you'd think it would have been Cassie – or rather, Sandy – who got her big break from this production, not Vanessa.

The last attachment is a screenshot of an online chat about actors and how they started out. Jay says he just Googled 'film stars lucky breaks' and a few came up. Goodness know how long it took before he found one with Vanessa in it, but there it is.

Vanessa Forsyth was spotted in a youth theatre production in Edinburgh when a casting agent saw her perform in Hairspray. The girl who was supposed to play the lead was ill, Vanessa stepped in at the last minute, and the rest is history!

There's a reply below it:

I wonder what happened to the other girl – she must have been gutted!

And there it is. Sandy's motive.

TWENTY-TWO

I read Jay's email again. Slowly. I've jumped to too many conclusions recently and I want to be sure that he's made the same connections as me. My body's tingling all over and I can feel my heart beating faster than usual, but for the first time in ages my thoughts are clear and I know exactly what to do. It was Sandy. It was she who wanted to act, not Ellie. She wasn't 'filling in' for anyone. She got that part through a long and tough audition process, and she'd never have got it if she wasn't good enough. She must have thought it was her big chance to pack in her course and act instead. Maybe she'd already packed it in, and that's why she had to go for teacher training instead. But she got ill and Vanessa took the part. And Vanessa impressed the agent, not Sandy.

It's Sandy who's the weak one, not Ellie. I can see it now. It was Sandy who left London in a hurry, ran away from her plans, buried her dreams. It's Sandy who depends on having her family around her. Ellie's fine – she had post-natal depression, but that's not a terminal illness. Ellie's the one who followed her dreams, who's ready to move out and make a home of her own. So's Nora, come to that: it's only Sandy who keeps insisting she can't cope on her own. She's built up this façade of everyone needing her so that we don't leave her on her own. She makes out she's the 'secret centre' that Gaby was talking about, but she isn't. We'd all be fine without her. If she's the secret centre it's in a sneaky, selfish way, not a loving one.

I snap my laptop shut and go inside. I'm going to the police. Now. I go straight to the study, grab a backpack and stuff the laptop inside. I can feel the adrenaline rushing through my veins, and with it comes the anger. How much of my life has been manipulated by Sandy? I was too young to think about it at the time, but why didn't Dad and Ellie set up home on their own in the first place? Did Alex really need to stop going to school, or was that another of Sandy's bright ideas, designed to tighten her web around our family? I can't imagine Dad wanted to spend over ten years living with his sister-in-law, never mind his mother-in-law as well. My phone buzzes again. It's Jay, wanting to know if I've seen the email. I sit down for long enough to reply, saying yes and thank you and I'm going to the police. He replies:

Good. Don't wait any longer. Message me when you get there xx

My thoughts are still racing as I pull on my Doc Martens, putting all the pieces together at last. Sandy must have overheard Dad and Ellie talking about moving out and about Vanessa. She won't have wanted them to do that, and it mightn't have been enough on its own to make her kill Vanessa, but it could have tipped her over the edge if she was already mad at her. She must have used Dad's shirt as a back-up plan in case the suicide thing didn't work. Didn't Ellie say it was Sandy who told her to look for the slug pellets on the day they found the shirt? There probably weren't any slugs at all. But why all this talk about it being Dad; why not Dean? Does she really hate him so much? And why leave it so late to 'find' the shirt?

I'll go by bike; I want to get there as quickly as I can, like Jay said. Phone, bag, tobacco pouch – I'm all set. I sling the bag onto my shoulder and head out to the garden to borrow Alex's bike. I've got as far as the kitchen when I hear a key in the front door lock. It must be

Ellie, Alex and Nora, back from their swim. I'll have to think of an excuse to be going out – Gaby might be the best option. The kitchen door's just swinging to behind me when I hear her.

'Is that you, Billie?' It's Sandy. I freeze. What do I do now?

'Yes.' I put my backpack under the table and open the kitchen door. 'Did you forget something?'

'Yes. One of my library books is due back today and I forgot to take it with me. I'll pop upstairs and get it.' She pauses, looking past me and through the kitchen door. I'm trying to block it, but my body's not big enough to stop her spying my backpack. 'Are you off out too?'

'Um, yes. I'm going to meet Gaby.'

'Well, the front door's that way,' Sandy says, tilting her head towards the hall.

'I… I'm going by bike. We're meeting at the climbing wall. The one near Hull.'

'That sounds fun.' She's not moving, but it'll look weird if I ask why she's not going up to get her book. 'Is that bag big enough for all your gear? It doesn't look like it holds much more than your phone.' Why am I such an idiot? I could have made up a hundred different excuses, why did I have to pick that one?

'Gaby's giving me some of her stuff. She's had a clear-out too, and she's got some gear from when she was younger. She said it'll fit me. I can't afford any new kit right now, so she's bringing it along today.'

'Well, I hope it fits, or you'll be spectating rather than climbing,' Sandy says. She turns towards the staircase, and I let go of the breath I've been holding inside as quietly as I can. I pick up the bag and fill my water bottle at the sink. My mouth's as dry as a bone, and I don't want to choke to death before I reach the police station.

'Before you go, Billie—'

I jump about a foot in the air. 'Good grief, Sandy, why did you have to creep up on me like that?' There's water everywhere and I look for a tea towel to dry my bottle with.

'Before you go, Billie,' she's not even close to apologising, 'I need to ask you something.'

'Can it wait? I'm already late for Gaby.' This at least has a ring of truth to it: Sandy knows as well as anyone that my timekeeping's rubbish.

'No, it can't. Sit down, will you?' Sandy takes the tea towel from me and puts a hand on my arm as if to stop me running away. I'm starting to feel nervous – can she read my mind or something?

'You were in the garden all morning, yes?'

'No, I went for a run first and I had a shower, you know that. I didn't go out until at least—'

'Yes, I know that. I mean after then. After I came back inside. You didn't go back to the study after that?'

'No. I brought in my breakfast dishes but I went straight back out. Why is it so important?' It'll look suspicious if I don't ask why she wants to know, so I do, even though I'm scared of what the answer might be.

'I was expecting a parcel. I didn't hear anyone ring the bell but there was a card to say they'd tried to deliver it. I thought it odd you'd not heard.'

'No, I wouldn't hear from outside. It's a shame Alex was out,' I say, trying to lighten the atmosphere, which feels like the crackle of electricity you get before a thunderstorm.

'Yes, it is,' she says. She lets go of my arm, and I can tell she wants to know if I heard her talking to the police but there's no way she can ask. Her discomfort suddenly gives me a buzz, and I decide it's time to go. She'll be in big trouble soon and I'm looking forward to seeing her try to wriggle out of everything I'm about to tell DI Twist. I get up and head towards the back door, feeling almost giddy with excitement and anticipation.

'What were you waiting for, anyway? To be delivered?' I ask over my shoulder. 'A new blouse, perhaps, to replace the one you gave away?'

Sandy crosses the space between us like lightning, putting herself

241

between me and the door. 'What do you mean? Why would I need to replace it?'

'Well… they've not given it back yet, have they?' I stammer. 'At least, it doesn't look like they have. I thought maybe you'd ordered one for me to give to Poppy… as a surprise.' Oh God. What have I done? I'm not there yet. I've not told them yet, I'm still here, not at the police station. My confidence has run far ahead of my circumstances, and I'm here on my own. With a killer.

'And why would I do that?'

I can't think of anything to say. I look at the floor in silence, hoping that if I'm quiet for long enough she'll calm down and let me go.

'Billie?'

'I… I don't know. It was just a mad idea. I only thought of it because of Gaby clearing things out and me doing the same, and looking for the blouse on that same day…' I'm gabbling, it's pathetic, I know it is, and Sandy clearly thinks the same.

'Or did something happen recently to make you think of it?'

'No!' It's too quick. I don't care what Gaby says, being an actress doesn't make you a good liar, and Sandy knows it too.

'You were inside, weren't you?'

'No, I wasn't.'

'Listening. Listening to me and the police. Don't deny it, Billie, you've always eavesdropped, ever since you were a little girl, creeping around trying to listen in when the grown-ups were talking. You never could tell when you weren't wanted.'

'Sandy—'

'Worming your way in here with your oh-so-wonderful father, trying to take Ellie away from me.'

'I was ten years old, I didn't know what was going on!'

'Oh no? I heard you – asking why you didn't have a house of your own, and even now, you're still whinging about having to sleep in the study. And it worked, didn't it? Your father nagged at Ellie, nagged and nagged at her to move. And she gave in, didn't she?'

'No, that was only to get away from Vanessa. When she died, it all changed.'

'So you *have* been sneaking around again. How else would you know about that?'

'Ellie told me herself. How did *you* know, Sandy, if it wasn't by sneaking around too?' The injustice of it all is making me angry, and being angry is giving me courage. I pull myself up to my full five feet and lift my chin in the air.

'I'll tell you what I think. They didn't just want to move out because of Vanessa; they wanted to get away from you. From you telling them what to do, bossing everyone around, putting Ellie down, crowding out the house by making Nora live here too, even though she doesn't want to. It's all about you – it always has been. You make out you're so kind and helpful all the time, but you're only doing it to keep us all here with you.'

'And why on earth would I want to do that?' Sandy snarls. 'Nothing would give me more pleasure than to see the back of you right now. I've just about had enough of sucking up to you, playing happy families with your father and pretending that Alex is anything other than a complete nuisance.'

'I can't believe you just said that,' I say. 'Not about Alex.'

'Well, I have said it,' she says, and she sits down abruptly at the table. 'It's what I feel. I haven't told anyone what I feel for nearly forty years.' There's a sense of wonder in her voice, although I'm not sure if it's because of what she's said or the fact that she's admitted it to me. Suddenly, despite everything, I'm flooded with sadness for her. I sit down too. I want to take her hand but think perhaps it's better not to.

'I'm sorry, Sandy. We didn't mean to spoil things for you.'

'It wasn't your fault. You were only ten years old, remember?' She gives me a grim smile. 'But Ellie and I... it was us against the world, you know? It was just the two of us for ten years, it was working, I thought it would be like that forever...'

'And then Dad came along. And me.'

'Yes.'

'Did you always… well, dislike us?' I'm struggling to get my head around the fact that it was all an act, those cosy evenings in Sandy's room, her lessons with Alex, so many years when she almost felt like a mother to me.

'I didn't dislike you. And I didn't like you either. I just didn't want Ellie to leave.'

'They've been together a long time, they only want a home of their own, it's not about you. It's natural, isn't it?'

'No, lots of people live together in extended families, why shouldn't we? It's worked so far, hasn't it?' It may have worked for Sandy, but I'm not so sure Dad would agree.

'I expect you're right. And they haven't actually said they're moving out, have they? I'm sure it will all be fine.' Agreeing with her seems to be the safest thing to do, and Sandy appears to have calmed down now. It's been super-awkward, but at least she's stopped talking about the blouse, and I decide to make a cautious break for it.

'Look, Sandy, I'm really late for Gaby,' I say, easing myself slowly out of my chair. 'I'll see you later, okay?'

'Okay.' Sandy's staring at her hands with a faraway look on her face, and I can't help feeling sorry for her. 'Why *did* you mention the blouse, Billie?'

'I don't know. It just popped into my head. It was totally random. I… Poppy messaged me about something else today, so I guess it was in my mind.' I can't believe how many lies I've told her today. I can't wait to get out of here and tell the police the truth for once.

'Billie… perhaps don't mention that blouse to the police?'

'Why would I? What's it got to do with them?'

'Nothing… I'm getting paranoid, I suppose. This whole affair is making me so very tired, more than usual, even at the end of term. I'll be glad when they close their investigation and we can all get back to normal, won't you?'

'Of course.' I've got my hand on the door handle, but I've been brought up too well to leave while she's still talking.

'I think they'll have to accept it's suicide, don't you?' She looks up at me. I'm still angry with her, despite my attempts to stay calm, and my physically superior position, even if only temporary, gives me my courage again.

'I don't know, Sandy. I was under the impression you thought it was Dean. Or even Dad. You seem to have plenty to say about his lack of alibi.'

'I told you, that was a joke. And I never said anything about his alibi. At least…' At least not to me. But she did say it to the police. When I was supposed to be in the garden. She's up again, and smashing my hand off the door handle.

'You *were* listening. You heard everything those detectives said this morning, don't try to deny it. Why else would you be thinking about that blouse?'

'No! I don't know what you're talking about. What detectives this morning? Did—'

'Oh, stop denying it, Billie. You think you know everything, don't you? Hanging about listening to people's private conversations and putting two and two together to make five?'

'I—'

'You think I killed Vanessa, don't you? I expect you've dreamt up some ridiculous motive about with us being rivals in a play that I wasn't in, with a blood-spattered blouse that I never wore. That's it, isn't it?'

'No, I—' My mind's racing – have I got it wrong? Has Jay got it wrong too?

'You're not going to see Gaby. Are you stupid enough to think I'd believe she was meeting you in the middle of the day when she works full time?'

'She—'

'You're going to the police, aren't you?' She's grabbed both my arms this time, and she starts pulling me across the kitchen.

'No, I—'

'Don't lie to me,' she hisses. 'You're as bad as Vanessa. Telling lies, wheedling, getting your own way. She was nothing but trouble when she was young and she was even worse when she was older.'

'But you said you didn't know her when she was young.'

'Don't pretend you believe that, it's obvious you don't. You were clever, saying you'd keep quiet about it, but you've not been very clever today, have you?' She puts my wrists together and squeezes them together in one of her big, capable hands. 'They've seen that photograph and I've told them it wasn't me. They don't have any names, and it's so long ago they're not likely to find them now. The last thing I need is you stirring up trouble talking about plays and blouses and goodness knows what else. You're all the same, you actresses, you can't cope without drama in your lives.'

'I don't want drama in my life, I promise you I don't. Please let go, Sandy, you're hurting me.' I might as well not have spoken for all the notice she takes.

'First Vanessa, then you – if it wasn't for you, there wouldn't be all this talk of Ellie moving away. And if it wasn't for her, I'd never be in this—'

'In what, Sandy? What did Vanessa do to you?'

Sandy's reaching behind her for the cutlery drawer. I've got a horrible feeling she's about to do something awful, and I have to keep her talking.

'Please tell me, Sandy. I won't tell anyone if you don't want me to, but please tell me. Vanessa tricked us all into liking her, she was a dreadful person, I can see that now, so tell me what she did. I want to understand.'

I've rabbited on long enough to calm her down a bit, and I can feel a miniscule loosening of the hand around my wrists. She looks at me as if surprised I'm still there.

'Tell me, Cassie. What did Vanessa do?'

The gamble pays off. She doesn't question the use of her childhood name, and there's a change in her voice. It takes on a slightly higher pitch, giving her a hint of youthfulness, although the bitterness still comes through loud and clear.

'She stole my part. We were in a play together. I was the lead; she had a bit part. She was jealous. I was prettier, I looked right for the role and she didn't. I was the better actress, anyway.'

'How did she steal it from you?'

Sandy's still holding my wrists, but she's stopped grappling for the drawer. She doesn't appear to register my question, carrying on as if there's been no interruption.

'I fought hard for that part. It was my only chance to break free. My parents wouldn't let me act at home; I started doing it secretly as soon as I got to London. When I got the role, I wrote to every casting agent I could find, and one said he'd come and watch me. He was looking for someone to play the lead in a film, an unknown. I knew it was a long shot, but I knew I'd be right for it; I pinned all my hopes on it.' She's looking out of the window, the shadow of a smile on her face, as if remembering a time when she could allow herself to feel hopeful. I take my chance and start to cough, just a little at first but then a full-blown coughing fit, and she has to let go to let me have a drink.

'I promise I'm not going anywhere,' I say. 'Please, Sandy, can I sit down for a bit?'

She nods towards the chair that's furthest from the door, staying by the cutlery drawer, which means she's blocking my way should I try to make a run for it. I'm not sure it's much of an improvement, but at least I've got my hands back.

'So what happened? Didn't the agent come to see you after all?'

'Oh, he came. But he didn't see me act.'

'Why not?'

'I thought Vanessa was my friend back then,' Sandy says, and it almost feels as if she's telling me a bedtime story. 'We'd auditioned together, done a summer school course together, acted together in small parts. I told her about the agent. I made her promise not to tell anyone else, I thought it would jinx it if anyone else knew but I couldn't resist telling her, I thought I'd burst with excitement if I didn't. She said she was pleased for me...'

'And then...'

'It was the fifth night of the run. We'd bedded it in, it was going really well. I'd had a good review in the paper, I'd called the agent to make sure he was coming... and then...' Her face darkens. 'And then I got ill. I couldn't go on. Vanessa said she knew the lines, she persuaded them to let her do the show and the agent saw her instead. By the time I was better, he'd gone back to London. Vanessa left Edinburgh early to do a screen test.' Sandy's voice is flat, but her eyes look as if they could bore through glass. She turns to me. 'And the rest, as they say, is history.'

'But that's dreadful,' I say. 'Were you very ill?'

'Oh no, I was better the next day. Everyone said it must have been food poisoning, but I knew it wasn't. It was Vanessa. She'd made a habit of bringing me a cup of tea in the mornings while we were in Edinburgh and she put something in it.'

'No! How could she do that?'

'Oh, some people will do anything to get what they want in show business,' Sandy says briskly. 'The sooner you learn that the better, Billie, if you haven't done so already.'

'I suppose it was a bit awkward, her turning up here,' I say tentatively. Now that her story's over, she's turning towards the drawer. It's where Ellie keeps her sharpest knives, and I'll say anything to keep her away from it.

'She didn't recognise me at first.' Sandy lets out a bark of a laugh. 'Too full of herself to notice me, and she knew me as Cassie, of course.'

'Did she ever find out?'

'She did. She told me her parents had visited with a pile of photographs from when she was young. There was a picture of the show, the one Heidi showed you, and she spotted me and remembered.' Sandy's pulled a carving knife from the drawer. She's looking at it with interest, turning it slowly in her hands as if trying to remember what it's for.

'When did she tell you?' I can't believe this is happening. Is she really going to use that knife on me?

'Oh,' Sandy sighs. 'I went over there to try and persuade her to leave Mike alone. She laughed at me. She denied poisoning me, can you believe it? She said half a dozen people got ill, and we'd all eaten mussels the night before. It was a lie, a filthy lie, she always was a liar, I should never have trusted her in the first place. But she didn't lie about Mike. She said she loved him and he loved her too. She said she'd take him if she wanted, just like she'd taken my part in the show. Only it wasn't just a part, it was a film contract. And a career. And a life...' Sandy tips her head to one side, like a bird. 'A life that was different. Where I was an actress, not a failed academic, teaching in the sticks and living with her sister.'

'I can see why you were mad at her,' I say quickly.

'Oh yes, I was mad at her but not quite mad enough to kill her.'

'So why did you?' It just pops out; my brain's forgotten I'm supposed to be pretending I don't think it was her.

'She'd gone too far. With Mike. I couldn't let him move away, take Ellie away from me. I killed her to stop her splitting up the family. You should be grateful, Billie, it's your family too.'

'I know.'

'But it turned out it wasn't just her. Spoiling everything. Your *father*,' she almost spits out the word, 'wanted to move out anyway, even after Vanessa was dead. Hiding in the studio with Ellie where he thought I wouldn't hear them, telling her it was time to live their own lives. Poisoning her mind against me, telling her she didn't need me. How *dare* he? How dare he think he can split up my family, take my sister away from me, ruin my whole life?'

'So that's why you put the shirt in the shed for Ellie to find. To make it look as if Dad did it.'

'Yes! A clever idea, wasn't it? Taking one of his shirts to kill her in? Rather neat, I thought, and a very useful insurance policy as it turned out.' Her expression has switched from venom to triumph, which is slightly less scary but equally disturbing.

'Such a shame you found out too much, Billie. You're coming with me now. I've got the car parked outside the front door. I had to wait ages for someone to move out of the space this morning, but it was worth it.' She takes a step towards me, the knife raised.

'Where are we going?'

'You don't need to worry about that. You won't be spending very long there.' A horrible giggle escapes her mouth as she pushes me up and out of my chair. 'I'll tell them you left for London in a hurry. Maybe I'll say Jay came back early and you rushed down to see him, that will sound nice and romantic, won't it? Or maybe you'll have decided to elope? We can discuss the options on the way… I might even let you choose.' She elbows me towards the kitchen door.

'This way, Billie. Oh, and bring your bag. It might look a bit odd if you leave it behind.' The knife's less than a foot from my face, and I keep my eyes fixed on it as I bend to get the bag.

'That's right, nice and slow. All right, get out your phone and turn it off.' Her voice is low and calm, but there's a tautness in it that tells me to be careful. I do as she says, feeling my hopes fade with the screen. Why isn't Ellie back yet with Alex and Nora? It's gone one o'clock, surely they'll walk in any minute now. Sandy catches me glancing at the clock and laughs.

'Hoping the troops will return to rescue you? They're going out for lunch after their swim and to the cinema. I mentioned that the new *Star Wars* spin-off is on over breakfast, and Alex wouldn't take no for an answer. I think Ellie might have been saving it for the weekend, but she gave in eventually. Mike's meeting them at the restaurant, I believe, so we don't need to worry about being disturbed.'

It's as if she can read my thoughts, and she's thought of everything. She must have planned this last night, while I was talking to Jay. Was she hiding somewhere in the garden, listening in? Or did she only make up her mind for certain once she knew I'd heard her talking to the police this morning? *Okay, Billie, don't panic*, I tell myself. *There's got to be a chance when we get outside. She can't walk out of the front door holding a knife in broad daylight.*

'And don't try anything once we're out there. I'll have a jacket over this, but it won't be more than a few inches away from you.

You're driving. You'll slide in across the passenger seat and do exactly what I say. Got it?'

'Yes.' My mind's refusing to give in. There has to be something I can do – maybe crash the car? If I do everything she wants now, perhaps she'll relax enough for me to take my chance when it comes.

'You first, Billie.' Sandy points at the kitchen door with the knife, but before I can take a step there's a ring on the doorbell. Sandy grabs me and puts the blade to my neck, and it's there, filling my nostrils, the floral fragrance from the dressing room, the perfume she always wears but which my weak sense of smell couldn't recall.

'Leave it,' she hisses into my ear. 'Leave it and they'll go away.' I can't even nod for fear of cutting myself, and I hope that my silence is enough for her. We stand, rigid, while the bell rings again and there's a loud banging on the door.

'Police! Open up! We know you're in there!' It's just what they say on the TV, and I can't believe I'm hearing it in real life. Half my brain's collapsing with relief, but the other half knows it's far from over.

'Don't. Move.' Sandy must know that she can't get away with her plan now, and what good would hurting me do her? But she's past thinking rationally, and I can't afford to antagonise her. The banging starts again, and out of the corner of my eye I can see a flash of something in the garden. Sandy's eyes are on the knife, and she edges towards the back door, pulling me with her.

'Slowly. Slowly. Turn round.' I do as she says. 'Open the door. We'll go out the back way.' I push the handle down slowly, hoping that whoever is out there will see it. I look down, the glimmer of an idea coming into my brain, and walk slowly, slowly down the steps and into the garden. I hesitate on the top step. The sun's in my eyes, but I don't dare raise my hand to shield them. If I can just get down these steps, I might have a chance. I can't see anyone yet, so perhaps they're hiding behind the studio or the shed, but I'm sure there's someone out here, and that's all I need. I can't believe the police are knocking on the front door without sending someone round the back as well.

'Keep going,' Sandy says, and I move gingerly down the steps. She keeps the knife at my neck, and a firm grip on my shoulder. I don't want anyone to appear suddenly and give her a shock – she'd more than likely cut me accidentally, even if not on purpose. I could easily dislodge her grip, I could end up cut, perhaps badly, but I can only think of one thing to do and it's now or never. I stamp my Doc Marten down hard on her foot, harder than I've ever stamped in my life. Sandy's stylish sandals offer no protection from anything, and I hear the crunch of bone a split second before her agonised shriek breaks the silence. The knife clatters to the ground, something hot runs down my neck, and I hurtle down the path and straight into the middle of Sergeant Carter, who scoops me up and out of the garden before Sandy even notices the handcuffs on her wrists.

TWENTY-THREE

There aren't happy endings to stories like ours. Dad meeting Ellie didn't mean Mum hadn't died, and Sandy being brought to justice didn't bring Vanessa back for George and Heidi. It couldn't have ended differently, even if I'd wanted it to. The police were already on their way to arrest Sandy when Jay finally got hold of them saying he was worried about me. They'd been on her case for a while, although she'd been careful to keep her dealings with them secret from the rest of us. They'd been looking for the cast list ever since they saw the photo, and it came through soon after they got back from interviewing her that Tuesday morning.

I never watched many cop shows, but I do know that they don't tell you what it's like afterwards. For the people left behind. The interviews, the reporters, the social media trolls. Even worse, seeing someone you thought you knew, someone you thought loved you, put away for murder. I don't know how Ellie held it together, but she did. She had Dad on her side, of course, and they say it helps having someone to look after, so Alex must have made a difference too. Nora's been amazing. She said she wouldn't let it break her, and she hasn't, although I think it was a near thing. She's had her op and moved into her own place now. She visits Sandy, although she said not to tell anyone; they wouldn't understand.

Alex is back at school and loving it. He's extended his model-making skills from planes to landscapes, so he and Dad stripped Sandy's room bare and they're recreating Middle Earth in there. Ellie's paintings are selling better than ever and I'm working in a café to pay the bills while I wait for the next acting gig to come along. Jay's still my hero, and I've gone cold turkey on social media. It took a murder to make it happen, but suddenly I've got masses more time to do other stuff. So no happy endings, but – maybe – some new beginnings.